Silver Dreams

Linda CHAIKIN

HARVEST HOUSE PUBLISHERS
Eugene, Oregon 97402

Scripture quotations in this book are taken from the King James Version of the Bible.

SILVER DREAMS
Copyright © 1998 by Linda Chaikin
Published by Harvest House Publishers
Eugene, Oregon 97402

Library of Congress Cataloging-in-Publication Data

Chaikin, L.L.
 Silver Dreams / Linda Chaikin
    p. cm. — (The trade wind series ; 2)
   ISBN 1-56507-756-3
   I. Title. II. Series: Chaikin, L. L.,   Trade wind series ; 2.
 PS3553.H2427S55 1998
 813'.54—dc21   98-15188
                                                              CIP

Printed in the United States of America.

98 99 00 01 02 03 / BC / 10 9 8 7 6 5 4 3 2 1

❧ 1 ❧

On the Spanish Main

From the end of the earth will I cry unto Thee...

—Psalm 61:2

The raging wind of the hurricane had at last grown still. The trade winds sent the thickly growing palm trees bending toward the Caribbean Sea, which sparkled in the sunlight like a blue-green jewel. Devora Ashby bent low in the saddle of the high-spirited mare, while her satin skirt, somewhat tattered from two days of hard riding, billowed behind her. Her legs were protected by a pair of leather jerkins she'd received from the darkly handsome Captain Bruce Hawkins while aboard his buccaneering vessel, the *Revenge*. He had taken her captive from the Isle of Pearls before unexpectedly putting her ashore in the care of Friar Tobias and telling her goodbye.

She galloped the mare beside the edge of the wet beach, the horse's nimble hoofs kicking up the fine white sugary sand as she followed fast on the trail of her escort and unlikely bodyguard, Friar Tobias Valentin. He was a few lengths ahead on a black stallion, leading her to Cartagena to a politically arranged marriage with the ruthless Don Nicklas Valentin, son of the powerful viceroy.

The sea-sticky breeze tossed Devora's long, honey-colored hair, making it shimmer. But the blowing trades did little to dry the lavender ribbon-laced waistcoat that clung to her, making her feel uncomfortably wet.

In the trees above, squawking parrots nested in dried-up fronds hanging against pillar-straight trunks. While airborne, they circled above the fringed green crowns of the palms looking like halos of red, yellow, blue, and green. But Devora, caught in a whirlwind of events, was not greatly affected by the tropical beauty that splashed about her. From a discussion she'd had with Friar Tobias earlier that morning as they had dined on a breakfast of roast crab and plantain fruit, they were within an afternoon's ride of the queen fortress-city of Cartagena, the heart of the Spanish colonial empire in the West Indies.

She handled the borrowed mare with a horsemanship that heartily pleased Tobias Valentin. "The Valentin family will be proud of you. They live and breathe horses. They own some of the best bloodlines from Spain." Tobias was an unlikely escort and body-guard, a good man of the faith who seemed shrouded in a mystery concerning his loyalty to the English pirate named Bruce.

The mare she rode had been borrowed from secret friends of the friar at a small fishing village between the Isle of Pearls and Cartagena where Tobias had brought her two nights ago—surprisingly because of instructions from Captain Bruce Hawkins. After Bruce had "rescued" her from the governor's mansion on the Isle of Pearls and mocked her unwanted marriage to his enemy Don Nicklas Valentin, he had promised to bring her safely home to Barbados and her Puritan uncle, Barnabas Ashby. Barnabas, a goodly physician on the Ashby plantation, had allowed Devora to work with him in medicine. Then, quite suddenly, with no explanation, Bruce had landed her and Tobias on an isolated section of beach, ordering Tobias to bring her to the viceroy. Bruce had promised to find her again in Cartagena, but she entertained small hope of that ever happening. Any English pirate daring to scale the walls of Cartagena would soon be caught and turned over to the inquisitors. For his sake she hoped and prayed fervently that he would *not* come, despite her feelings for him, feelings that were now tinged with bitterness over the fact that he could so easily betray her to the viceroy on a whim.

Her own fate was as precarious as the pirate's. Marriage arrangements conceived by the will of her English parents, the Earl and Countess Radburn, awaited her at Cartagena. She was to wed the king of Spain's prized soldier, Don Nicklas Valentin, son of the powerful viceroy. The fate was sure, unless she managed to either escape by her own wit or Viceroy Maximus rejected her as an unworthy bride for his knighted son. There was also the possibility that the arrogant Nicklas himself might take one look at her and send her out of his sight forever. She prayed it might be so.

Devora galloped the mare along the beach through the densely growing palms, following hard on the trail of Friar Tobias Valentin, that enigmatic confidant of the equally enigmatic Bruce Anthony Hawkins. The friar was an ally of the English buccaneer, and he seemed now to be the primary source for her quest to learn the truth about Bruce. What bond or shared belief bound their loyalty to each other so confidently? Where had he met Bruce? When? But thus far Tobias had said little to satisfy her curiosity.

"Suffice it to say we share a common goal," he called over his wide shoulder, his silver hair whipping in the wind like the glossy mane of his stallion.

"What goal? To capture the annual treasure fleet? Foolhardy, indeed! Does he expect to wield the sword of Sir Francis Drake?"

"Ah, never speak boldly of such daring escapades, my child. If you cannot whisper them, say them not at all. A little bird may overhear and fly to the bedchamber of the viceroy. Nay, nay, Bruce is too clever to attempt so great a blunder as to pirate the galleons hauling Peruvian silver."

"Then what is his plan?" she spoke into the warm desolate wind, brushing a strand of hair from her eyes.

"Bruce's plans are none of my own."

"Yet you are loyal to him. Tell me, what binds you and him together?"

"We near Cartagena. Like a well-behaved woman of Spain, you must bind your tongue and retire placidly behind the alabaster latticed windows of the Valentin mansion and wait for further word from him."

"He must not come!"

"Ah, but he will."

"And if he does, then what, Friar? Will he attack the city? I've not forgotten the horrors when his pirates ransacked the Isle of Pearls."

"Nor has the Spanish governor. But you must remember it was not his crew that sacked the city, but that of Captains Jago Quinn and Jean le Testu."

"How can you befriend him when Don Nicklas is your nephew? Will you not also face trial before the Dominicans if they find out you were with him when the Isle was attacked?"

Tobias laughed unpleasantly. "The Dominicans have long wanted me to stand trial, but not for piracy or knowing Bruce Hawkins." He surged ahead, putting an end to her questioning.

Three days had passed since they departed from the *Revenge* and neared Cartagena, bastion of the Indies, a city whose walled strength could not be matched. They came along the coast almost as far as the Boca Chica Channel. She could see the sails of the native schooners as they plied over the surface of the water.

Tobias, noticing her interest, pointed. "You see that area over there? It was once a flowing river called the Boca Grande, meaning 'big mouth.' It is now filled up by sunken ships and mounds of rock, while those two forts you see in the distance have a great iron chain stretching between them, protecting the 'little mouth,' the Boca Chica Channel."

"Why did they fill it in?"

"As a defense against pirate raids. The channels once protected the Bay and town from invasion by pirates. Cartagena thought itself invulnerable to attack. Then one night Sir Francis Drake slipped through the Boca Grande. The city woke the next morning to find his ships in the Bay and his cannon pointed toward the walls. After that unpleasant surprise they decided to fill in the Grande."

She wondered if there wasn't a trace of irony in his voice since he was an ally of a bold adventurer little different than Drake. "Then the city was plundered?" she asked.

"Plundered, ah yes," he said, as though remembering something he had seen with his own eyes, though he could not have known Sir Francis Drake. "Drake made off with hordes of silver. Pirates of many faces have made devastating raids from Cartagena's earliest years."

From her upbringing on Barbados, Devora knew such men belonged to several distinct groups, from independent but legally commissioned privateers, to outright pirates. They formed what was known to the English, French, and Dutch colonies as the Brethren of the Coast, making their home at Tortuga and Port Royal.

"Of all the ports here on the Caribbean, Cartagena de Indias is a prize every buccaneer most longs to capture," said Tobias. "Founded in 1553, it is one of the earliest and most important Spanish cities. It has markets where merchants can trade with other Spanish colonies, and it is one of the chief treasure ports. The yearly mule train from the mines brings silver bars down the Gold Road from the mountains, and the Magdelena water highway brings in tropical produce and goods from all over the interior, all destined for the king of Spain."

Devora saw that the defenses of the city were reinforced with tremendous bastions and towered fortresses, so that Cartagena appeared to be a fortified medieval town.

"The narrow streets have witnessed more than enough bloodshed these many generations. If one listens," he said, musing, "the streets yet echo with sailors' brawls, battles with buccaneers and pirates, and the clink of armor-clad Spanish soldiers. Yes, Señorita Devora, the city has great wealth, much of it owned by the nobles. But even more is destined for the king of Spain. At certain times of the year, when the galleons arrive, treasure such as can hardly be counted awaits here, stored in the warehouses until the galleons leave for Spain. Such abundance naturally tempts every adventurer and pirate who looks upon those great walls with fire in their bones."

She thought of Bruce and was troubled. What did he have in mind?

Sir Francis Drake captured Cartagena in the previous century. Devora had heard the glowing tale from the English on Barbados of how he had demanded an immense ransom in gold and silver before he would leave.

"Now, no enemy ships can enter Cartagena Bay without first passing under the cannon of those military towers," he said.

Devora surveyed those towers bristling with heavy cannon. The gray stone walls of the fortress-city were wide enough for two coaches to ride abreast on top, Tobias told her. She saw other gates and towers looking down on the seaward entrance to the lime-green waters of Cartagena Bay, which was crowded with galleons and other vessels of varying size. The yellow and crimson flag of Spain flew with disdainful arrogance, as though daring any pirate to try to storm the city.

"Then how can Bruce even entertain the notion of coming here?" she asked incredulously.

Tobias' dark eyes flared with heat. "Bruce is no typical buccaneer. He has his ways. Ways that no other buccaneer will ever have."

She studied the side of his hard, brown face, many questions on her tongue, but Tobias seemed not to notice. He went on to point out what he called the Fortress Lazaro and a mighty hill that seemed to grow right out of the Caribbean, looking misty in the heat haze. The hill supported the great Cathedral called the La Popa, which looked down on Cartagena. There was what appeared to Devora to be a separate outcropping fortress pointing directly toward them that alerted her interest. "And that?"

"Ah . . . 'that,'" said Tobias soberly, "is the Tenaza. Inquisition trials are held there, my child, and executions. There are dungeons, to say the least." He pointed. "See that dome rising above the city walls? That is the Templo de Santa Domingo."

Devora's skin tightened on her scalp. Tobias looked at her gravely. "That is one of the reasons why Bruce has vengeance stirring in his heart. That is why my conscience bids me to help him." His eyes softened. He read her horror as she pondered the gray castlelike structure. "There will no harm befall you, my daughter. I will see to that. Neither I nor Bruce would have seen you come here if there were any chance of such a thing. Surely you know by now I do not support the way the Dominicans treat the Incas and those of the Reformed faith. Not," said he darkly, "that the Dominicans have much to do directly with the treatment of the Incas. That cruelty comes mainly from the conquistadors and their grandchildren, the nobles. It is something I would heartily put an end to if I could. It is one of the reasons why I have returned; I go to Lima to do what I can to stop the horrors going on in the silver mines. I expect Maximus to do something to help this time. I bring a letter from the archbishop of Madrid."

"You were in Spain recently?" she asked, curiously scanning him.

"I was there some months ago," came his easy reply. "To see my nephew Nicklas knighted by the king. Come," he said kindly, "the sun grows hot. Rest and victuals await you at the Valentin mansion."

Devora rode beside him toward the city gate, having much to ponder. She glanced at him, studying the rugged side of his creased face, seeing his gray hair moving in the wind. She liked Friar Tobias. What was his brother Maximus like? She had heard hard things about the dauntless viceroy of the Main. More importantly, what was his son Nicklas like? Was there anything of his Uncle Tobias in his blood, or was Nicklas like his unyielding and ruthless father, Maximus?

The sky was blue and clear, utterly cloudless, with a fresh breeze that brought a moment's relief from the heat. The day grew hotter still, the sun shining relentlessly above the pale-green waters of Cartagena Bay, where many galleons put in and out of the city.

"Cartagena is not as invulnerable as it deceives itself into thinking," Tobias said thoughtfully. "The city has been ravaged more than once by English and French pirates from Tortuga, but only when taken by surprise." His robust, dark eyes glinted, reflecting his troubled thoughts. "We now deem to think ourselves invulnerable to future attacks by those seadogs." He shook his silvery head. "The pride of a man takes false solace in solid stone walls. In cannon-mounted fortresses encircling a sheltered bay." He sighed, his wide chest heaving beneath the friar's brown cloth, where also, beside a silver cross, she saw a dagger. "But alas, how God oft surprises our false securities that proud men may learn how feeble they are apart from His grace."

"Pride does not belong to one race," she said. "The English cloak themselves in it also."

"Aye, we all have blood of the same color under our skin." He gestured toward the bay, and she followed his gaze to a great triple-decked galleon from Seville.

"In a few months the annual fleet of treasure galleons from Seville will arrive loaded down with goods to bring to the annual fair held at Portobello. They winter here at Cartagena, then the mule train arrives from the Peruvian mines near Lima, bringing silver bars. The cache of silver, emeralds from inland, and gold from Vera Cruz are stored in the galleons until they sail back to Seville. Don Nicklas will see that the flota of galleons sails safely to the king."

Devora turned her head and looked at him, wondering at the slight smile on his face. She couldn't tell whether he felt pride or amusement; yet there was something else too, a troubled look in his eyes. Was he worried about his nephew Nicklas because Bruce might have plans to try to attack those treasure galleons?

They entered the gate of the city at last and proceeded to ride down the stone street. Devora looked about her with keen interest but also with caution, her nerves taut. Though she could speak Spanish fluently and had accumulated much information on Spain, its culture was foreign to that of English Barbados. Would she ever feel at home? Certainly her mother had adopted Spain to her heart, but perhaps that was due more to having Spain meet her expectations for ease and comfort.

But as Devora rode with Tobias down the streets of the city toward the viceroy's mansion, she saw little of ease among the common people on the street. The crooked, narrow streets were alive with the coming and going of people. Africans and Indians and poor half-breeds made a living as street vendors, carrying their wares in large round baskets upon their heads, crying out their goods in musical chants. Slaves ran to and fro on errands for their masters, beggars whined from doorways, priests and monks trotted along, showering blessings on pious folk who hastened to kiss their hands or their robes. There were tiny, hole-in-the-wall shops of Indian weavers, gold and silver smiths, barbers, and sellers of hats, drugs, and commodities.

"The dons and other nobles from the great families of Spain are spoiled and rich, it is much to be lamented." Tobias told her that Maximus was one of the wealthiest, with mansions in all of the key cities along the Main, and the richest holdings in all Lima. Devora learned that Maximus possessed a luxurious hacienda there, and another also in Cuzco, once the royal city of the Incas.

"He owns mines as well," Tobias was saying, "in Cali, Muzo, and Zipaquira, as well as in the greatest silver mining town of all, La Plata. And horses, the best from Andulusia—such horses!" He gave a pat to the sweating black mane of his mount. "These creatures are not to be compared. Nicklas was raised on horseback. He can outride the best cowboy. A swordsman of excellence too. Favian is jealous, sadly so. It will mean much harm in days to come, I fear."

"Favian? Who is he?"

"Ah yes, I forget. You have not met his half-brother. But you will," he said, then changed the subject back to his brother Maximus. "The viceroy has indigo, sugar cane, bananas, and," he said fiercely, "slaves—over a thousand."

"You do not approve," she said. "Good. Neither do I."

"There is little that can be done about it."

Devora was too overwhelmed with the sights all about her to make any further response, but it was gratifying to know Tobias disapproved, even as Uncle Barnabas had disapproved of Spain's tyranny under the guise of "rights" to the New World granted by the pope.

Her gaze rapidly flitted over the populace—handsome Spanish nobles and vain hildagos, with fine features and ribbon mustaches, wearing rich apparel. Their sleeve cuffs and velvet vests were dripping with cream lace, and they wore either silver ornaments or gold. She saw soldiers in gaudy uniforms of yellow and black, or red and blue, and Africans wearing the winsome livery of their masters, the satin cloth molded over huge, muscled bodies. And there were the lowest of the low—naked or half-naked slaves of both sexes, boasting nothing more than chains and healed scars. There were half-breeds of various ethnic groups: Indians, Spaniards, and Africans. But all possessed an eternal soul in great and desperate need. She flushed when she saw painted women garbed in an Indian dress called a saya—some were cut too low. Obviously these were women of the street who belonged to no one or to any man who wanted them. She felt both pity and disgust at the same moment, then she rebuked herself. Could not such a fate also have been her own were it not for the grace of God? Suppose she had been the illegitimate baby of one of these women and left to survive on the squalid streets of Cartagena where the gutters ran deep with the city's filth? Just then a window above in one of the tall stone houses opened and a slave shouted a warning in Spanish and then emptied her washpot to splat below. Someone shouted up at her angrily and she banged the window shut; obviously, the pedestrian was no one important.

Devora maneuvered her mare through the crowded street just behind Tobias, who had warned her that the area they must pass through before coming to the Valentin mansion would be shocking.

"I have seen such things before," she told him. "I worked with my uncle among sick slaves on Barbados. I am not shocked easily, Tobias."

But she was wrong. Tobias held out his arm to halt her on the hot, crowded street where the sun beat on ancient stone. Ahead there was a ruckus. Squealing pedestrians ran for cover as sleek black and white stallions ridden by wealthy nobles came tearing down the cobbled stone. An old woman had been trampled down and a boy in a knee-length, tattered, gray-white shirt was crying and dancing around her as though his bare feet were on burning coals. "El Niño! El Niño!" he was bawling.

The lead capitan escorting the nobles shouted impatiently in Spanish, but when the boy either refused to leave the dying woman or could not move fast enough to suit the man's temper, he spurred his horse forward ahead of the coming caravan.

Devora turned a frozen face toward the soldier, who looked grim as he uncoiled his whip from the side of his Cordovan saddle. She saw the snake-like black whip rising against the hot, pale sky. Then it whistled downward, coiling itself halfway around the boy's thin, brown body. When the soldier drew it away, the tattered cloth of his long shirt had been cut through and the sight of blood froze Devora's heart. Her hands gripped the leather reins until marks were left on her palms. Both horror and anger seized her. He was only a child. Perhaps the old woman had been his grandmother. Such injustice! Such—

The boy's scream cut through her. The soldier brought the whip down a second time, the fierce, godless lash singing with cruel laughter through the suffocating stillness.

"Stop it!" came Devora's shout, and oblivious to all else, she was about to ride forward when Tobias caught her reins and stilled the prancing, nervous mare, the muscles bulging in his arm. Sweat stood out on his grave face streaked with dust and there was pity and anger in his eyes that sobered Devora. All at once the energy spilled from her as if from a broken vessel.

Tobias shouted in Spanish to the soldier, his voice barking and growling like the lead wolf in a pack ready to lunge.

Unexpectedly the soldier stopped, his whip falling powerless beside him. The next moment someone broke rank from the nobles and edged his white horse with silver decorations past the soldier, past the woman and boy lying on the dirty cobbles.

Devora stared at the noble astride his ornate saddle. He wore a haughty smirk on his lean, handsome Mediterranean face, showing clean, even white teeth beneath an arrogant mustache. He was young, garbed in a tight-fitting black suit with pristine white lace. A pale pink feather spiraled above his wide-brimmed hat and a gold ring was looped in his left earlobe.

"By Saint George! I see you have made it safely from the Isle of Pearls, Uncle Tobias. And that you bring the fair English blossom who is to wed my gallant brother."

Devora stared at him, feeling the sweat running down her throat. The young man spurred his horse closer until he stopped in front of them, the leather of his saddle and boots creaking. His dark, earthy eyes swerved over Devora, then back to confront Tobias.

"And I see you are as undisciplined and as haughty as ever Favian," said Tobias.

"My apologies, Uncle. Had I known you were ahead bringing Doña Ashby I would have stopped Don Sebastian from using the whip."

He said this, thought Devora, *not because the matter troubled him, but only to please Tobias.* She scanned the young man who must be a Valentin and heard Tobias saying—

"This is my younger nephew, Don Favian. Beware of him; he is a rogue with the oiled tongue of a snake."

"My Uncle. You assassinate me before I have been able to greet my future sister-in-law," and with a mocking air of grievance he removed his hat and bowed. "Do not listen to my uncle, Señorita Ashby. Tobias is but a wounded bull, and wishes to take out his temper on me now that Nicklas has escaped his tutorage to be knighted by our illustrious king." He smiled. "I am dedicated to your happiness. But it is a shame I did not first enthrall Countess Radburn with my charms before Nicklas did so. Then I would be blessed to have you coming to Cartagena to meet *me* instead."

Devora sat still, hearing a fly buzzing at her ear and meeting his bright gaze with a coolness that might have been born in the Andes. Favian Valentin's brow formed an arch as he looked at Tobias. Tobias snorted a laugh. "You will not woo this one away from Nicklas. She's too smart for that, and too good for the likes of you."

"Then she has not met Nicklas," said Favian with a smirk. "Pardon, Señorita, but if Tobias has not yet warned you, it is my brotherly duty to do so."

"Warn me?" came her brittle but leery question in a low, tired voice.

Favian smiled. "That while Tobias may favor Nicklas, as all suddenly seem to do in the Valentin family, he is a ruthless scoundrel who can hardly be said to be half the gallant that I am."

"Bah, out of our way, my boy Favian," said Tobias with humor. "If anyone smells of ruthlessness, it is you, despite your lace and perfume. Where is Maximus? Am I to believe by this entourage that he has ridden to meet Señorita Devora?"

"He has sent me. Whom else would he need?" He smiled and gestured ahead. "Come! The English bride-to-be of dear Nicklas must needs be escorted in style. Welcome to Cartagena, Doña Ashby," and he rode ahead of them to where the entourage of nobles formed a grand escort, which surrounded her and Tobias and led them down the cobbled street. The populace had drawn back in a crowded line and the din of voices in odd snatches of dialects and awe rippled through the heat waves. The smell of the sea, of ancient stone, of flowers, and garbage accosted her nostrils until her senses felt sickened.

"Viva Valentin!" came the shout.

Devora looked back at the old woman on the cobbles and the bleeding boy now sitting beside her. His barren-looking face would forever haunt her nights in Cartagena. The old woman and the boy were only two of thousands of the same, and a picture of many more in even worse situations. There seemed to be no answer to the dilemma. Devora lifted the two faces in prayer to the throne of God, and told herself her prayer was not in vain. The Lord was aware of them, just two more little brown sparrows among the flocks of the world. The burden of their need, too great for her to solve, was left at His merciful feet.

He knows when a sparrow falls. How much more, these?

❧ 2 ❧

Don Maximus Valentin

I will trust in the covert of Thy wings.
—*Psalm 61:4*

Don Favian rode ahead with the escort of nobles sent to bring Devora to the Valentin residency, while she and Tobias took refuge from the heat and dust to ride in comfort within the viceroy's gilded coach.

They had arrived at a far more ostentatious section of Cartagena, one she would not have guessed existed. She looked with awe out the window at the magnificent thick-walled stucco houses with great wooden street portals, studded with iron, which opened into courtyards surrounded by galleries. Through those galleries she could catch glimpses of women in the large stone courts built according to Old Spain. The courts, though walled, were open to the sky, and along the second-story galleries she could see many grand rooms belonging to the aristocrats. She could hear dogs barking and the loud cawing of a host of tropical birds. Every house seemingly possessed a garden where hundreds of tropical flowers bloomed and scented the air.

It also appeared every goodly Spanish house had exquisite balconies, which overhung the cobbled streets from under tiled roofs. She noticed that all the lower windows had iron grillwork, probably to keep thieves out—or was it to keep the women in? She saw little paned glass, and there were no chimneys in the houses.

17

Like Barbados, she suspected the weather was much too hot for indoor cooking. The Countess had told her that the houses all had large rooms, wondrously decorated with goods brought from Spain.

"Cooking is done outside by the meztiza slave, or they boil coffee and cocoa indoors over braziers made of silver, heated by charcoal. Just as it is done in Seville and Madrid." Her mother had gone on to tell her that life for the Spanish aristocrats was much the same in all the cities on the Main. Indolent and proud, letting time slip through their fingers in the manner inherited from Spain, they enlivened the days and nights with fiestas, with processions in honor of viceroys or saints. "There are always wondrous spectacles of all sorts enjoyed by the families of the dons as well as the peasants. There are gorgeous processions for the saints for Holy Week and Carnival. Fiestas of all sorts! Music, dancing, even fireworks. The whole population comes to the streets for enjoyment."

Devora suspected it was the festivals that her mother liked about having lived in Spain.

But what of me? she wondered uneasily. It was also true that Spanish life on the Main consisted of a world that would shut her away from all outside contacts.

What dangers might await me here? If it hadn't been for my mother—she halted—*mother? Hardly!* She struggled to arrest her thoughts from proceeding. Her fingers plucked at the limp, frayed feathers of the fan in her lap. All of her Puritan teaching arose to warn her that she must not nourish the seeds of bitterness. *Still,* she argued with herself, *if Catherina had cared about me—what mother would send her daughter to Cartagena to marry a ruthless don—*

No, she would not nurture these rebellious thoughts.

Her strong will wrestled with resentment, as though combating a weed that demanded to flourish in the hot, tropical earth of her garden-heart. *It was my heavenly Father,* she thought, *not Catherina that sent me here.*

Did she believe it? She must. If she did not believe God to be in control of her circumstances, with loving, good purpose in mind, she would doubt to the point of bitterness. There was more than her future at stake; there was God's holy character. He had promised in His Word that His plans were good, were for her welfare, and that His love remained ever true and faithful. Therefore, whatever befell her here must be sifted through the sovereignty of God in allowing it all to happen.

But am I that strong in my faith?

"We are almost at the Valentin house. You could use a sound rest, Señorita. I fear from your countenance that you could use a very long one."

The husky voice of Friar Tobias shook her awake. She managed a smile and made an appropriate comment that she was, indeed, exhausted.

They turned onto a paved carriageway where the coach driver stopped the white horses beneath the shade of a mammoth, lacy-leafed pepper tree. The nobles, too, stopped, resting in the lazy noon heat as Don Favian left them to ride ahead through a large gate to announce their arrival to the viceroy.

Devora's cautious gaze studied the magnificent mansion of stone and wood. Like many of the others she had just seen, it too boasted wrought iron decorative work and a double wood door strapped with leather and more iron. *No pirates or enemies would be breaking through that door*, she thought. The house looked just as she had expected it would, Mediterranean, overpowering, with the dark, rich flavor of Spanish intrigue.

"I have never seen such a great house before. The work is costly with intricate design."

"It is but one of several strategically located on the Main, or as the Spanish call it, the *terra firma.*"

"Was Don Nicklas raised here?"

His eyes flickered. "No, but in Lima, near the mines."

She wondered at the troubled tone. *Why the mines?* He too must have noticed his tone for he went on, "The most lavish mansion to behold is the Palace of the Viceroys in Lima," Tobias explained. "Lima is the official seat of the Viceroyalty of Peru. You will see it also, once Nicklas arrives and we journey there.

Unfortunately, the trip inland will bring us through difficult terrain."

She had heard of crossing the mosquito-infested Isthmus of Panama and the steamy jungle river. She would not even think of that now.

Tobias mentioned that the general term "Peru" was used to encompass far more than the mountainous region near the Andes. "Peru is a relative term in the mind of many Spaniards. From the time of the conquistadors it has grown to include the entire Main. The citizens of Cartagena and Portobello are considered Peruvians."

"Then your brother is viceroy of all the Main?" she asked with uncertainty, beginning to realize the strong will she was up against.

"There are viceroys in New Granada and Havana, but Maximus is greater in the extent of his authority. In Europe he would be looked upon as a monarch of a small kingdom."

She took note of the inflection in his voice that told her Tobias did not approve.

"Why is the seat of authority in Lima? Why not Cartagena or Portobello? Both cities have harbors, do they not? And look upon the Caribbean? Is the inland location at Lima a refuge from pirates?"

Tobias smiled. "It was no refuge from Sir Francis Drake. He sailed right into Callao Harbor at Lima and made off with a shipload of silver. No, Lima is the seat of the Viceroyalty because it was the region the early conquistadors first located the Inca silver and gold treasuries. Cuzco, near Lima, was the mighty capital of the Inca Empire. Eventually the greed of the conquerors brought fighting between them, and King Philip sent a viceroy to settle matters. He did, and the government was established there."

She saw his rough scowl. "You do not approve of the conquistadors. I know little of the Incas," she admitted. "Uncle Barnabas mentioned them, but the history surrounding their lost kingdom is vague."

"What happened then, and what happens now, is not a pretty history, my child. Greed and cruelty do not make for me good and honorable heros. But explanation is best left for when we arrive at Lima. Then, if you are interested, I will make it my duty to show you Cuzco, the ancient city of the Incas, and the mines."

She had no wish to travel inland, to cross the Amazon, but wondered if she might not end up in Lima anyway. She had little hope that Bruce would come to Cartagena.

"I will remember your offer," she told him.

She wondered when Nicklas would arrive, but since the thought did little to please her she preferred to push the unpleasantness to the back of her mind. *There is enough to worry about now*, she thought, frowning, looking about the strange new world she suddenly found herself in.

"You may say Don Maximus is one of the most powerful men in the New World." Tobias did not appear either proud of his younger brother, or pleased.

"You do not agree with his policies?"

He shrugged his heavy shoulders. "They are no better nor worse than the viceroys before him. Power, authority, ruthlessness, and pride—it is the way of the nobility of Spain. The common people and the Indians are considered tools to be used to promote their cause. It is the way of a world without the mercy of Christ in their hearts. Believe me, Señorita, it is the teachings of Jesus and His doings while on earth that uplifted the fallen, the forgotten, the weak, the poor, the women. Apart from the influence of Christianity, the bent of all powerful civilizations has been to glorify the mighty and to ravish and steal from those who cannot fight back." He looked at her, his brown eyes evenly meeting her gaze. "It is as Saint Paul wrote in the third chapter of Romans: 'Their feet are swift to shed blood, the way of peace have they not known.' Ah yes, one has but to look at history to see that mankind is sinful. And the conquistadors and Spain follow the well-worn path of the ancient Greeks, Romans, and Barbarians!"

Devora assented in silence. She was rather startled to think a friar in the Roman Church would be saying the same things that her Puritan Uncle Barnabas had taught her from childhood. She realized that Tobias could not be labeled. He grew in her esteem and she thanked God there was at least one man in her new world who was a friend and who represented the true Light which was Christ.

She opened her heart to him. "I am of the Reformed faith, Friar."

"Yes," was all he said.

She studied the side of his care-worn face, and unveiled a little more of the concerns beating in her heart. "I do not see how the Valentins will accept me as a fit bride for your nephew, Don Nicklas."

Tobias mused to himself, one finger beating against his broad chin. She continued. "I do not understand why Don Maximus would even consider the daughter of an English Countess worthy to marry Don Nicklas."

"There are reasons," he said. "As yet they are not revealed. In due time you will most likely understand."

She wondered. "Does Don Nicklas also share his reasons?"

He looked at her and his eyes twinkled. "No," he said. "I do not think so."

"Does he know about me? Does he understand I am here to meet him?"

"Yes, I think he does."

"How could he possibly agree to such a marriage?"

"You will meet him for yourself and I am sure he will give the matter grave consideration."

"What about Bruce, and your loyalty to him? How can you—"

"Now, my child, as I have said before, these matters cannot be discussed with openness now. You must not even breathe the name of Bruce Hawkins once we step from this coach."

Weary of getting nowhere, she swished her feather fan and was left to her own musings. Thus far, the pieces of the puzzle did not fit. She wondered if they ever would.

"You ask about how Maximus could even entertain the notion of your marriage to Nicklas. It is because your parents the Earl and Countess Radburn have remained loyal to the Roman Church during the upheaval of the Civil War. They have denounced Oliver

Cromwell and the movement begun by Martin Luther a century ago."

She looked at him worriedly. "Do you think of my uncle and me as heretics?"

"If I said no publicly, my child, I too would be branded one. I cannot risk it. Not in fear of my life, but because what I live to accomplish at the silver mines would immediately end with none to take my place."

"What is your work? Is it that you hope to ease the treatment of the Indians?"

"That, always, but more than that. It is to gain the support of those in authority to enforce the laws already issued to protect at least some of their rights as native Incas. It may surprise you to know it was never sanctioned by the king and queen of Spain to enslave the Indians and monopolize the assets of the land. It was to 'convert' the Indians to Christianity. But unfortunately, as it so often happens when it comes to the laws of royalty so far away in Seville, good laws get delayed enforcement. Some in the Church became puppets of the conquistadors. The door was left open for greed and brutality. Still, I choose with good conscience to remain in my official calling, to work within the Church rather than to break away and fight a battle against the House of Inquisition. I cannot hope to change them at this time when it would be deemed apostasy. So much time has elapsed, so much wickedness has been allowed by the grandees, who are all greedy dogs, that there seems little hope of undoing the ruin and rebuilding with justice." He sighed. "But it is my duty to try." He looked at her. "When I answer to Christ I will not be held responsible for the conquistadors, but I must answer for Tobias Valentin, for what *he* did with his life and time in an evil hour. May Christ have mercy."

Devora laid a hand on his arm. "I think, Friar Tobias, that you are indeed a good man. Barnabas, I am sure, would like you very much."

He laughed, a hearty robust laugh that also brought a smile to her face. "A Puritan—and a Friar. Perhaps, yes, perhaps so. And why not if we both stand firm on the only true foundation?" He sobered. "As for your Puritan belief, say nothing to Maximus until Nicklas has arrived. Should you need protection from the archbishop, he will seek to arrange the matter. I am beginning to be looked upon with certain suspicion."

"How so?" she asked nervously.

His bushy brows shot up. He reached inside his friar's robe and brought out a battered, leather-bound book. "Do you know what this is, Señorita?"

"A Bible?"

"No, though I have a copy—two, actually; a Geneva Bible and a King James translation—they were given to me as gifts."

"Gifts from whom?" she asked, for she wondered who had traveled widely enough to have recognized their value and risked bringing them to Cartagena.

"Gifts from a man of interesting travels," he said. He glanced out the coach window to see Don Favian just entering the house, an elegant and languid caballero.

Not Favian? she wondered incredulously, or had he been looking to make certain Favian was nowhere nearby to overhear? Not that she could believe a member of the family would turn against another of the same blood.

"This book, my child, is a *banned* book. All books are banned on the Main except those authorized by the Church officials." He patted it affectionately. "This book deals with matters of science. It rebukes the Church for accepting the Greek philosophy of Aristotle, and discusses its error in the unjust treatment of Galileo. Had we been more loyal to the Scriptures than to the works of Aristotle, we would not be in the controversy we now find ourselves." He replaced the book inside his robe. "I could be called up before the House of Inquisition to answer for my error in possessing a heretic book."

Her throat felt dry. "You must be careful," she urged in a whisper, yet within her bodice she too carried her own secret: a copy of the Geneva New Testament. As yet, she had told no one.

He reached over and patted her hand. "We will both be careful "

"What is Nicklas like?" she asked suddenly, boldly.

He smiled. "Nicklas is a difficult man to adequately explain in a short time. Look," he gestured, "we are about to enter the Valentin residence. Don Maximus will be waiting to meet you." He sobered. "You must forgive him in advance. He knows only the ways of arrogance and Spanish pride. There is not a humble sinew in his body. He is, sadly, a conquistador in spirit."

Devora, somewhat benumbed by all that was sweeping her away into a destiny that seemed out of control, found herself being escorted by Tobias into the square entry hall of the grandee. Don Favian had already gone ahead to announce her arrival to his father.

A grave Castillian courtesy smothered the atmosphere, yet seemed unreal. In her mind the house became the indomitable image of the powerful family itself: overpowering with an oppressive grandeur; stern, with a chilling desire to subdue all beneath its realm; squelching any rebellion as ruthlessly as one might squash an ant.

Her sweeping gaze took in the heavy wood beams of que-bracho wood; wood so dense that it sank in sea water and so hard that workers bemoaned that it blunted the edge of their axes. The furniture, which had been brought out from Spain, was carved from some other type of rich, dark wood, its thick leather upholstery dyed a becoming red.

Through the open arch inlaid with marble squares, Devora could see shimmering silver reflecting flickering light that spilled from wide candles which blazed in more silver sconces on the wall that illuminated yet more silver vessels.

Her gaze stopped abruptly.

Devora studied with internal qualms the austere wall hanging above the candles where a uniformed caballero returned her stare with stern and defiant superiority. The portrait could be none other than the Viceroy Maximus Valentin.

In that face she searched for what she anticipated would foreshadow the man she had come to meet, Don Nicklas. Yet she had no way to know from the portrait what Nicklas would be like. Nor did the tapestry portrait do justice to his father the viceroy, for at that moment the viceroy himself appeared and spoke. Devora turned toward the voice and saw the man who had considered with the Earl and Countess the possibility of a marriage arrangement between their daughter and his knighted son.

Don Maximus Valentin stood there like a statue in tribute to the conquistadors. The only thing missing was the steel armor and plumed helmet. His height and weight suggested a man of enormous strength, while his strong, granite features revealed an iron will. This was not a man growing soft with the mounting years, but a handsome soldier of rugged appearance. The sleeves of his black doublet were strained by his solid arms, revealing an outdoor activity, perhaps training horses or working cattle. A scar, long-ago healed, slashed his right cheek above a well-groomed, short, inky beard.

Devora wanted to shrink back as his bold, dark eyes beneath brows that nearly touched above a masculine nose studied her with cold scrutiny. At once she understood what Tobias must have meant when he informed her of the pride and arrogance of the Spanish nobility. For a moment she felt as if Don Maximus was like a breeder of well-blooded horses, considering a specimen which might be valuable enough to sire with his noble stallion.

Maximus came down the polished hardwood steps, continuing to study her. At that moment she believed she knew the demeaning shame of a Negress on the slave block surrounded by ruthless bidders. Everything within her that spoke of her dignity and value arose to stand against his evaluation. Unlike the African slave, however, she could not be whipped or backhanded for a spirit of insolence; she was a blooded daughter of an English countess. Still, she knew the Scriptures bade her in the spirit of Christ to render a blessing, a soft answer rather than evil for evil, knowing that in doing well she could entrust her soul to Him as unto a faithful Creator.

In obedience, she struggled to hold back a flippant attitude. *Lord, enable me to endure this until such a time as You deliver me*, she prayed, her anguish such that her cheeks burned.

Maximus, dressed in black leather breeches and calf-length boots, stopped before her and stood without a word. Was he forty-five, perhaps? A new question sprang to the forefront of her concerns; her gaze swerved from his to glance about. Where was his wife? Did he have a wife? The thought that Maximus, still a relatively young man, did not added to her alarm.

Maximus snatched up a gilt lantern from the table and turned to face her. "Turn yourself about," he ordered. "I wish to see what manner of woman has been brought to be offered to my son."

Devora's fingers clutched until the nails dug into her palms. Despite her best intentions the flesh was weak and her indignation surged. "I beg pardon, Your Excellency. I have not come as an offering to appease the gods, but as the daughter of an English earl and countess. In spite of what you may intend, I must also make a decision—whether or not I wish to have your son, Don Nicklas."

He stood as though insulted, then his eyes smoldered and for a dreadful moment she believed she had indeed overstepped her grounds and would know the force of his bejeweled, brown hand.

Tobias may have thought the same, for he moved at once to draw her away, his own demeanor swelling to confront his younger brother. The cross on his broad chest shone in the lantern light, as did his eyes, and it seemed that his esteemed religious position had a quieting effect on Maximus.

"Enough of this. Is this supposed to be the Valentin cordiality befitting the choice daughter of Countess Catherina?"

Maximus' lip twitched, but there was no humor in it. The heavy-lidded eyes swerved from Tobias to Devora. "Exactly so, when it comes to the countess. You forget I have met her in Madrid, and again in Seville—on several occasions."

There was something more in his suggestion than his words seemed to suggest. Devora flushed and glanced away. Her mother's character—or should she say lack of it?—left Devora with scarce opportunity to rush to her defense, which saddened and shamed her. She stood a little straighter and, though the steamy heat drained her, she drew her cloak about her.

Don Maximus noticed. He did not turn away until his son Favian entered the gilded room, keeping a certain distance as he loitered next to an intricately carved, black table set with all manner of elegantly designed Venetian glass bottles and goblets. He filled a glass and gave her a brief toast behind his father's back. Favian was tall and slim, and if Maximus was robust and rugged with a sense of ruthlessness to his physical presence, Favian was as graceful as a cat and carried languid airs of dangerous conceit. His fine bone structure gave him a boyish handsomeness. His dancing eyes watched her with unashamed appreciation. His long, dark wavy hair was oiled, and he wore a ring in his left earlobe, and more gold and emeralds than even the Countess owned. She had the misplaced thought that her mother would be envious. Favian still wore his sword, she noticed. Again, she sensed much danger in the Valentin house. The addition of Don Nicklas, she decided, would surely worsen matters.

Devora came alert, realizing Don Maximus was speaking boldly—

"Make no mistake, Tobias. It is my duty to know whether the Doña Devora Ashby from Barbados—an island of English intransigents on Spanish soil—" he added with irony, "is as interested in the glories of Spain as her mother, the Señora Countess Catherina Radburn."

Devora told herself if she showed intimidation now, there would be little hope for her in such a volatile household. "Am I to understand, Your Excellency," said Devora with muted tones, "that you are not as favorably inclined toward my introduction to your son, with view toward marriage, as the countess has sought to convince me? If such be the case, I would choose to trouble you no further and request to be immediately brought to a ship and returned to Barbados."

His dark eyes, equally muted like smothered coals that continue to burn, watched her relentlessly. "You do not come of your own will to the noble enterprise of marriage to a Valentin?"

Obviously he could not conceive of it. "In all truth, Don Maximus, and with no slight intended toward the Valentin name, I did not wish to come to Cartagena. I would be content, yea, more than content, to even now return to what you no doubt consider a meager life on Barbados. It is out of duty to the countess I am here; even so, I told myself many times on the voyage that I would appeal to both you and Don Nicklas when the time came and insist that I prefer to return to my own family. I wish to go back to my own English people. I am not pleased with this decision for a political marriage, nor am I the woman appropriate to become the betrothed—"

Maximus' mouth twisted and he waved his hand flashing with blue stones and heavy gold. "In reference to 'your own English people' Doña, you have nothing against the noble Spaniard do you?" His eyes sparkled maliciously.

She had not meant to imply that, but she believed he thought himself superior, and her sensitivity caused her to flush even more.

"I am waiting, Doña Ashby," he said too tenderly.

Friar Tobias cleared his throat, interrupting. "Maximus, cannot all this wait until we have refreshed ourselves, rested, and dined? It has been a long and arduous journey fraught with danger. The Señorita Devora must be very exhausted, as am I. A night's rest would go far to enliven all our minds before we come to important decisions about the future."

Devora glanced at him. Why did he not strengthen her cause to be sent away at once? It was not weariness that prompted Tobias, but an unwillingness to see her return to Barbados. Why? Surely he did not believe Bruce would actually dare come to this fortress of Spanish power and authority? Maximus might have dismissed her at once and the two of them might leave in the hopes of finding Bruce at Tortuga. Instead, Tobias seemed bent on urging Maximus to prolong her stay.

"There is no hurry," said Maximus to Devora. "As you will learn, Señorita, the Spanish are gravely polite and obliging hosts."

She was too distraught to smile her wry amusement, and it would have been impertinent to comment on the House of Inquisition. "I understand you can write," said Maximus unexpectedly, with a change of mood. He studied her, his eyes lingering on the thick waves of her honey-colored hair, now mussed.

"Yes," she admitted, but he showed no commendation, only disapproval.

"The mind of a woman of Spain is too fine a thing to be stained by worldly matters. They must be protected from reading things that are unfit, as well as their eyes from seeing what goes on in our streets. Nicklas will see to that."

Devora said nothing. She knew it was his way of letting her know she would not be free to ride and roam about as she pleased, as she had done on Barbados. She knew little of the lifestyle of the women of the dons, but her mother had told her that many lived lives as cloistered as the monks, and that they were like pampered doves in silver cages—but cages nonetheless.

"Do you not agree, Tobias?" demanded Maximus. "It is a sin for a woman to read and write, to enter the world of a caballero."

"Such ideas grow out of fashion, even in Spain, Maximus," said Tobias. "English women live more open lives than do our daughters. Knowing Nicklas, he will find the notion of freedom entertaining—"

Maximus chuckled. "Unfortunately, Nicklas is too daring." He looked at Devora and a surprising glance of appreciation swept over her, reminding her again that Maximus was not the fatherly don she had expected to deal with.

"You will keep your reading to your catechism and prayer book should you become the betrothed of Don Nicklas. Anything else, Doña Devora, is not likely to please the Dominicans of Cartagena."

She stood still, scarcely breathing, every fiber of her body wanting to revolt. Her nostrils flared slightly, and color again darkened her cheeks. She bowed her head subserviently, but said, "I do not think, Your Excellency, that your son will find an English woman a fit wife for his high and noble service to the king of Spain."

He gave a humorless laugh. "A ready tongue, I see."

"You must not find my father's manners troubling, Señorita," came Favian's languid tone as he lounged back against the table. "He wishes only to see Nicklas receive what is rightly due a son knighted by our Most Catholic Majesty."

There was sarcasm in his tone, perhaps loosened unwisely by the liquid in the goblet he drank. A spark of jealousy showed—or was it a long, slow burning fire between two siblings out to win the accolade of a father like Maximus? Evidently Nicklas had won, and Favian was not looking kindly upon his brother.

Maximus shot him a rebuking glance. "It is not my manners you need worry about, my son, nor what is due your brother Nicklas, who has a reputation as a strong caballero and a soldier. One you are too lazy to have yet matched," he said with a barb of cruelty.

Favian's mouth drooped beneath his groomed mustache. "For the sake of the Señorita who does not understand the trumpets—" and he turned toward Devora. "They sound forth the praise of Nicklas, our hero in the Valentin family, though at one time he was less than an illegitimate son of a jackal—"

"Silence!" Maximus' command cracked like a whip.

But Favian, relishing the red liquid in his goblet waved it in a salute. "To Nicklas. He who has done Spain a great service in ridding the Florida colony of a nest of heretics."

Devora froze, afraid of what Maximus might do. He walked toward Favian and for a moment she expected to hear the crack of his hand across his son's mouth, but Maximus only knocked the goblet from Favian's artistic, slim hand, causing it to clatter loudly as it rolled across the red tile floor, spilling its contents.

Tobias strode toward the two men and pushed them apart. He spoke in Castillian, but Devora had no difficulty in understanding his rebuke.

"You behave worse than two fighting cocks. What must the Señorita think of us? You, Maximus, rude. And you, Favian, killing your soul with drink. Where is the fear of God in both of you?"

Devora had turned away, grasping her wilted, pink feather fan. *Oh Bruce. Bruce. If only you would come. But how impossible.*

Was it her imagination, or had it been the mention of Florida that had brought the conflict to an outburst?

Favian, tight-lipped and pale, bowed precisely toward Devora. "You should know, Doña Devora, that our great father always gets what he wants in the end. We obey him without question." Turning on his polished boots, he marched out.

At the moment she could feel some pity for him, but his remark seemed an odd response to have made to her.

Tobias too looked displeased, but Maximus waved an impatient and unsympathetic hand. In that gesture she saw a man to be reckoned with.

Maximus walked up to her, unapologetic over the scene that had occurred, as though it was not uncommon.

"My mind is not yet made up concerning you, Señorita. It will take time. We will meet again, and talk. Nicklas too will have something to say of this when he arrives."

"It seems everyone, Your Excellency, has something to say about my fate. In the end, I desire to have the final word about the man I marry for life."

Maximus touched the scar on his cheek and his mouth twisted with wry humor, as though her remark afforded him amusement. She could guess as to what stringent lengths the dons usually kept their wives and daughters.

"We shall see," he said, and again his gaze took her in.

In those brief words and the response she saw in his eyes, she could hear in her mind the front door closing, and a heavy bolt just sliding into place.

Tobias watched thoughtfully, and as his gaze shifted to Maximus, a troubled look deepened the lines on his face.

"When does Don Nicklas arrive?"

"He is overdue," said Maximus, still looking at Devora. He caught the gold bell sash with one strong hand and pulled it, calling for the slave.

"You may go to your room now, Señorita Ashby. I will see you tonight at dinner." He bowed with a studious politeness that now contradicted his earlier rudeness, but whether he was aware of the change was not clear. She guessed that Maximus was a man of many contradictions that he himself had not come to reckon with.

A half-Indian girl entered wearing a saya. She bowed and beckoned Devora to follow.

Devora cast an uncertain glance toward Tobias, the one person she trusted. The sympathy in his eyes encouraged her to be strong. She would need to be, she thought, stronger than she had ever been before in her life.

She turned to Maximus and curtsied to him, showing herself the daughter of an earl, then followed the slave.

As Devora's slippers sounded on the cool tile of the house of the most powerful of the dons, she had never felt more isolated, or more in danger.

She was here, in this turbulent and volatile situation, because of Catherina's plans. Yes. Why not admit it to herself? It was her mother who had done this to her.

Devora's eyes smarted as she fought to hold her feelings inside. *Like the bones in a crypt. They must stay buried,* she told herself. *If you ever open that door. . .*

"I choose to trust Him," she whispered below the rustle of her skirts and the click of her slippers, as dark shadows from heavy furniture towered above her. Her hands clenched.

A great mahogany carved door opened and the half-caste stepped aside, bowing. "Your chamber, Señorita. May you find happiness here."

Devora stood in the archway, and with concealed anguish looked about at the grand room flashing with silver, crimson, and more red tile. Handsomely wrought grill work barred her windows, screening her from the voices and horse hoofs in the cobbled street. She walked through the chamber into a square garden floored with more tile, where caged birds hung and hundreds of tropical flowers perfumed the air. She stood there, a prisoner amid luxury and dense sweetness, in the home of the most powerful man on the Main.

If only Bruce— She turned at the rustle of skirts and saw a woman near her own age and extraordinarily pretty. Her mouth was faintly smiling, but her expressive chocolate-colored eyes in a face of soft ivory offered no welcome. Her blue-black hair was elaborately coiffed, bespeaking nobility, as did her lace gown, which was wondrously embroidered.

Devora was already aquainted with Doña Sybella Ferdinand. They had met briefly the night Bruce came to rescue Doctor Kitt Bonnor from the dungeon on the Isle of Pearls. There was no reason to think Sybella's dislike for her had changed since that chance meeting. If anything, Sybella would resent her presence in the Valentin home even more. Sybella's warning came to mind: "It is well you do not wish to marry Nicklas, because I hope to do everything in my power to prevent it from happening."

Devora surveyed the one person in the Valentin family that could become her greatest enemy, exceeding even that of Sybella's uncle, the viceroy. There was, however, a small chance to change all that. Since Sybella would have plans of her own concerning the arrival of Don Nicklas, she would not want Devora to stay should the viceroy decide in favor of the introduction. Should she enlist Sybella's help in returning to Barbados? Or would she risk Bruce's safety by telling Sybella she was in love with a buccaneer whom the viceroy wanted above all men to trap and hang?

❧ 3 ❧

The Buccaneer!

Receive My instruction, and not silver.
—Proverbs 8:10

Bruce Anthony, known as Don Nicklas Valentin among his cousins, the nobles of Spain, moved nearer the window inside the governor's council chamber overlooking Lake Nicaragua. The evening light reflected off the leaves of a small grove of ceiba trees, turning them into quavering silver. He listened gravely to the report on the sacking of the Isle of Pearls—as was expected of him. From his outward appearance, none would guess that he had led that buccaneering raid. Bruce was once again the son of the ruthless Viceroy Don Maximus Valentin, a powerful man in the West Indies, one to be feared by the lesser nobles.

Bruce's strong, tanned fingers tapped his leather bandolier loaded with gunpowder and two silver-butted pistols. He wore a stylish, wide-brimmed hat over hair as dark as ebony. His exquisite uniform was that of Seville's most elegant caballeros, with a wide black collar embroidered with silver and studded with pearls. A Latin cross encrusted with emeralds was deliberately displayed on a thick silver chain around his neck. It was worn for the benefit of two stoic-faced Dominicans, who sat across the council chamber on a hard bench. They were officials from the House of Inquisition located in Cartagena.

Beneath the handsome, tight-fitting black jacket he wore chain mesh from Toledo, home of the finest steel in the world and the origin of his own sword, which was sheathed in Cordovan leather graced with more silver.

Capitan Sanchez stood before the long, dark-wood table in the Hall of the Audiencia, his black eyes smarting as he faced the governor of Granada, His Excellency Davido del Campo. This grim offical looked worried as he slouched in his chair with its gilded arms and crimson upholstery. Beside him sat the commander of the Granada Provincial Cavalry. Present also was Archbishop Harro Andres, the newly appointed head of the Church seat at Lima, and unfortunate enough to be delayed in Granada. He had come from a previous position in Santo Domingo and was a friend of the viceroy. Bruce wondered that he watched him so thoughtfully, and because he did, Bruce did not trust him. The governor of Santo Domingo was friendly with the Chevalier Fontenay on Tortuga, a French governor who would talk for a bribe.

Capitan Sanchez slapped his strong, scarred hand down on the table for emphasis as he faced the officals.

"I tell you, caballeros, we cannot be too careful here on Granada. This English Hawkins is born of the same breed of jackal as Henry Morgan."

Nicklas turned his head and looked at him, his gray-green eyes flickering at the scathing denunciation; yet he felt confident he would not be unmasked. Although Sanchez had been at the Isle of Pearls, he had not seen him, nor had anyone else on Granada any idea who he was. What's more, no one would dare suggest so preposterous an identity even if they had reason to suspect. The powerful viceroy insisted that his son receive all the fawning and bowing he cultivated for himself. And, if that were not reason enough to treat Nicklas like a prince, he was now knighted by the king of Spain for what were considered great military victories against the enemies of the Spanish throne. Nicklas had arrived with sufficient credentials to more than safeguard his plans to detour the treasure fleet to Protestant Holland.

As he heard Hawkins being consigned to everlasting punishments, he congratulated himself on his victory at the Isle of Pearls. He had not only rescued members of his buccaneering crew from the inquisitors, but had "captured" the memorable and delectable Lady Devora Ashby. If his Uncle Tobias were able to accomplish his task she would be waiting for him at the Valentin mansion in Cartagena when he arrived. He tapped his chin and listened with mock gravity to the report about the recent pirate attack.

"This scurvy dog made off with the English prisoners that were held for your esteemed father, Viceroy Valentin," Sanchez said to Nicklas, who obligingly lifted a brow at this despicable news, "and also a cache of pearls worth many thousands of ducats."

The governor groaned and mopped his brow as though he was to be blamed for the loss.

Nicklas had grown accustomed to hearing himself labeled a devil in service to the heretics while continuing his ruse as the military grandee of the king. As he accepted the Cuban cigar offered him by the governor's servingman and whiffed the fragrant tobacco, he thought not of the wealthy planters but of the slaves and "heretics" who had been sent to the fields to cultivate the plants. He bit off the end and lit it from a glowing tallow candle, and as the smoke went up as evil incense, he relished again his plans to rob the mule train bringing silver bars over the famous Gold Road to the treasure fleet at Portobello. How Maximus would pale if he ever learned of his plans. He smiled to himself.

He looked out the window at the harbor. He wouldn't need to wait until he brought the mules over the Isthmus of Panama to strike another blow upon Spain. There would be a surprise attack here on Granada. He studied the wide harbor, seeing dozens of tartanes, xebecs, barcas, and canoes. The spars and rigging of several small ships lying at anchor, under the protection of a dangerous-looking battery, would be going up in flames tonight. *Had Morgan made the rendezvous with Kitt?* If so, they should arrive in small boats in the still, breathless night when Granada least expected an attack by buccaneers.

Sanchez had suggested to the governor that Granada must be alert. Did he know anything? Had he seen Morgan's ships in the Caribbean heading for the San Juan River? No. . . impossible. . . Morgan was too careful, and Kitt equally so. Yet anything could go wrong—and usually did. This was one reason Nicklas liked to work alone. But this time he needed others, just as he would need them to attack the mule train.

Kitt, a skilled physician as well as swordsman, had been an important prisoner, for the Spanish governor was to have turned him over to the viceroy. Maximus would be furious when told of his escape. He had expected to learn more about Bruce Hawkins from Kitt; for already, certain rumors were circulating that Bruce had another identity. Rumors also whispered that even his supposedly cut-throat crew of malcontents from the buccaneering stronghold of Tortuga were not that at all, but mainly soldiers from Holland.

He turned away from the window and scanned the stiff countenances of those present while Sanchez reported the exaggerated atrocities that Hawkins and his English pirates had perpetrated while on the Isle of Pearls. The crimes were such that Nicklas was hard put not to show his disdain. So he had robbed a convent, had he? And boiled a friar in oil! He might tell the good Friar Tobias about that, seeing as how Tobias was forever lecturing him that his notorious ways would end in doom. He would remind Tobias next time to be careful with his lectures lest he also boil *him* in oil as he had the fictitious friar on the Isle of Pearls.

Nicklas would have challenged Sanchez regarding his lunacy in reporting the events did he not fear giving even a hint of sympathy toward the pirates, no matter how absurd the reports against them were. Then, there were the waxen-faced Dominicans, who sat so ghostly still on the bench, two men who were known to show no mercy in a trial for condemned heretics. Nicklas had no desire to draw their attention, for they had too fine a memory to suit him.

He had left Kitt in charge of his ship *Revenge* in Monkey Bay, near the River of Nicaragua, where it was left hidden at anchor among the inlets and cays while Kitt and the crew boarded canoes and headed for the golden-brown San Juan River. There, according to plans laid at Tortuga, they would make the arduous journey by river and land to join Henry Morgan's expedition to the inland town of Granada. The strategy was all part of Bruce's carefully laid plans to collect soldiers from Granada, under the auspices of the king of Spain, that would actually be buccaneers posing as captured heretic prisoners.

After leaving Kitt in charge of the *Revenge* and its crew, Bruce had journeyed alone with a friendly Indian guide through the jungle on a secret route to Santa Marta. He had arrived at Granada three days later on a barca longa rowed by Spanish soldiers who knew him only as Don Nicklas Valentin. At Granada he was expected to take command of a hundred of Governor del Campo's garrison soldiers and proceed with them by ship to Cartagena. He had just met Granada's governor as Captain Sanchez arrived from the Isle of Pearls to report with anguish on the attack by that "Diablo Hawkins." Little did Sanchez realize he had come just in time for an attack upon Granada by the infamous Henry Morgan.

Bruce had been to Granada twice before, and the white-walled town was familiar to him. He had sketched the map that a member of his crew had delivered to Morgan while anchored off the Mosquito Coast. Granada was built at the tip of a short peninsula which jutted out into the comely Lake Nicaragua, where graceful palm trees and clouds of blue and yellow tropical birds made their nests. From inside the governor's official house he commanded a wide view of the vast jewel-blue lake with the cones of majestic volcanoes in the distance. He could see silver wisps from those volcanoes ascending like incense, sometimes flinging ruby hues against the pale, clear sky, warning of the presence of molten lava that might suddenly break forth with ruin and devastation.

But it was not the volcanoes that held his gaze. Beyond the twin towers of a large cathedral and seven other churches, and past the female convent and some monasteries, the military battery dominated the waterfront. His mind placed all eighteen carriage guns. The regular garrison numbered four companies of infantry and two troops of cavalry, and it was from these that he was to select soldiers to bring to the mines, but he had no intention of doing so. Kitt and the crew from the *Revenge* would be joining Morgan's men, which included some fifty native Indians— a mixture of fiery-eyed Oyates and Maribos. The Indians hated the Spaniards for the near extermination of their tribes and others in the region. They waited with anticipation to join in on the attack upon Granada. Even with his own crew from the *Revenge*, Bruce knew that Morgan was outnumbered by at least five to one. Unless the attack succeeded with the help of the element of surprise, his plans of bringing buccaneers to Lima, under masquerade as heretic prisoners to double the silver production, would fail. If that should happen much of what he had worked and planned for over the past six years could evaporate.

Bruce's gaze came alert. A tall and powerfully built Englishman with thick, brown hair and a reputation as a fighter emerged from the direction of the harbor, escorted by two armed Spaniards. His fine black camlin was stained, his shirt was torn, and his right arm was bandaged. It was Earl Robert Radburn, Devora's stepfather, who had been on the Isle of Pearls at the governor's hacienda when Bruce had fought to free his crew from the dungeon. He had left Robert and governor Toledo blindfolded and incarcerated. Just what would bring him here to Granada? Since Robert had been made Ambassador to Spain by King Charles, the soldiers must be escorting him to speak to the governor. About what?

Disturbed, Bruce watched as the ambassador strode forward. As he drew near the house his sword and pistol were evident. He'd been right; Earl Radburn was no prisoner, but he appeared to be on a private mission—no doubt one of personal benefit.

Robert was a skilled politician. He was also ruthless. Bruce knew of a sword duel in Madrid in which Robert had killed a man. He was now willing to use Devora for gain. He suspected Robert's interest in an Inca silver mine in Patosi, high in the Andes. The Radburn family was reported to also own ships that sailed to the African coast of Guinea for slaves which were sold to British-, French-, and Dutch-owned islands, but Bruce had learned that the shipping line was about to be claimed by debtors in London. Bruce did not like the man, though since meeting Devora he was inclined to cooperate with him and Countess Radburn, who were selfishly using her to arrange their introduction at Cartagena.

Bruce turned toward the door as it opened and Robert entered, his presence causing a stir as both the governor and his officials stood to their feet while showing surprise and dismay over his condition.

"Ambassador!"

Robert waved aside their concerns, showing he was a soldier at heart and a formidable opponent where Bruce was concerned. "I bring evil tidings which I know you will abhor, even as I do."

"If it is about Hawkins and the Isle of Pearls," said del Campo wearily, "Capitan Sanchez has already informed us of the treachery. Please," he gestured to a crimson chair. "Be seated. Cumana," he shouted to his servingman, "wine for the English ambassador." He looked at Robert with a frown. "Your injury, sir, it came from fighting the devilish pirates?"

"Unfortunately. And the one prisoner we wanted above all was taken from us."

"You speak of Kitt Bonnor, yes. Viceroy Maximus will be much displeased at the news that he has escaped." He gave Capitan Sanchez a sharp look as though he were to blame.

"Is it any wonder? Bonnor could identify Captain Hawkins."

"Yes, yes, dreadful news. You of course know the son of Maximus, Don Nicklas?" and he waved a jeweled hand toward Bruce.

Robert's head turned sharply toward Bruce, and he stared at him, for Bruce had not stepped forward when Robert first entered the room. Robert's countenance reflected his relief in seeing him, for he apparently suspected nothing toward the man whom he knew only as an avowed champion for Spain.

"Don Nicklas, this is indeed most fortunate finding you here. I feared you had set sail with your soldiers."

He came forward, his sharp, blue eyes taking him in somewhat too cautiously to suit Bruce, who smiled as though pleased to see his future father-in-law. "And what brings you to Granada, if I may ask?" said Robert.

He thought Robert already knew but played along. "Service to His Majesty in Seville, Señor Robert. I am under commission from the king to relieve Governor del Campo of half his troops. A tragedy, don't you think? Especially after the Isle of Pearls. One never knows when these pirates I've heard so much about may attack farther inland."

"I quite agree, Nicklas, but I am sure that under your command these soldiers will be put to good use."

"I assure you so."

"If I may disagree, Señors, the fact is that pirates are not known to attack inland, but to keep to the Caribbean shores, as the Isle of Pearls and Hispanolia sadly attest."

"Let us hope you are right," said Bruce easily, and turned back to Earl Radburn. "And your visit? From your injury it appears you have had a run-in with Hawkins and his vile crew."

Robert's handsome face hardened. "That is why I am here. I was informed you would be coming to gather troops for the silver mines near Lima. Waiting until you arrived at Cartagena might be too late."

"Too late?" asked Bruce with feigned curiosity.

Robert's blue eyes turned cold. "The mad dog has abducted my daughter Devora aboard his pirate vessel! Your uncle, Friar Tobias, was also taken with her. By now, anything may have happened. But I feel it is our duty to hunt down the *Revenge* and sink her."

"Your daughter," groaned Governor del Campo.

Bruce knew Devora was safe with Tobias. By now they should have arrived in Cartagena to be escorted to the Valentin mansion, but he could not reveal to Robert that he knew as much.

"You are sure of this news?" he asked soberly.

"Quite certain, Nicklas. A tragedy you had not been on the Isle of Pearls with a command of soldiers. We may have thwarted his attack and captured Hawkins himself. While I would be the last man to make anything yet of your meeting my daughter, you can understand my anger, and deep and abiding concerns. Lady Devora Ashby is aboard this madman's ship among it's blood-thirsty crew. I'll not rest until I have rescued her. I'm here to gain your support. Can you swear your ship and men will hunt down this scoundrel?"

"You have my full support, Lord Robert. I also will not rest until I have seen her safely delivered to Cartagena."

Robert looked satisfied, but a flash of anger turned his eyes hard. "If anything has befallen her I will personally see Hawkins delivered to the tormentors for this barbaric act."

"There may be no need of that. I assure you, I will find Lady Devora again if it is my last accomplishment on the Main or the Caribbean. I'll search out the *Revenge* until I find it and put matters of Hawkins and his crew to a just end."

"The only justice will be to see them all hanging on a gibbet in Cartagena," said Robert. "I'll not rest until it is so, nor will the viceroy. Your father is adamant about finding Hawkins at any cost."

"Rest assured, Ambassador, I intend to set sail as soon as His Excellency turns over to me the soldiers required to increase the silver production." He removed the silken letter from his jacket and handed it with fanfare to del Campo, who was bemoaning the fact that they would be left with less defense.

"But as you say, Excellency, the pirates are not known to attack so far inland. We all know their haunts to be in the cays and inlets on the coast," assured Bruce.

"Yes, yes, but do not forget the attack on Cartagena by a French pirate, and later by El Dragon," he said of Sir Francis Drake.

"But that was a hundred years ago, Excellency. I must have those soldiers. The silver mine production for the treasure galleons is the king's priority."

"Yes, yes, you are right, Don Nicklas. You shall have them at once." He turned to Capitan Sanchez, mopping his brow as he did so. "Have the commodore order a hundred soldiers to the beach. They will proceed under Don Nicklas' orders to Cartagena."

"Yes, Excellency!"

When Captan Sanchez had hurried out, Bruce noticed Robert watching him.

"It might be wiser for you to return to Cartagena to where I assume the countess is waiting for your return with anxiety," Bruce told him. "I wouldn't want to risk so important a man as yourself in the service of your king with this diabolical Hawkins."

"We will do far better to find him by pooling our resources."

Bruce was afraid he might say so and was prepared with a frown. "True, Ambassador, but separate we shall cover more territory. Being English you naturally have access to areas I dare not sail."

But he hadn't expected Robert's wholehearted support for such an idea, thinking he might limit himself to the areas around the Isle of Pearls.

"You are quite right, Nicklas. Being English I can land even in Tortuga. Perchance the notorious captain of the *Revenge* may have set his sail for that pirates' den. And if he has Devora, the sooner I go there to appeal to Chevalier Fontenay, the better off she will be."

Fontenay. Bruce did not look lightly on Robert nosing about Tortuga asking questions about Hawkins.

"It may be that a reward offered to the Chevalier could loosen his sly tongue," said Robert.

"This Frenchman," said Bruce, with a casual wave of his hand. "You know him?"

"Good fortune has seen to it that a friendship with the Chevalier was cultivated in Paris some years ago before either of us had come to the Indies at the request of our separate governments."

Bruce concealed his concerns. It was one thing to get rid of the ambassador, since Bruce had no intention of mounting a pseudo-search for a phantom named Hawkins. But Robert's words were troubling. A reward would indeed loosen the tongue of the greedy French governor, and anyone else on Tortuga who did not look with favor on Hawkins. Not that anyone there knew him to be Nicklas Valentin, happily not even the Chevalier knew that dangerous bit of information. It might not be too serious if Robert were to ask of Hawkins' appearance.

"Someone comes," said an aide to Governor del Campo.

Bruce glanced out the window and saw a *petacha,* a small boat, arrive with a messenger. The messenger threw the lines to a slave, then came running toward the governor's residence. Governor del Campo, already alert to danger, went at once to the door to meet him.

"What news?"

"Pirates, Excellency!"

❧ 4 ❧

The Sack of Granada!

*The refining pot is for silver . . . but the LORD
trieth the hearts.*

—Proverbs 17:3

The cathedral bells were clamoring and the alarming cry, *Los Inglesia!*, "the English!" rang throughout Granada's streets where, in a panic, Spaniards bolted for the hills to hide themselves and priests rushed about trying to protect their treasures from the oncoming onslaught of the pirates.

"Forward, you bully lads!" Henry Morgan's commanding voice bellowed above the tolling bells. "Did I not say Granada was yours for the picking?"

A wild and weird yelping filled the air above the crack of pistol shot, of steel clanging against steel. Sharpened pikes were leveled at the bellies of those unwise but courageous enough to stand and contest the onslaught.

Bruce heard the noise of shattering glass, of musket butts smashing door panels, of racing feet, and of voices shrieking in alarm. He fought back a quell of uncertainty that confronted his conscience. He had given orders to his own crew about maintaining restrained behavior as soldiers in time of war, but he knew the hundred men under Morgan had no such inclination, nor did he think Morgan was troubled by the need to enforce such laws.

Inside the governor's council chamber there was a moment of frozen alarm that such a fate could be theirs, then Capitan Sanchez reached for his pistol and ran toward the door. Bruce turned to the governor. He was escaping through a side door with his aides. Only the archbishop remained, his defiant mahogany features glistening, fingering a large gold and ruby-studded cross around his neck. He was a figure in black against a yellow-and-crimson tapestry embroidered with the arms of Castile and Aragon. He began to advance toward the front door, grabbing a crucifix from the two grave-faced Dominicans in brown and black tunics who had rallied to his side and implored him to escape with the governor.

Bruce moved swiftly to intercept his path toward the door before the archbishop could confront the onslaught. He took hold of his arm, but the religious man shot him a rebuke, looking down at his grip.

Bruce ignored his intimidation. "Step outside, Lord Bishop, and the first buccaneer to see you will rejoice to thrust you through the belly with a pike."

The bishop gripped the crucifix, his nostrils flaring with indignation. "Devils. They would not dare," and he pulled his arm free and strode toward the door. Capitan Sanchez had paused in the court as several pirates rushed into the area. Sanchez raised his pistol, but was fired upon. As he fell to the cobbles he held to his pistol, which emitted a small cloud of smoke and one of Morgan's men went down.

One of the Dominicans rushed past the archbishop to defend him and defiantly raised a crucifix toward the advancing pirates, only to receive a vicious pike-thrust that doubled him up and then tumbled him down the council chamber steps.

The archbishop stood dazed and stared as though such a thing could not possibly happen. Bruce grabbed his arm again and pulled him back into the chamber, slamming the door.

"Robert!" he shouted, but the English ambassador had already disappeared. Bruce led the archbishop to the side door and turned to the sweating Dominican. "Take him and depart at once. If you stay a moment longer you'll be responsible for your own deaths. Go!" He slammed the door behind them, and with sword in one hand and pistol in the other waited, watching Morgan's crew use a machete to break down the door.

Hoarse shouts of delight filled the air as the door cracked, splintered, and gave way beneath the final barrage of their muscled shoulders. They stormed through, a sweating pack of buccaneers. Their eyes blazed, and their faces and bulging arms were bloodied and scratched from the long and torturous trek through the sweltering, mosquito-infested jungle. A pirate named Hogan stepped forward with a leveled pistol, then stared as his grimace broke into a friendly, sweaty grin.

"Why its 'awkins 'isself! Stab me wormy innards!" He gestured his snarled red head toward him, glancing over his shoulder toward the others behind him, gaping, "An' dressed like a duke."

"Silence your tongue, Hogan," gritted Bruce.

"Aye, I fergit—"

"Forget again and you'll have no tongue left to babble with. Where's Morgan?"

"Comin' behind last I seen 'im." He wiped his mouth on the back of his hand and looked toward the door behind Bruce. "Be any silver idols 'hind that door, Capt'n—yer Excellency, I means?"

"If there is, you won't be knowing. I need those men alive in Cartagena, now take yourselves elsewhere. There's more than enough booty in Granada to sink a ship."

With a cry they turned to leave as Henry Morgan burst past them, using the flat of his cutlass to give a whack to Hogan. "Out of here, you vermin. I told you to get on to the Avenida del Alcalde."

Spurred by threats they knew were not idle, they turned and scattered.

In the moment of silence that surrounded Bruce and Morgan, shouts could be heard on the streets as the pirates fought their way down predetermined streets. According to Bruce's earlier orders, the crew of the *Revenge* under Kitt surged with cutlass and drawn pistol toward the battery and its row of formidable cannons, while two other groups under Morgan turned toward the Plaza Parada in the center of town.

Morgan, a robust figure in sweat-stained jerkins, stood with feet apart and a grin on his leathery face. His heavy, dark brows outlined shrewd, granite eyes while a wide mustache thick and slightly curling at the tips adorned a full, grinning mouth. His hair was groomed, cut straight across at chin length and paged smoothly under. He wore a brimmed leather hat which he removed, and laughed silently, his broad shoulders shaking.

"Well, we'll have Granada yet, thanks to your map—*Nicklas.*" And he laughed again. Bruce smiled and walked toward him.

"You're a fiend, Henry, you know that."

Morgan's bushy brows shot up with mock pain. "Ah, do not say so, my friend. My conscience is wounded."

"I'm sure that once your vessel is laden down with Granada's booty you'll find solace enough. But right now we have much to talk about, and we must not be seen here."

"Yes, and that scoundrel, Ambassador Radburn, was seen sniffing about the Caribbean after you left the Isle of Pearls. Be careful, it wouldn't take much to set him on your trail."

"Little chance of that," said Bruce with confidence as they skirted the governor's council chamber and made their way out of view toward the harbor where some smaller boats were in flames.

Morgan hissed under his breath. "The insubordinate rats. As if we couldn't have carted away those canoes for our own good use. But your crew, Bruce, are a fine lot o' men. I'd exchange the whole ratty passel of the others for 'em. Discipline, that's what's important. A hearty asset to the Brotherhood."

"I have chosen them carefully. And I'll need everyone of them, along with men of your own if you can spare them."

"Ah, that I could, but I've another mind after victory here at Granada. I'll be going to Port Royal to see Modyford," he said of the English governor. "I've the devil to pay since we've no commissions for this attack on the Main. But once his eyes sees this handsome purchase taken here, I'm thinking he'll have an answer to appease King Charlie."

"He has managed to keep your mentor, Commodore Mings, from the gallows in spite of his many raids. But I need to ask if you'll be interested in the silver mule train?"

Morgan sighed wistfully. "I'm always interested in so sweet an idea, Hawkins, but you know my rich plans for a raid on Portobello. But first I must attempt to convince Modyford it's useful for the safety of Jamaica."

"That could be made much easier. Panama's Spanish governor, Don Juan de Guzman, is adamant about an all out attack against Jamaica. If Governor Modyford learned what the Spanish governor was thinking, he could start feeling quite insecure. If you then arrived in Jamaica to ask for a commission, you would be well received."

"But if I told Modyford about de Guzman's plans he may not be convinced." He sighed.

Bruce smiled. "Governor Modyford can be informed through Kitt Bonnor. Just as soon as I can arrange to send him with an official paper from Cartagena."

Morgan chuckled. "You're twice the spy as that rat-toothed Ambassador Radburn. Let him squeal to the Spanish viceroy; a strike by my forces could be easily explained to King Charles, should it become necessary . . ."

"About the mule train—I've made careful plans about some of the buccaneers that I'm going to take to Lima who will substitute for soldiers from the garrison. This will enable me to have loyal men in the right places when the time comes."

"How can you? They will be instantly recognized by the Spanish."

"I'm going to tell them only part of the truth—that all the Spanish soldiers fled or were taken in the raid. And that after I got here I found it necessary to take a bunch of heretics that can work the silver mines."

Morgan stroked his mustache and looked toward the cannons. The barracks had been taken and hundreds of soldiers rounded up. "Aye, too bad. They'll make better slaves than soldiers for Seville.

I've got to hand it to you, Bruce. It's a wily scheme and fraught with danger. Will it work?"

"It has to. And all except for Kitt, who is known, the buccaneers can play their parts well as heretic prisoners."

Morgan laughed. "So you'll herd your English prisoners to the silver mines and crack the whip o'r their shamed heads. May luck be with you, lad. If not, the viceroy will skin you alive at the House of Inquisition, son or not."

Bruce believed Morgan to be right. If the scheme failed, he would be a wounded fox with a hundred of the hunt's hounds closing in on him.

"You'll meet with Kitt?" asked Morgan.

"Just as soon as you have these Spaniards rounded up and out of the way. If I'm seen meeting with you or Kitt like this it could bring my end."

"Not a one will escape—least wise, none that will be going to Cartagena or Lima." Morgan laughed and handed him a looted cigar. "To the mule train," he said. "To your success at Lima!"

Bruce smiled. "And to Portobello, friend Morgan—with only one request." And his gray-green eyes showed deep-seated conscience. "Leave the nuns alone—and the children. One can fight to destroy the power of Seville without cruelty to the innocent. If you cannot promise to control your men, I will not send Kitt to Jamaica."

Morgan's bristling brows shot up. "Am I a dog that I would do such a thing? Ah, you've heard false tales from that sly-tongued Esquemeling. He despises and lies about me. Nae once have I ever turned my brutes on the women and children. And Portobello will be no different."

Bruce heard cries from the town being looted and plundered and the unmistakable sound of women's voices contradicted Morgan; but the buccaneer king didn't appear to notice and was lighting his cigar. As the Cuban tobacco smoke spiraled up against the fiery sky like that from a miniature volcano, Morgan laughed, his teeth gleaming, and slapped Bruce on the shoulder. "Kitt's waiting. Ye best slip away while you can."

Bruce settled his fancy hat and turning, tipped the brim toward Morgan. Bruce did not see Robert Radburn coming out of the jungle thicket, more bruised and bloodied than before.

Earl Robert Radburn, English Ambassador to Seville, stepped back into the jungle shadows of deep purple and black contemplating the scene between Don Nicklas and the pirate Henry Morgan. Though many yards away, and unable to hear what had been said, he told himself that the rapport between them had not been imagined. Nicklas had appeared friendly with the rascally pirate from Jamaica.

Robert carefully considered. Could he have imagined that friendly slap on the shoulder from Morgan? Or that relaxed, smiling expression from the son of the viceroy?

If he managed to live through this night he had quite a tale to bring before Maximus at Cartagena. He would need proof, however.

Robert's pale blue eyes watered in the smoke coming from burning buildings as the trade wind blew it into his smudged face. His white shirt was blackened with ash and damp with sweat, and his light brown hair looked almost ebony.

Wait. He must think . . . let it all sink in deeply . . . to understand. . . .

His thoughts took an abrupt turn. Perhaps there was much to be gained. Perhaps there was more to this than he realized. His voyage to Tortuga to speak with the Chevalier was now more important than ever, as was further investigation among the infamous Brotherhood. He might also stop briefly at Barbados and even Port Royal before he returned to Maximus. There might be more than flames beneath the acrid smoke. Nicklas may need to do a great deal of explaining to convince the Spanish officials and inquisition judges that his tete-a-tete with Harry Morgan was harmless—especially while Granada was being raided.

Robert watched the buccaneers hauling their looted chests of treasure toward the boats in Lake Nicaragua. It may be that he had found the key to enriching his future in this chance meeting.

Bruce saw the mound of booty sparkling in the sunlight on the red-and-black pavement between the ornate pillars of the *cabildo,* the town hall. It could have been dangerous walking about in the garb of a Spanish don, but the roaming buccaneers knew him and word had been carefully circulated even before Bruce left the *Revenge* that he would be "masquerading" as a caballero. He encountered sly grins from some of Morgan's pirates as he located Captain Kitt Bonnor. Kitt, a physician and an enigma, bristling with pistols and a cutlass, carried a satchel of surgical instruments and bottles of varied mendicants, most of them gathered on his voyages with the help of friendships with native Indians. He was bending over a body. Kitt looked up at Bruce and wore no exultant expression over the carnage about him. He was now all physician rather than a buccaneer.

"We lost Mac," he stated sharply of McWhorten, the man at his feet.

Bruce held in the stab of anguish. "Mac," as they called him, had been the self-appointed chaplain aboard the *Revenge,* an old Scot they had both been fond of, a staunch Presbyterian who liked to quote from the Scriptures. At the same time Mac was trying to minister to the uncooperative crew he had also been the ship's cook.

"He warned us not to come," said Kitt, looking at the lifeless face. "'Have nothing to do with a callous pirate like Morgan', he said. And now—it's Mac who was killed, while the rest of us live." He placed a bloodied, torn shirt across the man's face.

It struck Bruce that despite the onslaught there was no horror on Mac's features, only a calm, peaceful countenance.

Bruce clamped his jaw. "I haven't heard of a war yet that could be fought without the innocent suffering. Only the gullible could think that it could be done in Granada."

Kitt looked up at him, a wry twist on his mouth. "What are you so defensive about? You didn't lift a cutlass against anybody. What happened to Granada rests in the hands of the sea dogs, most of them loyal to Morgan."

The irony wasn't lost on Bruce. He hadn't led the fighting, but he had drawn the map and laid out plans for attack. He pushed aside the sting and told himself he owed no mercy to the sons of the inquisitors.

"How many others?" he asked bluntly, feeling irritation toward Kitt.

"None. The others will recover quickly," he said of the men lying about, "all except for the boy Toby, over here. His hand's been blown to pieces."

As Kitt turned back to the lifeless form of the Scot, Bruce abruptly walked away. He went over to where his bo'sun lay and, removing his hat, stooped beside him, his handsome face sober. He gave a friendly ruffle to the boy's soiled hair.

The sixteen-year-old managed a too-brave grin. "It were nothing, Capt'n. Wouldn't amissed it—worth it seein' ye looking a fancy don."

Bruce stared down at the bleary-eyed boy, and if anything, his troubled spirits grew. "I told you to stay aboard the *Revenge* and keep my cabin ready for my return."

"It's ready, Capt'n. Top-shape. An' the sooner you move back into it the happier we'll all be. Ol' Kitt is worse to get along with than even yo—" he stopped as if realizing who he was addressing, and flushed, but Bruce smiled.

"What's the pay for a crewman who loses his hand in service for the cause of Holland?" he asked, knowing very well, but wanting to assure the lad it was for a higher cause they had fought.

Toby grinned, then winced as Kitt came up and poured a reddish liquid over the mangled hand and began to bandage it.

"Pay is a hefty purchase, Capt'n," said Toby.

"You're worth more than that. We'll see you rest at Barbados until we put you aboard the ship for Holland."

Toby's eyes lightened. "The ship bringing silver to the army? Can't wait for that, Capt'n," he whispered, trying to swallow.

"This may ease the pain a little, lad," said Kitt, giving the boy a drink from a wineskin. "We'll get you back aboard the *Revenge* before morning."

"Aye, Kitt, don't worry 'bout me. . . ."

The boy's eyelids trembled and shut sleepily. Bruce stood, holding back a frown. A moment later Kitt joined him and they walked aside from the others on the square to be alone. Bruce leaned against a pillar and looked off toward the jagged peaks which crested the Huapi Mountains.

Kitt sank down wearily onto the stone pavement and drank from the skin. Bruce looked at him. He was a rugged young man with mid-length, golden brown hair, a wide mustache, and a short, pointed beard. His keen, dark eyes were alert, his complexion tanned from the Caribbean sun. There was the same look to his countenance as Bruce's; a boldness and confidence that belonged to soldiers who had little doubt but that their cause was just, however painful or sacrificial to themselves or others, and who had little sympathy for the enemy.

"I saw Radburn," warned Kitt. "What was he doing here?"

"Seeking help to blow the *Revenge* out of the Caribbean," said Bruce wryly. "He thinks Devora and Tobias were hauled aboard as unwilling prisoners. He's on his way to Tortuga, where he thinks I may have brought them."

"Tortuga?" Kitt repeated meaningfully.

"Yes, you see the difficulty that could emerge if our double-tongued Chevalier de Fontenay decides to invite him to supper," he said of the French governor of the island. "Knowing Radburn, he'll offer an enticing sum for whatever information Fontenay has on me."

"Which is little, since you've been away in Spain these last two years. Fontenay can hardly blame my infamous reputation on you."

Kitt Bonnor had been captain of the *Revenge* since Bruce had yielded his ship to his friend while away on service for the king of Spain. But that was not what he worried about.

"Radburn is no fool. He may decide to ask what others thus far have overlooked," said Bruce dryly. "A careful description of Bruce Hawkins."

Kitt smiled. "And neither am I a fool, my good Nicklas. Every raid I've made these years was done as you suggested—using French periwigs: white, gold, and red." He laughed. "It became rather amusing."

"Very well done, but don't forget Fontenay saw me recently before my attack on the Isle of Pearls."

"True, and if he talks to Radburn I'll be the first to admit you're in trouble, since Friar Tobias was also with you. And what do you think Radburn might make of all that?" he asked gravely.

The answer was obvious and Bruce mused, weighing the circumstances and his options.

"I could always seek a duel with him on Tortuga before he has a chance to dine with Fontenay," said Kitt.

Bruce's black lashes slitted. "No. He's better than you. Best leave him to me if it comes to that."

Kitt's brows lifted with wounded pride. "I'll have you know I'm the best shot on the *Revenge*—including you."

"Debatable, but Radburn would choose the sword. Besides," he smiled easily, "he's Lady Ashby's stepfather. And I can't very well give orders to my chief lieutenant to end his life, now can I? No, the best thing I can do is proceed with our plans for the mule train as speedily as possible, and—" he stopped and looked at Kitt.

"And?" asked Kitt warily.

"You must delay him at Tortuga so that he will not be able to arrive before we rendezvous at the Isle of Pines, where the mule train is scheduled to cross the mountain. I'll be in touch with you there no matter how things go for me at Lima."

"Delay him? How?"

"That will be left to your clever machinations," said Bruce good-naturedly. Then he added evenly: "Just don't silence him permanently. I've no intention of needing to tell my bride-to-be that I'm responsible for the death of her father."

Kitt pulled at his mustache. "Then you truly plan on marrying Lady Ashby in Lima?"

Bruce's gray-green eyes flecked with warmth. "No. At Cartagena." And he straightened and swept up his hat. "I dare not stay any longer. It wouldn't take much for some lone Spaniard to notice I'm moving freely among the heretic crews. And speaking of heretics—where are my 'prisoners' that I'm bringing with me to Cartagena for the mines?"

Kitt stood and gestured across the square. "I've fifty of the 'worst dogs' fit for the inquisitors."

The "dogs", of course, were the hand-picked buccaneers that Bruce and Kitt had settled on before they had attacked Granada. The men all knew what to expect and the grave danger to befall them, including Bruce, if the ruse were discovered once they entered the stronghold of the Spanish Main, Cartagena, and then the silver mines in Peru near Lima.

"Let's hope their captain is not a fool," said Bruce of himself. He would arrive at Cartagena with a shipload of heretics. Could he convince both Maximus and the officials? He believed he could, else he wouldn't risk it. But with the risk came the danger of discovery. Knowing that Cartagena held the House of Inquisition, it was with somber mood that he went to meet them.

The buccaneers all waited, their mood solemn but determined. Bruce had been careful to choose men who were not only good with the cutlass and pistol, and were known to have discipline and an avowed hatred for Seville, but who also wanted to return to the Netherlands to join in the struggle against Spain.

Bruce faced them in the ruby twilight as silence and expectation fell over them.

"You know what we're about. I can't promise our plans will go smoothly. You are taking risks which threaten you with the dungeons of Cartagena, or even Cadiz. But I fare no better, though the son of Maximus Valentin. But if I did not believe our quest possible, I would be the first to tell you. We will lay in wait for the mule train crossing the Isthmus, even as Drake did, only ours will be a richer victory for Holland. And it will be your sacrifice that will make it possible. At the appointed time Kitt will be waiting for us with the *Revenge* at the Isle of Pines—the same location Drake held up when he attacked the mule train. However, unlike even Drake, we will load those silver bars aboard the *Revenge* beneath the very noses of the Spaniards."

He looked at them and their sweating faces were silent. "You have one last chance to return with Kitt to Tortuga or sail with Henry Morgan. But I warn you, having once sworn your allegiance to this cause, there'll be no turning back upon pain of death. All our lives will depend on each one of us."

One by one the buccaneers stepped forward, and while some hesitated, wiping their sweating faces on the backs of arms and looking with anguish on their cutlasses and pistols, all tossed them down in one mound, disarming themselves.

"We'd trust you anywheres, Bruce," said Kirby. "Our lives are in your hands. We're doing it for Holland."

"And to teach the Spanish devils a lesson they'll not like forget," said another.

"We can make it," said a third.

"Mines or no mines," added Kirby, "we'll keep the shining dream before our eyes and in our hearts. Lead us on to Cartagena, Don Nicklas. And may Christ have mercy on us all."

"And give us victory," said Bruce. He was deeply moved as the last of the weapons were surrendered and fifty valiant men willing to face the Peruvian mines surrendered themselves to him.

Yes, thought Bruce. *May Christ indeed have mercy on them, and myself.* The weight of their destiny suddenly pressed more on his conscience than all the bars of silver he could confiscate for the Netherlands army.

The Other Woman

Jealousy is cruel as the grave...
— *Song of Solomon 8:6*

"Ah, so you have come," came the indolent voice of Doña Sybella, as Devora was shown to her chamber inside the Valentin house at Cartagena. "I have ordered Cuzita to fill a tub so you can bathe. Afterward she will serve us refreshment on the patio. We must talk, Señorita."

Cuzita the meztiza slave girl was lifting the last large, pottery vessel, pouring water into a small, round tub lined with salmon-colored tiles sitting behind a screen of alabaster.

Sybella walked out onto the enclosed square garden of potted plants upon a tile floor. Devora looked after her, wondering how Sybella had arrived from the Isle of Pearls so swiftly. Did this mean her mother and Earl Robert had also come? Strange that Don Maximus had not mentioned her parents' arrival. Somehow Sybella must have traveled ahead of them, which was curious.

Cuzita waited near the screened tub with a large yellow towel. Devora, though cautious and curious about what Sybella would say, was even more anxious to wash away the dust and perspiration accumulated on the long journey.

Cuzita poured an ointment into the water that turned its color yellow but offered a pleasant aromatic yet stringent fragrance.

"What is it?" asked Devora, running her fingers through the warm liquid.

"Will make bites no itch," she said with broken Spanish.

"Thank you," said Devora with a smile.

Cuzita looked at her with surprise, as though her smile and gratitude shocked her. She bowed and left her in privacy. A meztiza, or cholo, was the name given by the Spanish to people of mixed blood. There were several other groups as well: mulattos, who were African and Spanish, and zambos, who were Indian and African. These slaves usually belonged to the wealthy families and served inside the houses. The Portuguese slave traders came yearly with ships from Africa selling Negro slaves to work the large fields of the dons growing sugar and tobacco, while Indians and prisoners, especially heretics, were sent to the silver mines.

A beautiful gown of white lace was laid out for her on the bed when Devora came out of her bath. After dressing her damp hair and pinning it up, she walked out onto the warm, dusky patio, feeling refreshed and believing that there might be some hope left in her life after all.

A myriad of tropical flowers perfumed the humid air as she joined Doña Sybella at the table with its newly laid Spanish lace covering. Utensils of silver glimmered, and a centerpiece of lush fruits adorned a platter. Parakeets and cockatiels scolded and squawked inside gilded cages swinging from gold chains near the high brick wall.

Cuzita moved as silently as a shadow between some orange and lemon trees to a silver brazier from which she returned, carrying two steaming bowls. As Devora held a bowl between her hands, she sipped the strong rich cocoa and watched Sybella, who appeared to be lost in reverie.

Cacao trees with their big colorful pods, along with bananas, grew wild in the lush lowlands and were profitable products. Many families depended on morning cups of thick, rich chocolate, and for the poor as well as the wealthy, bananas were served with every meal. They were baked, boiled, fried, or fermented into a beverage.

Sybella's henna-colored lips turned upward. "I heard Maximus and Favian shouting. It does not dawn on their insensitive minds that their behavior must offend a genteel Englishwoman. Tobias should have warned you what to expect in coming here."

"He did warn me," said Devora, wondering about Sybella's motives. She seemed almost friendly. "He knows I've been brought here against my wishes. That I would return to Barbados as soon as possible if permitted."

"I warned you too, at the Isle of Pearls, that the wishes of Maximus are not dismissed as one does of lesser lords. Believe me, he will not let you go home."

If she permitted herself to despair easily, Sybella's confidence would have weakened Devora's resolve. "I hope to prove you wrong. I would leave tonight if there was a ship willing to take me, and if I had heard from my parents. I assume the earl and countess safely left the Isle of Pearls even as you did."

"I have not heard. I was rescued by Favian, but that is another matter," and she waved her hand impatiently. "You do not understand Maximus. This marriage alliance is his wish, not Don Nicklas'."

Is that true? Or is blaming it on Maximus her way of dealing with her jealousy?

"I see you do not believe me," and Sybella's countenance took on an accusatory look.

"I've no way to know if you speak the truth, but I have no cause not to believe you or any wish to do so. There is no reason why we cannot be friends at least. As I've told you, I do not wish to marry your cousin. Tell me, what is it Don Maximus hopes to attain by his son's union with the Radburns?"

Sybella looked thoughtful. "I have not concluded yet. I have my suspicions, but that is not enough. If I say anything now he will find out I told you. He can make matters uncomfortable for me."

She could feel sympathy for Sybella. "The viceroy appears to be an uncomfortable man to be around."

Sybella's brow arched. "You do not yet know the worst, but lest I sound ungrateful, Maximus is indeed a great man. Stern and ruthless, yes, but he is an efficient viceroy. It was Maximus who established firm government in the large Viceroyalty of Peru. I was a small girl when he arrived in great state. My parents had died and I remember how his fleet arrived from Seville, bringing noble families and poor hildagos seeking their fortunes in the new world. Maximus brought prestige and glory to the Viceroyalty: tapestries, carved furniture. . . . Heavy silver came in ships to adorn the Valentin house, which is now the Palace of the Viceroys." Her eyes darkened. "Yet he is not satisfied."

"The eye is not satisfied with seeing, nor the ear with hearing," commented Devora. "What is it he wants?"

"Like his son Nicklas I do not think he knows— that either of them truly knows. Both see a giant to slay that no one else understands or can see. Neither man is at peace. And there is great animosity between them, though they will no longer admit it. Those on the outside do not see, but it is there."

Devora leaned toward her. "Nicklas and Maximus are at odds?"

Sybella looked as if she had said too much. She reached for the platter of sliced fruit, taking a juicy, white piece of chirimoya. "That should not concern you."

"You are right. If you would help me escape—"

Sybella's wearied smile interrupted. "No bird escapes the gilded cage—nor do the women of Spain. Most dare not think it possible. Women have been sent to the isolation of the monasteries in Spain for reading banned books. We are not to care whether we can read and scrawl our name. We must not voice our dissent, lest the bishops reprimand us. Yes, we are in lovely prisons in these fine houses. And you will be too, if you stay. For me, if I were with Nicklas I would not care. For you, an Englishwoman—" she shrugged— "you will find it unendurable, even as your mother, the Countess. Who knows? You may get by with more, even as I have."

I am in prison! thought Devora, looking about her as though seeing for the first time the details of the decorative artistry of iron grillwork that barred her windows.

"We live behind the shuttered windows of our houses in seclusion among our slaves, with no education and little to occupy us, while the dons have many illegitimate sons and daughters by every negress and meztiza they wish. Unmarried girls never leave home except to go to Mass or to witness the religious festivals—you will see many of those. But we are wiser than they think. We are not entirely shut away from contact with other men," Sybella smiled secretively, a gleam coming to her eyes. "We cloistered girls are experts in the language of glances and flowers."

"Flowers?"

"Oh you will see. When a señorita drops a rose at Mass, or from her coach when she is taken out for an airing, it is a signal for the caballero to follow her. He learns where she lives and comes at night to loiter beneath her lattice balcony. After several nights she may open the window and whisper down to him. And love is born."

"I see that you cannot escape your culture, but why do you come to me now? What is it you want me to do?"

"I did not say *I* could not escape. I have already broken their rules and have paid in kind. My deceased husband, Ferdinand, was a hero. My wealth and his name give me ways not offered to lesser señoras. Often I do as I wish and few can stop me. When the bishop comes, I give a worthy gift to the cathedral. Maximus, however, *is* one who can stop me. And so is Nicklas," she said, her voice mellowing. She looked at Devora.

Devora watched her curiously, finding her words both interesting and tragic. Whatever befell her here in the world of Spain, she would make certain her fate did not cause her to end up like Sybella, or the other Spanish señoras and señoritas.

"I came to Cartagena of my own will," said Sybella. "I might have stayed in Seville and married a gallant. It was not forced on me to come here. Eventually I will go to Lima, where I grew up. Maximus wants me to come, to marry his son Favian. If the Radburn name pleases him in a union with Don Nicklas, then the Ferdinand name means much also in an alignment with Favian.

Between us," she said flatly, "we will bring wealth, influence, and ties to Spain and England."

"But you do not love Don Favian," said Devora quietly.

"I have no intention of marrying Favian," she retorted. "It was a way to get here, to be around Nicklas. He will arrive soon to oversee the king's wishes at the silver mines near Lima and Cuzco."

As yet Devora knew little of what Don Nicklas would do at the mines. It appeared that even Sybella did not know the details.

"What is it you want of me? If you will not help me escape, there is naught I can do except to meet your cousin, since it is forced upon me."

"I did not say there was *nothing* I could do to thwart Maximus. And again, I say it is Maximus, and not Nicklas, who wishes this arrangement between the two of you."

"One would hardly guess it from the way he spoke to me earlier," said Devora, remembering his obnoxious ways.

"Maximus is not always easily understood. There are ways to thwart him," she said in a lower voice. "I am no fool. I learned much from the Ferdinands in Seville. I am no longer only a bird in a cage. I have wings now. I can fly places others do not know about, learn things in secret—as I did in Seville I bring back bits of information."

Devora tried to understand where her veiled suggestions were leading, but apart from suspecting her to be involved in intrigue while in Spain, Sybella was talking in riddles, perhaps as much to herself as she was trying to inform Devora. Sybella looked at Devora quickly, as if she had said too much.

"If it is true what you say, that you do not want Nicklas, then it may be I can do something. It will depend on help from Nicklas. He is not like Favian. Nicklas does not give in to his father as readily."

This bit of insight caused Devora to move uneasily. What was Nicklas like? What if he decided he *did* want a marriage with her? No. She would do all she could to see that he did not. He would not like a stilted Englishwoman. . . .

"If you refuse him, he will tell Maximus to return you to Barbados," said Sybella.

"And you think Maximus will listen?" scoffed Devora. "You said he wishes this political marriage for some purpose of his own."

"He does. Yet it will be of great consequence if Nicklas refuses to have you. Maximus will not like it, but he will have to accept it."

For the first time Devora believed that her freedom could come not in fighting Maximus, but in refusing the stalwart will of the ruthless Don Nicklas, who came at the wish of the king of Spain. And if he was in love with Sybella as she said, then he would not settle for an arrangement by Maximus.

"Then if that is why you've come, to ask me to refuse your cousin when he arrives, you have my assurance I shall do so," said Devora with conviction.

Sybella watched her for a long moment. She had finished her cocoa and set down the silver bowl. "There is another man perhaps?"

Devora hesitated, then admitted quietly, "I was to marry another on Barbados. Yet the countess disapproved. And—there is someone I have recently met. Someone I did not mean to love, but alas, it is so. Only I do not think I will ever see him again."

Sybella looked at her curiously but did not press for more information. They were interrupted by the shadow of the meztiza, who bowed.

"Yes, Cuzita? What is it?" asked Sybella.

Cuzita held a gilded box in both hands and knelt before Devora. "His Excellency sends."

Devora's response was one of wary concern. Sybella too looked surprised. She stood slowly, a new thoughtfulness on her face. She looked unexpectedly pleased, as though an occurrence she had never considered now offered her more room to maneuver her plans. Devora's unease grew when she saw her pleasure.

"I think I know what the gift is. Open it, Doña Devora."

"I am not sure—"

"He will be offended if you do not."

A moment later Devora held amethysts on her palm, at first confused, then troubled. It was Sybella who broke the awkward silence gripping Devora's heart.

"Maximus means for you to wear them tonight."

"I—I couldn't," she breathed. "I couldn't accept such a gift from a man I've only met—"

Sybella considered thoughtfully. "If I were you, Doña Devora, I would not offend him by refusing. He is rich and powerful. Maximus likes to give gifts. Such a gift from him does not mean what it would from the man you say you love. But it may be he has more in mind for the daughter of the countess than marriage to his son Nicklas."

Devora's head jerked up. "It is a mistake. I will send it back to him at once."

"I would not be hasty. Maximus may hold the key to your freedom. Treat him well, and who knows? We may both get what we want in the end."

Devora stood, holding back dismay and indignation. "I do not use the interest of men, whether they are powerful or otherwise, as something to manipulate to gain my satisfaction."

Sybella smiled, her eyes bright and mocking. "Then it is true that you are no daughter of the countess."

"Nor do I take kindly to remarks about my mother!"

"I meant no harm. A word of advice, Doña Devora, from one woman to another. I believe you, but you will yet need to convince Maximus. If I were in your place, I would not be hasty to alienate him, but I can see you do not think as I."

Sybella left her in the patio still holding the amethysts.

From the look on Devora's face, one could easily suspect she had received a box containing a poisonous viper from the jungles of Peru rather than amethysts from Muzo or Chiquinquira. She would discuss matters with Friar Tobias, she decided, but she had barely replaced the jewels into the box when Cuzita returned.

"Don Maximus say come down. Señor Alfonso is gone and Don Maximus now wait for you."

"Alfonso?" her concerns grew. "Who is he, do you know?"

"He is the general of all Cartagena soldiers. He brings big news to Don Maximus," answered Sybella.

What news might he bring? She turned expectantly toward Cartagena Bay, looking past the patio wall and the tops of distant palm trees. For a moment she thought she might see English ships in the bay flying the *joli rouge,* one of those ships being the *Revenge.* A rosy hue coming from the setting sun turned the peaceful bay into one great rippling ruby encircled with ornate Spanish galleons. She was not disappointed, since she hardly entertained the serious notion that Bruce could, or would, risk his life along with the lives of his crew on an impossible feat. Surrounded as she was, it seemed unrealistic to entertain the hope of ever seeing Bruce again. Bruce was not impetuous. He was daring, but not rash. What had convinced him that he *could* come to a place like Cartagena?

His plans and promises made little sense to her, and as reality set in with time she loosened her grip on his promise to come for her. Had it all been the result of a moment on a Caribbean beach beneath the palm trees? It would seem so. Yet his embrace, his kiss, had spoken of more. When he promised, he had meant it.

There is no time to think of him now, she thought sadly. Why had Don Maximus called for her so unexpectedly? What information did General Alfonso bring?

❧ 6 ❧

The Grandee!

Treasures of wickedness profit nothing...
—Proverbs 10:2

"Enter, Señorita," came the robust voice of Don Maximus Valentin.

Devora entered the sitting-room, shutting the door, and uncertain what to expect, she glanced about. He stood on the open balcony with black iron grillwork where the Caribbean trade wind swayed the palm trees and swept across the room. The damp tropics greeted her as boldly as did Don Maximus. Her white lace dress, loaned from Doña Sybella, stirred restlessly.

He was not looking at her but toward the Caribbean Sea. "Come here, Señorita. I wish to show you something."

She was curious, and cautious. Her muffled steps crossed the crimson carpet, keeping time with her heart.

"There," he stated, gesturing a tawny hand toward the Bay of Cartagena. "Look."

Uncertain, she followed his direction, more curious of the man than the sea. Her eyes feasted on the deep blue surface, darkening as the crimson-orbed sun appeared to dip into the horizon, casting golden beams soothingly along its surface. "It is a lovely sight, Your Excellency," she stated simply, giving him a side glance. Was this the reason for his call?

He gave a brief, hearty laugh. "The ships, Señorita," he corrected, "I point your attention to the warships. You see them?" The pride in his voice beamed. He handed her a brass telescope and again gestured. "Ah, the sight sends the heart pounding. I wanted you, an Englishwoman, to behold it. Appreciate what England refuses to submit to, the power and glory of Spain's might upon the oceans of the world."

The man was mad with pride and she had half a notion to thrust the telescope back at him and refuse. "It was Spain, Your Excellency, who was forced to bow her knee to the greatest Power of all when the winds of God blew King Philip's armada away from the shores of England and scattered her ships like broken toys upon the rocks."

His head jerked in her direction as though she had slapped him. For a moment she didn't know what to expect and was sorry for her quick retort. His dark eyes flashed, then he unexpectedly threw back his head and laughed unpleasantly.

"For such insolence I could have you locked in your chamber until you learn the submissive manners of the daughters of Spain, but I shall forbear, seeing you are a stranger to the better ways. You will learn. I bid you look, Señorita," and he gestured again.

From the balcony she had a wide, clear view of the Caribbean, and through the telescope she saw a small but formidable force of ships. Some half-dozen caravels guarded an ornate three-decked galleon sailing past the cannon of Santa Cruz Fortress. She could just make out the flag of Castile waving and rippling before the evening darkened its colors of red and yellow.

"The treasure fleet?" she asked, her voice tense. Was Don Nicklas aboard?

"No. Warships. The *Armada de Barlavento* has the task of policing Spanish sea lanes from the Windward Islands to Vera Cruz."

"For pirates?" she asked, too simply.

His mouth twisted with cynicism at her innocent question. "Pirates," he repeated in agreement, "English pirates."

"They are fine ships," she said.

"They were built in Havana, and are victualed and based from Vera Cruz to Santa Domingo. We on the Main pay for them with a special sales tax, the rate of which has doubled due to the vermin that prey upon the Main."

"Is this why you wished to speak to me? I assure you, I cannot speak for the pirates on Tortuga, Señor."

"Let us hope so, Doña Devora," came his too-gentle tone, and she feared to meet those unrelenting, searching eyes for fear he may have already learned that she had sailed aboard the *Revenge*. It was only a matter of time before he found out.

"I called you to speak of Don Nicklas." His voice changed to one of pride and pleasure. "For a time he will command this armada and set up base here at Cartagena. It will bring pirates like Hawkins and Morgan. It is my ambition to have these two diablos in my hands in a short time. The devils will hang in the Plaza for their unspeakable crimes against Holy Seville."

Devora was careful to show no emotion. If he supposed she held any sympathy for the buccaneers there was no telling the risks for herself and Friar Tobias. She remembered Tobias' words about his disagreements with the archbishop and the Dominicans.

"The fleet sails in search of Hawkins' ship?" she asked.

"The armada sails to meet Don Nicklas at Granada. The soldiers he gathers there from the armory will be transported back here and eventually to Lima to increase the silver production at the mines. When he arrives here in Cartagena there will be a great fiesta in his honor. You will be introduced to him at the masqurada ball. You will see then the gallant man you are esteemed worthy to marry, Señorita."

That was debatable. Tobias had told her little of what Don Nicklas would actually be doing, perhaps because he had not known. There had been little if any mention of working the infamous silver mines near the Andes, and the news greatly disturbed her.

"So his soldiers will be forced to work the mines near Lima," she said dubiously.

His mouth smiled, but his eyes mocked her. "You have much to learn. Incas work the mines. And—prisoners. Our soldiers guard and fight. They see that the work is done. The silver must be readied for the annual arrival of the great treasure flota, which comes to Cartagena and Portobello perhaps a year from now. And when they depart for Seville, you will see a great sight. The hulls will creak and groan with the burden of more silver bars than the eyes of your English King Charles will ever look upon."

"So I have heard, Your Excellecy. I have also heard other things, most unpleasant. How the Indians and prisoners work so long and under such adverse circumstances they die by the hundreds each season to fill the coffers of Spain."

His black eyes snapped. As if to show that her disapproval meant nothing, he lifted a heavy, opulent silver box from the balcony table, weighing it in hand. He removed a cigar and lit it against the wind from a candle, cupping his hand to shield the flame. He puffed with too much energy, all the while watching her.

"These lazy Indians and prisoners have seen nothing yet in the way of suitable task masters. Nicklas comes from the king with letters to see to it the silver production is doubled."

More brutality—more deaths, she thought. *Those slaving in the mines were of less value than even the poor mules who were also overloaded and whipped to pull the too-heavy burdens for their inconsiderate masters.*

"You are offended, Señorita. I am not, nor is the mighty king of Spain. Nicklas does what he must for a greater cause. That a few Indians must lose their lives is unfortunate but necessary."

"And Don Nicklas is the captain of these new task masters over the Indians, is that it? He brings soldiers to crack whips and to double the production. You and he see this massacre as honorable because it is draped in the flag of Spain's conquest!"

"Softly, Señorita, softly. Your feeble insults and indignation over the mighty rule of Spain accomplish nothing. Nor will your displeasure put an end to plans already arranged for your marriage to Nicklas."

He extinguished the flame on the candle with his fingers and a curl of smoke drifted on the wind.

Her eyes searched his, her confusion growing. "Am I mistaken, Señor, or did you not tell me earlier that you had doubts of my suitability for your son?"

"You were not mistaken," he said ruefully. "I have many doubts. Too many. I could wish you did not possess what I fear is a crusading spirit."

"You could always send me back to Barbados on one of your caravels, Señor."

"I could wish so. It is impossible. My doubts as to your suitability are as nothing when weighed against the benefits of such an arrangement."

She began to protest but he gestured her to silence. He leaned against the iron grill and smoked his cigar. "You look confused, even angry. I suppose you hoped your opposition to the mines would upset me. You wish to return to Barbados, yes. My apologies, Señorita. Your future lies with the Valentin family in Lima."

She watched him with frustration. "And if I do not cooperate?"

His smile turned into a grin below the dark mustache. She flushed.

She tried again. "What if the wishes of Don Nicklas conflict with your plans?" He may refuse me outright, in favor of Doña Sybella."

"So she has told you already. Naturally Sybella would hope to end the arrangement, but the love between her and Nicklas is no more. Sybella was sent to Spain five years ago to marry Don Marcos Ferdinand."

"But she has told me Don Marcos is no longer alive. Sybella is a beautiful woman, one who feels she has claim to your son. Who is to say he will not agree?"

"I will say it, I know him well enough. No one has claim to Nicklas, except he allow it." He smiled, scanning her. "He will allow you, Doña Devora."

She was too weary to find his bold compliment a reason to blush. "In saying so, you also make it clear that I too will wish it so. I will not, Your Excellency. For many reasons important to me. I wish for one thing, and that is to go home to my own life, my people, my own cause."

"You have my apologies," he said, his tone denying it.

"My cause, Señor, stands in contrast to the desires of your king and of you yourself."

"Careful." His eyes narrowed. "For your own sake."

"You say you do not wish trouble. Then is it not easier to find a bride for your son who agrees with your cause, and his?"

"It would," he agreed wryly. "Unfortunately, the luxury is not mine, nor his. As for your private cause, yes, I know of it. The Countess mentioned of your working with an uncle in the practice of medicine on Barbados. Medicine is of great benefit, naturally, Señorita. But we will leave such work to our male physicians, and the art of showing mercy, to our priests. You, as a woman, must learn that such matters do not set well for the daughters of Spain. You are to please Don Nicklas."

His arrogance was beyond endurance. "And if I refuse outright to marry your son or to obey your rules?"

Maximus watched her above the glow of his cigar. "Surely, Doña Devora, you do not need me to answer your folly? You have no choice. It is the will of the Earl and Countess that you fulfill the cause for which you were brought here. In fighting me, you fight your parents."

She stood staring at him, trying to breath calmly. She knew he was right, that there was little she could do in the end. All her protestations now were accomplishing nothing and perhaps making her situation worse.

"You will learn. And in time you will be happy and content to belong to Nicklas. There are many women who would eagerly exchange places with you. He is a man of prestige. A great fighter, a magnificent swordsman."

"I am not impressed with such things, Señor. It is a grandee's character and honor, his humility before God that I hold dear to my heart."

He behaved as though he did not hear her. "Nicklas will become heir to all I have. You may count yourself favored and blessed to have the Valentin name."

"I must count myself little better than a slave," she said, her voice shaking. She turned away.

"If you were considered a slave you would not be speaking so boldly to me, a viceroy. I could have you whipped for insolence, but—" his voice lowered with restraint. "You are far too beautiful for that. And Nicklas would never stand for such treatment."

She whirled toward him, her eyes pleading for understanding. "Don Maximus. Can you not see I am not right for Spain? That I am not the woman for your son? As you say, there are others more fitting than I. Señoritas of the Spanish nobility who would, perhaps, gladly throw themselves at his feet for the opportunity to become his bride. Of what value is it that you will accept an Englishwoman into the Valentin family?"

He flinched, and the reaction stunned her. Why such a strong response when she had said even bolder things and he had scoffed at them with smooth indifference?

"It may be you are not the first of English blood in the family. I will ask you again to mind your tongue."

She remembered then; the countess had said Don Nicklas had an English mother. She stared at him, the silence enclosing them, the wind blowing about them. It tugged at his silk doublet, stirred his coarse black hair. His eyes took on a distant look as though remembering something painful. For the moment Don Maximus appeared vulnerable and all her fury spiraled downward until she felt only exhaustion.

"I am sorry, Señor," she said gently.

He looked at her, coming awake from his private thoughts and now his face was hard again. "It is precisely because you are an Englishwoman that you have value, Señorita. If you wish to know why, I shall tell you." He threw his cigar over the balcony. "The earl and countess make it possible for me to be granted a patent of nobility, carrying with it the title Count Lemos of the Realm, a decree from His Majesty."

She stared at him in dismay. "I do not understand how—"

"Do not misunderstand what that title means on the Spanish Main. It offers much more than a title of *Count* does in Europe. Nor do I wish this title because I long to receive flattery from any who fawn before me to gain petty favors." He strode to the other side of the balcony and poured wine into a gemmed, silver goblet.

"It may surprise you to know I do not care what others think of me. It is power that matters most, Señorita. When one has power, one has control. Yes, power, and riches. With these, a man may be a diablo, but his flatterers will still insist he is an angel. His treasuries are full and overflowing."

"I will never tell you that, Señor."

"I believe you, Señorita, and your goodness has certain charms. If it were not that I wanted you for Nicklas—ah," he emptied his goblet and smiled mockingly. "But we must not discuss that."

"You are wise in that, Your Excellency."

He laughed and went on: "The title Count of the Realm carries with it a grant of *mayorazgo*. I see by your expression you do not understand the word. Let me explain. It says that my extensive lands, and other holdings here in the West Indies and in Spain, cannot be sold or divided after my death. What grandee would not wish that? My possessions will belong to the Valentins forever. All that I have must be passed down in unbroken succession from my eldest son, Nicklas, to his eldest son, and so on and so on, forever, like the royal family." He set the empty goblet down. "You see why you are necessary to me."

She turned seaward, and the water was now a pool of glossy ebony with starlight dancing on the gliding surface. The lanterns on the ships shone golden.

"I do not see how I aid you in this. My parents' titles mean little except in England. And I have been told many of the Radburn holdings have been ruined in the civil war."

"The Radburn title may be of little consequence, true, Señorita, but the privilege it brings him in London offers opportunity for information considered of great value to the king of Spain."

She looked at him, her suspicion growing. Was he saying her stepfather was passing him information from the chambers of the Privy Council?

"The Earl has chosen to share that information with me, and I, with Madrid."

"Are you accusing my father of being a spy?"

"Accuse? No. I affirm that he is—*my* spy, Señorita. I pay him."

"You pay him," she said, astounded, then insulted, telling herself it wasn't true.

"In return for the information passed to Madrid, I expect to be rewarded by the coveted title of the Count of the Realm."

"Are you not afraid to tell me this? What if I unmasked both of you to King Charles?"

He laughed. "You will not be seeing Charles anytime soon, Señorita, if ever. And since you are likely to mellow with age within the walls of the Valentin hacienda in Lima—I do not fear your knowing. The knowledge of what you are up against should convince you your wings are clipped—permanently. Any flitting about must be confined to the Valentin patio garden."

"Your arrogance disturbs me greatly, Señor. You take much for granted."

Don Maximus smiled. "It is getting late. Dinner will be served soon."

"And Earl Robert?" she asked, with barely concealed rage. "How much does he receive from you?"

"You will need to ask the countess." He gestured inside the sitting-room. "Don Favian is due to arrive at any moment with news. You had best sit down, Señorita, and gather your scattered wits. I have upset you." He turned away.

"Wait—" she said. "Even if all this is so, and the earl is important to you, I still do not see why I am needed."

"Do you not? It should be plain. The earl and countess have dreams of silver. Your marriage to Don Nicklas will grant them their wish."

She should have been shocked by this, but she felt only a merciful dullness. Her mind said it wasn't true, when in her soul she suspected Maximus of having told her the blunt truth. Yet there were many questions left unanswered about her parents.

She would find out, she promised herself, when she saw her mother and discussed the issue.

One thing was clear; she would do all in her power to keep from marrying this ruthless Don Nicklas. If worse came to worse she would seek to escape on her own. Anything but endure the attentions of such a man.

So he was coming to double the production of silver. And perhaps her parents were involved in the tragedy and sacrifice of human life to follow. How could she honor such a man?

Don Maximus was interrupted by the arrival of a soldier bringing him a collection of papers from the Fortress Santa Cruz. As the viceroy skimmed through the information she could see that he was not pleased. "Send for Don Favian at once!"

❧ 7 ❧

Confessing to an Abduction

*Understanding is rather to be chosen than
silver . . .*

—*Proverbs 16:16*

Devora sat in the sitting-room in a high-backed chair facing the open balcony. The trade wind blew in from the Caribbean and swept across the balcony into the sitting room. Don Maximus strode back and forth restlessly before the crimson drapes where the hems billowed.

Don Favian was there too, looking more subdued than he had earlier, and dressed extravagantly for dinner in stiff velvet with cunning red embroidery. He looked on in silence as Maximus seethed with some internal storm. There was an alert suspicion in Favian's manner that set her on edge. The information brought by the soldier was another report from General Alfonso. She assumed it concerned the Isle of Pearls, although Maximus had not said so.

She broke the silence herself, asking hopefully, "You have heard from my parents, the earl and countess?"

Maximus ceased his pacing and turned to look down at her. The red and yellow glow from the flickering weave of the lantern cast his handsome but brutal face with a smoldering glow. He lifted the military report from General Alfonso.

"We shall get to that, Señorita. But first—"

The doors opened and Friar Tobias came in, causing Devora to breathe a silent sigh of relief. The presence of the dauntless man whom she considered to be equal in will with the viceroy gave her hope, reminding her that she was not alone in her cause in the Valentin home.

"Was that not a soldier from Fortress Santa Cruz I saw leave minutes ago? What ails you, Maximus? Why do you hold Doña Ashby here to discuss military matters?"

The mild rebuke was plain. Why hadn't Maximus also called him when he summoned Devora?

Maximus did not look upset over the question, but over the report. He held it up with disdain. "You know what ails me. This! If she knows anything about the pirate's attack on the Isle of Pearls—"

"She knows little to aid your search for the Englishman. I can attest to it. I was there."

"She does not leave us yet," said Maximus stubbornly. He dropped the report back on the table with disgust and made a hissing sound between his teeth. "General Alfonso assures me there is no doubt who the English diablo was who led the sack of the Isle. It was Hawkins. He attacked Governor Toledo's residence and made a daring escape with the heretic Kitt Bonnor!" Maximus walked to the balcony and looked out toward the darkening sea, hands on his hips. "The audacity of the dog! To attack under my nose. He deliberately insults me."

"Come, come, Maximus, such anger does your health little good. Perhaps you make too much of it," said Tobias. He sank into a chair near the balcony, where a breeze blew, and chose a cluster of deep purple grapes from the glittering silver platter.

Maximus looked at him as though his brain were fevered. "Too much? When a meager, despicable pirate mocks the glory of Spain, and taunts me, the viceroy? It is my duty to see these scurvy sea rats preying on our coasts eliminated, even if I must attack Port Royal and Tortuga."

"Well said, my Father," echoed Favian indolently, toying with a crimson rose, and now and then lifting it to his nose as he watched Devora.

Devora sat in the chair, holding her breath each time the viceroy looked at her, hoping the report did not mention that she and Tobias had been aboard the *Revenge*.

"Comfort, my brother. His Majesty has commissioned Nicklas to rid the Caribbean of these piratical fleas. We shall soon have him here to care for these matters."

"These piratical 'fleas' as you call them have made off with the entire cargo of pearls destined for Seville," said Maximus.

"Patience, Maximus. Has not Nicklas already proved his worthiness in handling English intransigents in the straits of Florida? He will handle this Hawkins well enough. I have no question in my mind but that he will prove himself very cunning in this matter."

Tobias could not possibly mean what he was saying, thought Devora.

Favian looked scornful over the confidence Tobias showed in Nicklas. He tapped his jeweled scabbard with its *V* for Valentin, engraved in gold. "You speak of his worthiness. Was it cunning that proved Nicklas so dauntlessly loyal and courageous in the straits of Florida, my Uncle?"

Devora sensed tension again over the matter of Florida, but had no way of knowing why.

"You were there, my son," said Tobias in a quiet voice. "Do you not agree your brother served Spain nobly?"

"I was not there. I did not arrive until afterward. There is some question—"

Maximus frowned. "We are not here to discuss Florida. Nicklas was knighted for his honor."

"Perhaps too hastily."

"Was not the rage of envy the sin of Cain?" asked Tobias. "Guard your heart, my son Favian. You do not grow less because Nicklas grows stronger in the eyes of the king of Spain. It is the eyes of God that matter when all is said and done."

Devora looked at Tobias, pleased, but Favian smiled wearily. "Perhaps instead of Father making too much of the pirate Hawkins, you make too much of Nicklas. His gallant and heroic deeds may not be as epic as his allies wish us to think."

It was Don Maximus who turned on him. "You are the expert on heroics are you, my son? You who wine and dance your life away with the caballeros and *pretty* Señoritas in the plaza day and night? Do not speak scornfully of your brother when you have done little to equal him. And mind your tongue when your godly uncle points out your sins, lest you find yourself under the scowl of the Dominicans."

Favian flushed angrily and straightened from where he lounged, his lean fingers tightening on his sword belt. "I do not waste my time on wine and song. This is Doña Sybella's scheme against me to convince you of my unworthiness as her suitor."

"Sybella has no part in this matter."

"She wishes to scorn my reputation because she intends to have Nicklas when he arrives."

"Foolish talk! A waste of time." Maximus waved a muscled arm of dismissal and turned to Tobias.

"You speak well when it comes to the arrival of Nicklas, but I cannot wait in Cartagena while Hawkins creates havoc on the Main. The Isle of Pearls may not be the only location he intends to ravage."

"Cartagena, you think? Impossible," said Tobias. "General Alfonso is on alert. And what pirate since Francis Drake has successfully entered the walls of this great city of His Majesty?"

Maximus walked to the balcony and was looking out toward the deepening violet sea. "I was not thinking of Cartagena."

"What, then?"

Devora looked from Maximus' rigid back, sensing uncertainty, to Tobias. Was he trying to discover how much Maximus knew of Bruce's plans? Favian too stirred from his morose state to pay attention, but Tobias merely studied the cluster of grapes.

"You speak in riddles, Maximus," continued Tobias. "You give this pirate the cunning of the diablo himself. Hawkins cannot be in two places at once. He cannot be lurking off the coast of Tortuga and Cartagena at the same time."

"Yes, if he is at Tortuga," said Maximus thoughtfully.

Devora was trying to understand what was actually being said between the two men. Tobias appeared to be trying to lead Maximus into thinking Bruce was at Tortuga, but Don Maximus was suspicious. Why?

"Did not the governor of Santo Domingo send word to you? Surely the word of one of our own Spanish governors can be trusted. Did not the Chevalier Fontenay swear to him saying Hawkins had not left the accursed island of Tortuga?"

"Perhaps the Chevalier lies."

"What reason to lie?"

Maximus turned on Tobias impatiently. "How do I know, my brother? Am I everywhere at one time? It is a thought, only. A suspicion he has something more on his mind. . . . It is a concern that keeps me awake at night—that somehow Hawkins is nearby. Far closer to me than I dare guess."

Devora dared not look at Tobias, and picking up her fan, swished it.

Tobias sighed. "It is you who worry me, Maximus. This compulsion of yours to catch one inconsequential pirate like Hawkins. He is only one among hundreds."

"Inconsequential! He made a fool of Governor Toledo. He looted, stole away the prisoner I wanted—Kitt, and made off with pearls from the fleet."

"I said, 'inconsequential,'" repeated Tobias calmly. "Is not Henry Morgan more dangerous to the well-being of the king's colonies on the Main? And what of that Englishman, Christopher Mings? Those two have nettled us far more than this petty pirate, Hawkins."

"Mings was recalled to England to fight the Dutch."

"Morgan is more dangerous than Hawkins."

The muscles flexed in Maximus' jaw. "You make light of him, but I do not. There is more cunning to this Hawkins than you suppose. The next raid may be an attempt to rob the mule train of Peruvian silver."

The mule train. Devora sat tensely, hardly daring to move as she watched the interplay between the two men and where it was leading. Tobias had deliberately led him to disclose his suspicions.

"These pirates are sea dogs," soothed Tobias. "They may raid the towns along the Caribbean, but the mainland of the viceroyalties are too remote and completely out of their reach. So too, the mule train."

"Nevertheless I shall be careful," growled Don Maximus, "or I too will be called to Seville to answer to the king. I have reason to be suspicious of Hawkins, not I alone, but also the new archbishop of Lima, Harro Andres."

"Ah? A new archbishop? I have not heard of him. When does he arrive?"

She could see the masked interest in Tobias' face.

"Soon," Maximus told him. "He will be arriving from Granada."

"What information does the archbishop have?"

Maximus frowned and gestured for Favian to bring him a goblet of wine. "He has not told me everything yet. He wrote me from Santa Domingo. He was close to the governor who knew Chevalier Fontenay of Tortuga." He waved his goblet. "More important to me than pearls is the prisoner that was within my grasp, but now has been taken aboard Hawkins' ship."

Tobias set aside the cluster of grapes as though his concerns had unexpectedly been altered, but Maximus seemed not to notice.

"There is more cunning to this Hawkins than you suppose. I have reason to suspect him of a second identity."

"Ah yes, that. Interesting. A physician perhaps, like Kitt Bonnor."

"He blindfolded both Toledo and the English ambassador," said Maximus. "He left them bound in the dungeon. Then dares to leave a message for *me*. He sends his greetings and writes that he is *aggrieved* to have missed me." He turned, his eyes like coals.

"Insolent. I shall have the mad dog yet. And when I have him, by the saints, his death will be slow and painful."

"You forget a lady is present, Maximus," said Tobias. "Your speech distresses Señorita Devora."

Don Favian picked up Devora's fan and solicitously cooled her face. "Uncle is right. The Señorita grows pale, my Father. Perhaps you should not discuss his burning as a heretic. She may have personal cause to see the pirate live. They are both English." He bowed. "No insult intended, Señorita. I happen to find English women very attractive."

Devora's gaze locked with Favian's. She snatched the fan away. *He could not know. He could not possibly know*, she thought, and yet she could see how Maximus was struck by his casual suggestion. He stopped his pacing, turned and fixed her with a searching gaze. Tobias rose to his feet.

"What do you mean to say, Favian?" snapped Tobias.

Favian became indolent again, lifting a white rose from the table to smell, his feet crossed at the ankles as he leaned against the table. "One merely wonders why Hawkins found it necessary to blindfold Governor Toledo and Earl Robert, but the others he did not worry about. The Señorita may tell you what this pirate looks like, since both she and Uncle Tobias were aboard his ship when it left the Isle of Pearls."

Maximus' complexion turned a ruddy brown. "What is this he says? You know this pirate?"

"Now, Maximus, it is no great concern as I can bear witness," interrupted Tobias.

"Bear witness?" he looked at him, astounded. "You actually *have* seen this dog of a pirate?"

Tobias spread his hands. "We had no choice. We were both taken captive aboard his ship when he departed the Isle of Pearls. At sword point, no less."

Maximus stood as though struck. "And you but now tell me this?"

"Is it not in the report?"

"You know it is not in the report," growled Maximus, "or else I would have mentioned the infamy first thing. Speak, Tobias! I will have all the truth. Now."

Devora's heart was thudding. Tobias looked at Favian. "Favian can tell you, since it was he who brought it up."

Maximus turned to him. "What do you know of all this?"

Shifting Maximus' full attention on Favian conveniently gave her and Tobias time. She believed it was why Tobias did so. *He is not an ally of Bruce for naught*, she thought.

Neither she nor Tobias could deny having been aboard the *Revenge*, but that Favian knew surprised her as much as the information apparently stunned Don Maximus. If she did keep back the truth it would be a lie and make matters worse in the end. *Lord, enable me to do Your will*, she prayed briefly.

There was a hint of moodiness about Favian's mouth. "I too wrote a report of my voyage to the Isle of Pearls, my Father. I gave it to you yesterday. I told all I knew. You have ignored it. Now, you make much of this report by General Alfonso—" he gestured to the papers on the table—"when all it contains is stale news."

Maximus' eyes flickered. "Well taken. I ignored you. I shall do so no longer. Now explain."

"As I said, Hawkins sailed away, apparently toward Tortuga. Though if that is what he did his plan lacked wisdom, since he first brought the beautiful Señorita and my esteemed Uncle to Spanish shores. He cannot be at Tortuga now unless his ship sprouted wings."

"Never mind that.When you arrived, what did Toledo tell you?"

Favian gestured his hand in its lacy cuff toward Devora. "That both the Señorita and Tobias had been taken as prisoners."

As prisoners. Devora's breath slowly released and a stolen glance toward Tobias revealed his pleasure. If they had been forced aboard as prisoners, then things did not look so dreadful for either of them. There was no way Don Maximus could ascertain from this that matters thereafter had turned friendly between them.

"You were prisoners to this diablo?"

"We were," said Tobias soberly. "Perhaps Governor Toledo's report failed to mention it since he knew Favian would report it to you," he suggested, as though the matter was of no consequence.

"But you, Favian," and he turned to his nephew. "How is it you know? You spoke to Governor Toledo of the Isle of Pearls?"

Before Favian could answer, Maximus interrupted. "It was I who sent Favian to the Isle of Pearls," he admitted with some reluctance in his voice. "He went in my place—a mistake on my part. I should not have sent him."

"He is angry that I did not capture Hawkins single-handedly," complained Favian. "But I do not live the charmed life that Nicklas does."

"Mind your envious tongue. Had it been Nicklas I sent instead of you, I would have my enemy in chains by now."

"Perhaps," came Favian's retort, suggesting doubt. "I should like to have seen my illustrious brother do the impossible. It could not have been done as you insist, my Father. I did the wise thing, the—"

"Yes, you saw the battle and kept to a safe distance," came the biting snarl. "My son—a Valentin—withdraws. Knowing it was Hawkins attacking the Isle. Knowing the man in the dungeon was Kitt Bonnor. Favian withdraws."

Favian flushed, tossing down the crumpled crimson rose.

Devora felt sympathy for him. Maximus was being cruel.

"Would you see my galleon blown to pieces?" asked Favian. "The flag of Spain floating in the Caribbean?"

"Spare me your anguish for the flag. Better it is dragged to the bottom of the Caribbean than see it shamed on your galleon standing back from the battle. Was not the flag torn down from the fortress La Gloria, guarding the bay? Why did that infamous sight not affront you enough to attack Hawkins?"

Favian grew tight-lipped. "I was out-shipped, out-gunned."

"Bah. If you had used the guns when Hawkins was first attacking the fortress, you may have captured him and made a name for yourself."

"I had but thirty men aboard when Hawkins had a hundred! Had I attacked unwisely and the galleon sunk you'd have up-braided me for recklessness. Now you accuse me of caution."

"I would accuse you of more than that if you were not my son. As it is, you make a poor captain, Don Favian. You are not Nicklas. One wonders how a father could spawn two sons more contrary."

"It was useless. Governor Toledo swears to the same in his report."

"Bah. Toledo says he would have run for the hills himself had not Earl Robert demanded he stand and guard the dungeon. "Even if unable to defeat Hawkins, you would have given Governor Toledo and Ambassador Robert time to bring Kitt Bonnor to the hills. At this very moment I might have had the English heretic in the inqui-sition chamber making him talk. We would know the identity of Hawkins."

"Nicklas! Nicklas! I grow weary of his name. There was a time when you disowned him."

"Silence!"

Favian's mottled face stiffened. He whipped about and walked across the room, flouncing into a red velvet chair and stretching his long legs in front of him. He rested his chin in his hand and stared moodily at his father.

Devora felt ill and lowered herself into her chair as well. The outburst between father and son had at least given a reprieve to her and Tobias, but she would not have wished Don Maximus' tirade on anyone. Having undergone the whiplash of the countess' disappointment in not meeting her expectations, she could under-stand the pain Favian must be feeling. She was beginning to dis-like Don Nicklas more and more. Undoubtedly he was the favored son, the one who had grown up indulged by Don Maximus. But there was little concern to spare for Favian's woes now; how would she stand up under Maximus' badgering that was sure to come now that he knew she had seen Bruce?

"Enough, Maximus," warned Tobias. "You deal more harshly with your blood sons than you do with the lowliest soldier."

Maximus must have realized he was out of control, for he poured himself more wine and went to the balcony where the trade wind cooled his perspiring face, downing the contents before tossing the goblet aside with a clatter.

"Favian, are you certain it was Toledo who told you Hawkins abducted Doña Devora aboard his ship?" asked Tobias.

At the word abduct, Maximus dark head turned sharply and his eyes squinted as they ran over her. She flushed, knowing the first odious thing that was likely to come to his mind. Already, she could see that he was rethinking his plans where marriage to Nicklas was concerned.

Well enough, she thought, satisfied. Perhaps she would be sent home to Barbados after all. Nevertheless she was careful not to show her feelings and maintained an outward calm under the dark, moody scowl he fixed upon her.

"Earl Robert informed me of the danger to his daughter," said Favian, looking at her. "He was beside himself with concerns, Señorita, to say the least. At his bidding I set sail at once to overtake the *Revenge*, and we were once within sight, but a storm arose and by morning we were blown off course."

"Did you speak with Earl Robert when you arrived at the Isle to see the governor?" asked Tobias. "The Señorita is concerned for her mother, the countess."

"She is alive," Favian said, smiling at Devora.

Maximus turned and looked at his son. His countenance softened. "Why did you not tell me you went in pursuit?"

Favian looked at him defensively. "Your insults were such that you did not give me opportunity."

Don Maximus scowled. "Proceed. What happened?"

Favian looked down at his polished boots. "The *Revenge* got away," he said grudgingly. "Through no fault of my own. The storm did havoc to my ship, as Robert will attest once he arrives. I was forced to take refuge in Monkey Bay and do minor repairs. Once the storm blew over, Hawkins had disappeared." He smirked. "One might hope his vessel has sunk, but it is too much to ask of the saints."

"What of my father?" pressed Devora. "He did not return with you?"

"No, at his own wish. Governor Toledo, who was also with us, arranged for a galleon to bring him to Granada to locate Nicklas," he said stiffly. "I would have joined Robert at Granada to engage my brother in aiding in the search, but it was your father's request that I return to the Isle to bring the countess to Cartagena."

"Then my mother is here?" asked Devora, surprised, standing to her feet. "Why wasn't I told sooner?"

"Pardon, but she is not here. She remains at the Isle. And your father and Nicklas search in vain for you."

"One might think their vain attempt causes you satisfaction," said Maximus wearily. "Perhaps Nicklas will yet find Hawkins and sink the *Revenge*." He turned and paced. "So Robert engaged Nicklas at Granada. That was wise," and he looked pleased with the decision, but Devora noted that Friar Tobias did not, as though there were something about Granada and Nicklas being there at this time that disturbed him.

"Then this explains why Nicklas has not arrived," mused Maximus. "He and Earl Robert both think the Señorita Devora and Tobias are prisoners aboard Hawkins' vessel. Naturally they will be out searching for the pirate. It will be like his gallantry to make certain of your rescue," he told her.

A cold fear began to throb in her heart. What if they overtook Bruce? What if they sank the *Revenge?*

"One hardly thinks he will find Hawkins," said Favian.

Devora looked at him quickly, wondering at his confidence. Maximus must have wondered too.

"Why do you think so?" he asked shortly.

Favian lifted a brow as though it were obvious to all but his father. "Hawkins is crafty. He attacks and disappears again, leaving no clue to where he has gone. It is odd that he knows the Spanish Main, the ways of our people, and the routes of the galleons so well. Nearly as well," he added, "as our most illustrious of commanders, including Nicklas."

A moment of silence settled over the room. Did she imagine the tension? It was curious, for she found nothing in Favian's remarks to warrant it.

"A spy among the capitans, is that what you suggest?" asked Maximus shortly.

Favian shrugged. "Who knows? Does it not seem strange that Hawkins comes and goes on the Main at will?"

"I do not see it at all," said Tobias. "So he attacked the Isle of Pearls. Does Morgan have the capitans on his side because he successfully sacked Rio de la Hacha? These pirates seek out all information on a locality before they risk attacking. It is the same with Hawkins. I see no cause to suspect a spy."

Favian stood impatiently and looked at Maximus. "Uncle is too trusting. It is to be expected of a friar, but you, Father, are the one who first suspected that Hawkins may have another identity. What if he has friends among us?"

"It was not I, but the archbishop," said Maximus darkly. "That is why we wanted Kitt Bonnor. He could have been made to confess all he knows of Hawkins to the inquisitors."

Devora masked a shudder.

"Even without Kitt as a prisoner it is not too late," urged Favian.

"No, you are right. When Nicklas arrives we will ferret out this spy who mocks us."

"Come, my Father, why wait for Nicklas? Does the sun rise and set because of him? Give me authorization to seek and search and I shall do much to discover just who this spy may be."

Maximus looked at him, his eyes shining with satisfaction as though Favian's passion pleased him. "I have half a heart to grant your wish."

Favian crossed the room to him, his fingers enclosing his scabbard. "Grant me papers of power and I vow I shall bring you the spy and maybe Hawkins."

Devora's breath paused, but she sat very still. The room went silent as Maximus appeared to be tensely considering the request. Tobias stood, unsmiling, looking from Maximus to Favian.

"You shall have the authorization you need," Maximus told him. "But whatever you may learn must first be brought to me, not the archbishop."

As Don Favian looked satisfied, Maximus turned to Tobias, changing the subject.

"How is it then, my brother, that you and Doña Devora managed to escape this pirate fiend and arrive safely today?"

"Because the fiend, as you call him, behaved a charming gallant," said Tobias, showing calmness.

"You scoff."

"I tell the truth."

"He abducted Devora."

"Truly, but later he relented. He agreed to bring her unharmed to Barbados, myself included, though I would hardly have been greeted with open arms," he said wryly.

"He would release her for ransom," suggested Favian with scorn. "What else?"

"But how is it you arrived in Cartagena?" persisted Maximus, doubt in his voice.

"The storm," said Tobias, " was just as Favian said earlier. We could not go on, so he let us depart to the Spanish coast by longboat. There, we managed to spend the night in a friendly village with peasants, where we also borrowed horses. We arrived this afternoon safely. We are here by the grace of God, but also in part because of this buccaneer's gallantry."

It was clear Maximus did not want to accept Tobias' explanation of Bruce's actions, and he frowned, dismissing the matter as a mere bewitchment.

"Whatever the cause, we are safe, and have reason to be grateful," said Tobias.

Maximus turned to Devora. "Is this how it was?"

"Yes."

He watched her evenly. "Your opinion of this heretic pirate?"

"I do not know what to make of him," she admitted truthfully, also aware of Favian's watchfulness. "I was on the Isle of Pearls with Doña Sybella when the attack took us all by surprise."

"Why did he not take Sybella a prisoner?"

Devora fanned herself. "Your niece and the other ladies had already escaped through a secret passage that brought them and their jewels inland."

Maximus' eyes narrowed. "And you did not go with them?"

"No. No one could tell me where my mother was. They had not seen her. I did not wish to leave without finding her first. As it turned out, she had already escaped with Sybella, the governor's Señora, and their ailing daughter."

"So you stayed behind."

"Yes," she repeated reluctantly.

"And you were seen by this pirate and were abducted by him?"

"Yes...."

"How do you judge him?" he repeated.

She hesitated. "I do not condone his piracy, Your Excellency. I saw both good and evil among the men who followed him and the other two captains."

Don Favian chuckled. "One would think this diablo has won you over."

She turned to him indignantly. "I also saw the horror to which members of Captain Hawkins' crew had been confined in the governor's dungeon. I cannot blame a captain's wish to rescue them and to see their miseries alleviated."

Maximus frowned. "Perhaps. And yet such words, Señorita, are not wise to speak in Cartagena. The archbishop is careful when it comes to heresy."

"Heresy? Because I told the truth about Captain Hawkins?"

"I will overlook your ways, Señorita, for now. I well understand the trauma you have been through these last few weeks. But as Friar Tobias will tell you, we do not look kindly on insubordination, whether in Cartagena or Lima, which will be your home if Don Nicklas approves of you."

"You asked her opinion," said Tobias. "Frightening her now will accomplish little."

Devora said nothing, and the moment eased when Don Favian announced he had further news to deliver.

"You persist in tardiness," said Maximus. "One would think you had a cause for such oversight."

"Only much on my mind, my Father."

"Yes, your cousin Sybella," he said with weariness. "Between your blind attraction to her and her attraction to Nicklas, I have little peace. Go on, what further news?"

"It is news for Doña Devora," and Favian bowed toward her. "It was your father's wish I dock at the Isle of Pearls on the way home to Cartagena to bring Countess Catherina with me aboard ship, due to her health."

"Governor Toledo has already informed me of more recent events," said Maximus tiredly. "There is no need to be alarmed," he told Devora, but she was, nonetheless, and stood. "Then she is still at the Isle of Pearls?" she asked anxiously.

"It was necessary to leave her. She had been taken with grave ailment, along with Governor Toledo's daughter. She will come when her strength is better suited for the voyage."

Devora recalled how ill Governor Toledo's daughter had been, and her concerns grew. "I should like leave to return to the Isle of Pearls and care for my mother," she said quickly to Don Maximus.

"Ah, that," said Maximus. "There is no need. Governor Toledo is on his way back tomorrow. I have taken the liberty, Señorita, to send with him my own private physician to see to her recovery. I am sure you will see Countess Catherina in a few weeks, arriving with Earl Robert and Don Nicklas. The air* is unhealthy here. Once we journey to Lima her strength should improve. We wait only for the arrival of Nicklas. Soon, he will come."

"If I am not a prisoner here," Devora said to Don Maximus, "I wish to take my leave of your hospitality and return to the Isle. I too have medical skills and wish to attend my mother."

"And naturally when she is strong enough to make a voyage you would return here willingly," he said with irony, as though he knew she would seek to escape to Barbados.

---

* A common, indirect reference to mosquitoes carrying malaria.

"It is my mother's wish I return, is it not?" she asked flatly. "She would see to it."

He smiled his doubt. "After our discourse earlier on the balcony, Señorita Devora, you will forgive me if I question your good intentions."

"The Countess will see to it I return with her."

"There is no need for you to go to the Isle of Pearls. Your parents will join you here soon and once Nicklas arrives, we will all journey home to Lima."

Lima. How would she ever escape?

A small hope remained. If her mother improved enough to sail here to Cartagena, she may not want to go inland to Lima but return to London to recuperate from the tropics. In which case, she would need Devora to accompany her. If she could manage to convince the Countess to delay marriage into the Valentin family, then, thought Devora with new courage, *I might somehow manage to contact Bruce again.*

It was a slim hope; but in dark desperation the tiniest and feeblest flame burned brightly. *Yes,* she told herself firmly, *there is hope in the arrival of my mother.*

Countess Catherina

A fair woman who is without discretion..
——*Proverbs 11:22*

Spain held a lifestyle far more rigid and secluded than England, especially for its women. And in the days and nights that followed Devora's arrival at Cartagena, though she lacked nothing in the way of ease and comfort, she sighed for the less restricted life she had lived at Ashby Hall in Barbados. There, when restless, she could simply walk out the front door of the Great House, stroll to the stables, ask old Percy to saddle her mare Honey, and go riding through the tall, green cane fields. Here on the Spanish Main, her every move was watched by house servants reporting to Don Maximus. The strict cultural and religious severity of portentous colonial society kept her bound like the tight bone stays in her corset that stifled her breathing. The iron grillwork on her windows and balcony reminded her daily that she was a prisoner of luxury, of Spain.

She was not the only one. The haughty noble families who sat in the chief seats of government positions held in social disdain all those considered below them, including full-blooded Spaniards called Creoles who were born on the Main.

But the Creoles were equally proud and indolent, believing that physical labor was below their dignity as aristocrats. Work was reserved for the meztizas—the half-breed Spaniards and

Indians who were the tradesmen and artisans. At the lowest section of society were the hard laboring masses of full-blooded native Indians as well as Africans brought as slaves from the Gold Coast.

From the upper-class point of view the native Indian population were born to serve the whim of the ruling dons of Spain.

"No sacrifice is too great," Tobias told her. "Many Indians living in the inland regions have steep mountainside farms to care for, but there is a law from Seville allowing the hildagos to round them up at will during certain times of the year to serve instead on our plantations, cattle haciendas, the mines, and weaving shops called obrajes. The shops are little more than slave-operated during the season when large flocks of sheep are sheared."

Devora knew about the expertise of the Indians in spinning, dyeing, and weaving fine cloth. She could see how the merchandise would be coveted, and how the goods could be sold in Spain's shops.

His face had darkened. "But you can be sure the Indians get little, if any, profit. Maximus is one of the worst offenders in this. As in the mines, society on the Main is based on the labor of the native Indians."

She had been in the Valentin residency two weeks when her mother unexpectedly arrived from the Isle of Pearls, having made the last stretch of tedious journey from the bay to the Valentin residence in the viceroy's gilded coach. The slave girl Cuzita came hurrying into Devora's chamber to inform her.

Devora ran to the balcony and through the lattice saw the glorious team of white muscled horses prancing through the gate into the wide, cobbled courtyard.

Countess Catherina Radburn was more of a stranger to Devora than a pillar of motherly strength. Devora had lived most of her years separated from her mother, who had seen her small daughter demanding too much attention from a heart overcrowded with court life. After Devora's father had died in the Civil War in England and her mother married Earl Robert Radburn, matters did not change for the better where closer family ties were concerned. King Charles had appointed Earl Robert as his ambassador to the

Court of Spain. Catherina had gone with her new husband to Seville, and once again Devora had found herself locked out of her mother's life.

As for Earl Robert Radburn, Devora found him as much of a stranger as Viceroy Don Maximus. She didn't know her stepfather well enough to judge whether the unflattering things Don Maximus had said about him were true or not. If he was, as Don Favian had told her, worried enough about her supposed abduction by Bruce Hawkins to be out searching for her, she preferred to think it was out of fatherly concern rather than the perceived threat to the arranged marriage that meant so much to him.

Devora had been raised by her grandmother in a large house in the suburbs of London, and then sent to Barbados to live under the guardianship of Uncle Barnabas at the sugar plantation, Ashby Hall. While growing up, Devora had often struggled with emotional isolation, out of which grew feelings of resentment toward her mother. Those feelings still grew, though pushed back into the far corners of her heart. Though born into a Roman Catholic family, her Puritan Uncle Barnabas had taught her the doctrines recovered by the Reformers—that of salvation through Christ by grace alone, through faith alone, through Scripture alone—and she had come to a personal trust in the finished work of Christ.

Until recently she had thought her godly pursuits had uprooted any resentment toward her past. But she had learned differently when the Countess arrived unexpectedly in Barbados, with plans to change Devora's life forever by arranging a marriage against her will to the viceroy's son. But now in Cartagena in an unfamiliar culture, alone in her dilemma, the news that her mother had arrived from the Isle of Pearls brought surprising relief. For the moment it mattered not that her dilemma was due to the selfish plans of her parents. It was enough that her mother was here.

Adorned in Spanish lace, Devora hurried down the outer steps to wait in the courtyard to greet her mother.

Liveried slaves ran to the coach and opened the door. The first to step down was Don Maximus, regal and severe, garbed in black and gold. A woman followed, a tall olive-toned attendee with high

cheek bones and still, black eyes. Devora remembered the personal serving woman named Isabel who had traveled with her
mother from Spain to Barbados. Next followed the woman's husband, Luis, a man loyal to Earl Robert who had left him in charge
of the ailing countess. The tall, sallow-faced Spaniard with narrow
chin and over-sized, black eyes wore a scabbard and looked sourly
about him as though expecting to be attacked from the oleander
bushes. Evidently satisfied, he aided the countess down from the
coach while the viceroy's slaves rolled out a red, gold-fringed carpet
across the cobbles to the front door.

The countess stepped down weakly, looking ill and pale in
crimson- and -black lace, carrying a dyed ostrich feather fan of the
same crimson as her gown, sprinkled with rhinestones. For an
older woman she had retained her outward beauty, though her
once slim figure had grown. Her hair remained dark, and was
drawn away from an oval face into elaborately done braids that circled her head like a crown. With fair skin and unusual eyes of
violet color, which Devora had been fortunate to inherit, the
countess had left her mark on the heart of one too many men.
Devora feared that her loose ways had also included Don Maximus.

The countess cast her eyes toward the masculine Don
Maximus, looking helpless, and he obliged her and came to her
side. Leaning on his arm for support, she walked across the court
to where Devora hurried to meet her.

"Mother, I'm so pleased you've recovered enough to travel."
They embraced lightly as though meeting for the first time.

"Don Maximus told me what befell you. Thank God the pirate
released you when he did."

"I'm fine, Mother. I would have returned to you as soon as I
was told of your illness but was forbidden," and she glanced
toward the viceroy, silently naming him the culprit, but her mother
seemed to take no concern and wanly smiled, stretching fingers
with nails tinted with henna to caress her cheek. "I would rather
have you safely taken care of here." She looked at Don Maximus.
"Thanks to the viceroy for sending his physician, I was able to

come to you. There is still no word from your father, though Maximus assures me he will do all he can to locate him."

"Yes, Countess, and my sons Nicklas and Favian are also out, searching. It may be we will hear from your husband, the ambassador, soon. Of that I am sure you will be pleased."

Devora glanced from her mother to Maximus and saw the subdued glint of irony in his black eyes. She felt shamed, but her mother gave a tinkling little laugh and thanked him as though he had performed some great deed of gallantry.

"You must be very tired," he told her. "I will see the serving woman attends to your needs at once."

When Maximus turned his gaze to Devora, her eyes fell, for she believed she saw something in his face that spoke of his attraction to her mother.

It was evening before Devora saw her mother again, this time without the viceroy. Catherina was propped up in a large bed with many pillows edged with lace. Lanterns glowed golden, flooding the room and illuminating the beauty of the heavy teakwood furniture and Mediterranean tapestries.

Catherina gestured a pale hand of dismissal toward her serving woman, Isabel. "Leave us, and do not forget my goblet of Madeira wine before I fall asleep."

"Yes, Madame."

Isabel bowed her head and joined her husband, Luis, in an antechamber, closing the door on them.

Lines of fatigue had deepened on her mothers pale, damp face. Tremors of weakness were visible in her fingers as she reached for the glass of water that Isabel had placed by her bedside. "Water," she said with a grimace. "It tastes dreadful."

Devora moved quickly to her bedside to aid her, helping to steady her head so she could drink.

Sighing wearily, the countess leaned her head back against the pillows, her long black hair fanning about her. "This miserable air in Cartagena is positively unhealthy. Outbreaks of typhoid are common this time of year. So many people here are buying and selling. Call Taffy to fan me," she said of the Negro child she had brought from Barbados, then must have changed her mind. "On second thought, it's best we talk alone now. Hand me that fan—I shall soon melt."

Devora picked up the large fan and cooled her mother's face. The countess smiled wanly and closed her puffy eyelids. "You are a good child, Devora. . . . I admit the Puritan teachings from Barnabas that I loathe so much seem to have tempered your personality for the better in some instances. You have little of my spoilt ways—'tantrums,' your father used to call them . . . ." and at the mention of Devora's blood father, now dead, her mother grew reflective. "He was good to me. . . I miss him. Robert is, well, as shallow as I am sometimes. You are much like your father. Wise and serious."

Devora smiled ruefully, thinking of Bruce. She had fallen in love with a buccaneer, a man she was not likely to see again. "I am not always as wise as I need to be." She grew sober. "Mother, you must leave for England to recuperate."

"I will, but not yet. There is much to be done. Do not worry, the cooler air of Lima will help me recover faster."

"Lima!" whispered Devora. "I thought surely you would wish to sail for England as soon as Robert arrives."

"Everything must wait until my plans come to a successful end."

Devora assumed she spoke of her marriage to Don Nicklas. She tried to reason with her mother—"But your health is far more important than my marriage. Once we meet," she said uncomfortably, "and if he is in agreement, can it not wait a year as I voyage with you to London to announce it to grandmother? I think not of myself only, but you, Mother. Once you've contacted tropical fever there's little chance of full recovery here on the Main."

"That is why I will recuperate in Lima," she said firmly. "Maximus has already arranged our travels for just as soon as Nicklas arrives. The air there is much cooler and healthier," she said again wistfully, moving uncomfortably in the bed. "Such miserable heat here."

Devora cooled her with a wet cloth. The countess gave a pat to her hand. "Travels to England can come later. It may be, once the marriage has taken place, you will find that neither the viceroy nor Don Nicklas will care whether you stay in Lima or go to London indefinitely. But we cannot leave yet. There is more involved than even your marriage."

Devora's heart recoiled from the indifference with which the countess assumed the Valentins considered the marriage contract. She was able, however, to push aside her displeasure long enough to consider what was meant by her mother's simple statement that "more was involved."

"What more could interest you in Cartagena than my marriage to a Valentin?"

"I have no interest in Cartagena, but Lima holds the fulfillment to my dreams, and Robert's. Yours too. You shall see in the end how I've done you good."

Devora could hardly believe her ears. "Lima," she repeated with surprise. "What could there possibly be in Lima to hold your heart—" she stopped, and the fan ceased its swishing.

Catherina's sweeping black brows shot up. Then, she laughed weakly. "No, dear, I have no romantic interest in Maximus, though he is a virile man isn't he? And it's true," she sighed, "I do not love Robert. I confess I married him for his title and supposed wealth. The title I received, but it turns out the rogue was not as wealthy as he told me."

Astounded by such an open confession and her lack of shame, Devora was speechless. She had suspected her mother had married Earl Robert for the Radburn inheritance, but to hear her admit it was painful.

The Countess' eyes widened, and she looked almost innocent as she took in her daughter's silent censure. "If I don't secure my future, who will? You think I am unfeeling to arrange your marriage to a wealthy don, but at least you will be rich and safe. What more could a woman ask for in our time? And I have seen Nicklas. Believe me, he will be no disappointment to your romantic inclinations."

"It is not my way, Mother. I should rather have less in life and be able to live with my conscience than to marry a man I do not love." She might have said more, but it went also against her conscience to rebuke her mother. No matter that she lacked character, the countess remained her mother and for that she owed her a show of respect.

The countess wrinkled her nose. "Yes, I know, dear, you are scandalized by my wicked ways. You are trying to hide it, but Barnabas has taught you too well. The shock is written on your face." She let out a deep breath. "I must say, I am scandalized myself at times over the things I must do to survive."

"But not enough to change your ways," said Devora softly.

Her mother took the fan from Devora's hand and swished herself. "Not that Robert lied to me about his wealth," she said, ignoring her words. "He was as devastated as I was when after the war we returned to London thinking the king would restore the Radburn fortunes and lands, only to learn they were consumed by debt."

"You mean Robert lost his earldom?"

"His title remains, of course. It always will, and we do have a few pieces of property, but it doesn't offer us the manner of life we want. No one knows it, but the Radburn family is nearly destitute. The king has done what he could to help us, including giving Robert the post as ambassador that he asked for, but Charles has no real money yet to repay those loyal to him during the exile. So Robert goes without."

Devora suspected that the viceroy did not know of their financial status in England. *When Don Maximus learns of this, he may decide I'm not worthy of the son he takes such pride in*, and she wondered suddenly if the Radburn penury might not be a way out of her dilemma, but the countess appeared to read her mind.

"Maximus expects no dowry to come from this marriage alliance. It will interest you to know that it's the inheritance coming to Nicklas from his English family that interests us all."

Devora had all but forgotten that Nicklas had ties to England. Thus far, she had heard precious little of who they were, or their status.

"Maximus knows that Nicklas should be heir of Duke Anthony in London, since his mother, Lady Marian Bruce, was the duke's granddaughter. Nicklas will be linked with both family houses, the Valentins and the Bruces, increasing his greatness."

Devora sat staring at her mother. That name! It *must* be a coincidence—what had Bruce told her aboard the *Revenge?* Her memory reverted back to the deck of his ship where they had stood facing each other.

"I've heard Nicklas had an English mother—the granddaughter of Earl Anthony, a close ally of King Charles," he had said.

"You've not always been Captain Hawkins have you?" asked Devora.

He had watched her, his gray-green eyes taking in her face, as though measuring the depth to her question.

"Why I don't know what you mean, Madame. I told you in the governor's hacienda that I was Bruce Anthony. Hawkins is a name I picked up. It suited me."

Devora was jarred back to the present by the voice of the countess: "Don Maximus believes a marriage to a Radburn would please the duke. But what he wants for himself in return is title of Count of the Realm."

Duke Anthony . . . Lady Marian Bruce . . . Bruce Anthony— Don Nicklas—

"Devora," demanded the countess. "Do pay attention."

"Yes," she said breathlessly, her heart pounding. "Don Maximus told me about the political information Robert is passing on to him. . . . Mother, about Duke Anthony and Lady Marian Bruce—"

The countess cocked a brow. "He told you this? Beast. Folly! I'm surprised he would. Did he mention the title Count of the Realm he expects to receive from the Spanish king?"

"Yes," said Devora wearily, dragging her mind away from the bewildering names of Duke Anthony and Lady Bruce. "As a reward for the information he will offer the Spanish king. Mother, how can you involve yourself in treason?"

She sighed. "Yes, yes, I know, quite tasteless isn't it? I'm ashamed of myself too, at times, and concerned for Robert, should any of this find its way to the court of King Charles. Not that it will, I'm sure of it. If there was a chance it might, he wouldn't have done as I suggested."

Devora started with shock. "What! You can't mean this. 'You' suggested? This was *your* idea, not Robert's?"

"Why not? I had to do something, didn't I? When I learned the truth about the Radburn inheritance—or lack of it," she said bitterly, "I knew Robert was too gallant to demand payment from the king of what he owed him. I needed to fatten our family coffers or I'd be selling the Ashby family jewels for both Robert and I to live on. I wasn't about to do that. My ruby brooch has been in the family since the time of Queen Elizabeth. It will be yours after I succumb, and much more if things go as planned. Not that you'll need it after marrying Nicklas. Ah dear Nicklas, so handsome, so *rich*. After Robert told me the dreadful news about losing the Radburn lands, I met the viceroy at a dinner in Seville. When I learned Nicklas was heir to the viceroy's small silver empire, and would also be awarded the inheritance as the son of Lady Bruce, well—I devised a plan to enrich the Radburn purse."

Devora did not know if she should feel horrified by this crass confession or allow herself to slip deeper into a daze. Little her mother did actually surprised her for long.

"But in Barbados you said some of the family jewels from Radburn hall would be reclaimed. That you and Robert would make a trip to England to get them and meet King Charles again."

She fanned herself, her mouth thinning. "A few family jewels from his great-grandmother remain, yes. But when I return to England, dear, I expect to do so as a far wealthier and powerful woman. If there's any treasure seeking to be done, it will be carried out near Cuzco, the royal city of the Inca Indians."

Devora's alarm grew. She remembered overhearing something strange in the conversation between her mother and Barnabas at

Ashby Hall the night she arrived to bring her to Cartagena. Uncle Barnabas had accused her mother, saying that Robert had sponsored Don Favian Valentin to trick the Inca Indians into leading Spanish adventurers to their mountains of silver. At the time it had made no sense to Devora, nor did it now, but her mother had denied knowing anything about it to Barnabas.

Barnabas had also said that ships which brought slaves and prisoners to work the silver mines belonged to the Valentin family and Robert. But if Robert was in such penury, where had he obtained money to invest in the ships? Did her mother know about them?

In the lapse of silence that had followed her mother's disclosure, she had grown weary from her fever and Devora listened to her labored breathing. The feverish flush on her throat and face warned Devora that she must not pursue the matter now. She wrung out the cloth from the bowl of cool water and applied it to her mother's face.

"You need to take the medication Doctor Cortez left you, then sleep. We'll talk again tomorrow if you like."

The countess turned her head to and fro on the pillow and whispered feverishly, "Maximus promised me—Robert can search the Inca tombs around Cuzco—tombs left—left undisturbed by the conquistadors . . ."

"Madame! It's madness. You cannot believe this?" whispered Devora.

"Maximus promised. . ."

"You cannot trust Don Maximus," Devora insisted. "He has plans of his own. He is ruthless. He will think nothing of betraying you and Robert if at any time your wishes conflict with his."

The countess opened her eyes and they glimmered. "I have risked everything to come to Lima, even my health. The trail Robert has taken follows the road of the conquistadors. The conquistadors found cities of gold, mountains of silver. And the royal Incas were buried with their personal treasure. Maximus knows of tombs yet undisturbed. Silver, gold, all manner of jewels will be mine."

Whether her fancies were real or fever induced, Devora could not say. There might be Inca tombs unmolested by the Spaniards' thirst for gold, but if Don Maximus was the man she thought he was since meeting him on his terms, neither her mother nor Robert would be returning to England with a chest of gold, silver, and jewels.

"Robbing the Incas can hardly be said to be any different than the work of the Caribbean pirates."

"Don't be silly, darling, what good does the gold and silver do anyone locked away in musty tombs? Not when I can save the Radburn earldom with it."

"I'm sorry, Mother, but I don't see that stealing from the Incas is any different than Henry Morgan raiding the Spanish Main. It's very unfitting how Don Maximus can storm about his balcony over Captain Hawkins being a pirate and a diablo when Maximus is stealing from the Incas."

"Maybe so," murmured the countess with a sleepy sigh, "anyway they won't know the difference in London. I shall be a rich and happy woman, whose silver dreams have been realized at last."

"Rich, yes, but happy?" Devora laid the palm of her hand on the burning forehead. *She's delirious,* she thought. *All of this tale of an Inca burial tomb is the result of it.* She might ask Don Maximus if he had baited her mother with such sweetly luring lies. *It would be like him,* she thought. All the while mockingly amused at her mother's gullibility. *Tobias might know,* she decided. She would talk to him about it. Tobias knew all about the Incas. What's more, he cared about their souls, not their silver and gold. Yes, she would go to Friar Tobias.

Her mother was asleep and breathing heavily. She stood watching her for a long moment, feeling regret that matters had turned out so badly. There was no hope for herself or her mother. They would both, most likely, become trapped on the Main, even as they were now. Bruce would not arrive. How could he? Marriage to Don Nicklas loomed before her.

She might try to escape, but how could she leave her ailing mother? The countess had abandoned her at an age when a child needed her mother, but she could not bring herself to walk away and leave her.

Then she remembered that the Lord had not left her alone; there was one friend, Friar Tobias. Again she wondered why Tobias had spoken so little about his nephew. Now is the time. She must have answers. Not just about the Inca tomb, but there were other questions she must ask Tobias as well. She wanted to know more about Don Nicklas Valentin.

⊸ 9 ⊷

Captured by the Dominicans!

For I said in my haste, I am cut off from before Thine eyes . . .

—*Psalm 31:22*

Devora prayed, then wisely waited for the moment she believed was given by the Lord. When the friendly meztiza slave girl, Cuzita, brought fragrant, steaming tea called *yerba-de-mate*, she inquired about Friar Tobias and where she might find him. Could Cuzita have a message brought to him?

"The good friar is not in the house, Señorita, but I know where in Cartagena you can find him. If it pleases you, I will bring you to him."

Devora whispered: "Is that possible? Can you leave the Valentin house freely?"

Cuzita's brown eyes shone with mischievous humor in the lantern light. She glanced over her shoulder toward the open door into the hallway. "I can leave no more freely than you can, Señorita, but together—who knows?"

Devora studied her earthy face and saw in it the signs of adventure and risk. "You would try?" she whispered.

"For you? Yes, Señorita, I would see to it. I have friends," she boasted in a whisper. "The stable boy Juan and the maid Maria who serves Doña Sybella. We help each other. I will bring you to Friar Tobias."

Even though she had prayed for just this answer, when it came she doubted. Why would Cuzita be willing to risk getting caught to bring her to the friar? "If you are caught, will it not mean punishment?"

"Florenzia will beat me, yes. She loves Don Favian and hates me because he told me I was pretty. But I am too wise for *him*. I do not listen to his lies. I see what he did to Maria. Maria loves him, but he no longer sees her alone. Now that Doña Sybella has returned, the master's son has eyes for no one but her."

"You are wise to avoid Favian. But tell me, why are you willing to help me?"

"Because you are different from Doña Sybella. She speaks bitterly to me, but you are gentle. I do not think you would ever have me whipped because you were in a dark mood."

"That such things happen brings me pain, Cuzita. We can behave beastly to one another, but God would have believing slaves and masters treat one another with grace."

"I knew you were like Friar Tobias," she said victoriously. "I told Maria so, but she said no, you would soon be as prima donna as Señora Sybella. Tonight, if God wills, I will bring you to the friar. He is a good man. He teaches us to pray to the Father through His Son only, only Jesus." She held up a pointed finger. "One savior between holy God and unholy people on earth, says friar."

"Yes," said Devora, and smiled. "Tobias has taught us both from the Scriptures. The Son of God invites us to come with outstretched arms."

Later that night Devora waited until the household was quiet, and Maria was speaking softly to Cuzita in the outer hall. A baby cried in one of the far off rooms and Devora was reminded with surprise that Sybella was a mother. Maria hurried off to attend while Sybella readied herself for bed, and Cuzita slipped into Devora's chamber with shining eyes.

"Don Maximus has left for business in town, Señorita. It is his custom to be out late each night. Now is our chance. Juan has a coach waiting down the street. If we are quiet, we will have success. All the slaves are for us and will keep silent."

"What of Don Favian?" she asked, thinking the cynical younger son of Maximus might still be up and taking wine in one of the rooms.

"Oh he will not know, Señorita, did you not see he was not at dinner?"

"Yes, but I thought I heard him leave for town earlier and then return."

She shook her head. "It must be someone else. Maria has learned from Don Favian's servant that he leaves for the harbor. He goes with others to escort Don Nicklas back to Cartagena. He will not return for how many days we do not know. Come quickly, Señorita."

Moonlight flooded the patio below, and the olive and banana trees cast ink-black shadows on the stone courtyard. Cuzita led her down a path between fragrant rosebushes to the other side. There was a low wall and a gate, and they passed through in silence, little else stirring but Devora's silken skirts. Beyond the main house there was a higher wall facing the alley, and an arched, black iron gate.

Cuzita went first to the gate, looking both ways through the grill, then whispered. The sound of scuffling footsteps was heard, then a boy of fifteen wearing an Indian poncho appeared and whispered. Cuzita swung open the gate and beckoned for Devora to follow.

Out on the street the boy led the way and Cuzita ushered Devora down the empty street where they turned left into a smaller, narrower alleyway where a dark, high wall hemmed them in. The outline of a small coach waited. A moment later Devora and Cuzita were inside, and the boy climbed up to the seat and flicked the reins. The coach gave a lurch as the horse trotted ahead. "He does not know how to drive so well, but he can be trusted."

Devora relaxed a little and tried to see her surroundings through the small window. She could smell the sea. Little showed on the cloistered, narrow street except dark outlines of buildings, lattice work, and trees. Soon, the full, ripe moon crept out from behind the ridge of palm trees and the sky brightened.

When they reached the main streets of Cartagena, torches flared from sconces on the walls. Juan brought the coach to a jerky stop in the shadows across the street from the cathedral. Devora climbed out, Cuzita behind her. "This way, Señorita," she whispered.

In the Plaza Square named after the great cathedral, a bell tolled and Cuzita stiffened, grasping Devora's arm.

"What is it?" whispered Devora worriedly. "It is only a bell."

"Oh Señorita, my sin! The hour of curfew!"

Curfew! Devora glanced about. The citizens of Cartagena were drifting away from the plaza.

"Anyone caught by the guardia civil," said Cuzita of the legal patrol guarding the streets, "could be arrested for breaking curfew. I forgot, for I do not come to town often."

"It's all right, don't blame yourself. We've come too far to go back now. You wait in the coach with Juan," she whispered. "If anyone notices me, I can surely appeal to Friar Tobias."

Cuzita did not look satisfied, and glanced about with alarm. "But news will reach the viceroy—"

"I will bear full responsibility. You have done much good. Wait in the coach."

Cuzita shook her head and her braids danced. "No, I cannot fail you now, Señorita. As you say, we have come too far. I must show you to the friar's chamber, for there are many and you could get lost. May the Christ bless our way."

The square crowned by Cartagena's largest cathedral was now deserted. The faint sound of horse hoofs and turning wheels receded in the night. Cuzita, leading the way, pointed ahead and Devora followed in silence.

The first building she saw with intricate stonework bore the arms of the Inquisition. Cuzita paused beside her in the muggy heat, looking up at the building with frightened eyes, then hurried past as though the diablo himself lurked above the steps between the porch posts.

In the blue shadows of the night, Devora neared the great church, the Templo de Santo Domingo, its dome rising higher than the walls of the city.

"Friar Tobias has a chamber office in back. When he comes to Cartagena to visit Don Maximus, he stays here," said Cuzita. "Though he has a room there, Friar does not like big house. There is no key, here. All are welcome to see him, or go inside to pray, to think."

Cuzita waited in the stone cubicle, while Devora tried the heavy door and found it unlocked as she had said.

The chamber was small and sparsely furnished with a desk and chair. Manuscripts and some leatherbound books were neatly stored on a library shelf. Tobias would need to be extremely careful as to what books he kept here. To possess one forbidden book smuggled in from Europe could mean his call to answer before the archbishop, and worse. She saw the typical items one would expect to see from a man of the cloth; a silver cross on the wall— this one plain and simple, some candles, some images carved of alabaster. An arched door was on the other side of the chamber. She decided it must be a private sleeping quarter. She loathed to awaken him but there was no choice now. But a quiet rap brought an answer of silence.

"Tobias? It's me, Devora."

Still, there was no reply and her heart sank with disappointment. She decided neither she nor Cuzita had planned this venture very wisely. They had arrived at curfew, and probably in vain, since it didn't appear as though Tobias was even here. Unless he was elsewhere in the cathedral, in prayer perhaps?

Still, she didn't want to leave without making certain he wasn't fast asleep, so opened the door a crack and peered in. The bed was undisturbed, a lantern burned, and there was a book open on the nightstand. A friar's cloak hung on a peg on the wall. Then he was here after all and would return soon. Relieved, she entered, leaving the door open and noticed, to her surprise, an item that did not belong inside a cathedral. A dagger in a leather sheath—lying on the floor.

Had she seen it before on the journey? Tobias had one like it, but was it the same one? Who else could it belong to except Tobias? She wondered that he left it boldly in plain view. Why was it on the floor? Did the priests also carry weapons? She paused, horrified, then decided that Tobias must have accidentally dropped it in his haste. Cartagena could be dangerous, she knew that, and Tobias was no ordinary friar to be sure. He was a close ally of Bruce, and so a dagger was fitting after all, she told herself.

She glanced over her shoulder into the outer chamber hearing male voices and sandaled footsteps enter from another alcove. Startled, she could see the two robed men, and Tobias was not one of them.

"You are certain?" the tall priest with a broad-boned face was saying. "Look in his cloister."

If they found her here—

She turned in a panic to bolt, but realized she couldn't; nor could she lead them to Cuzita and Juan. She glanced about wildly for a place to conceal herself and was prepared to dart into the tiny alcove that hid a washpot when her gaze tripped over the dagger. If they found it—

She snatched it up, darting into the semi-dark alcove and pressed hard against the back wall as the footsteps of the priest sounded.

She heard the door squeak as it was pushed. The men entered and all was silent. She could just hear garments rustle and sandals scrape on the stone floor before one of them said something in Latin to his fellow cleric. The door shut behind them and Devora's breath released. She leaned her head back against the wall and closed her eyes. *Thank you, God. Please, do not let them notice Cuzita*. Perhaps she had heard them coming too and had taken precaution to hide herself.

She waited until she was certain they had left, then stepped from the alcove back into the small cubicle. She listened at the door but heard no one moving about.

Where was Tobias now? Why were the clerics searching for him, or were they? Could someone other than Tobias have lit the lantern? Would Tobias even return tonight? She didn't think so. She glanced about and could see now that he must have departed in a hurry, even as she had darted into the alcove. Otherwise he would have taken his robe and the dagger—the dagger. That's why it was on the floor, he must have dropped it in his haste and not realized it until he was out of the cathedral.

Should she bring it with her and return it to him at the Valentin house, or hide it here to find when he returned? For she was sure he would return, at least long enough to gather his precious manuscripts.

She hesitated. If she were caught with a dagger, she would need to answer difficult questions, where she had been tonight, and why. Don Maximus was already suspicious about her dealings with Captain Bruce Hawkins. She dared not cast further suspicion on Tobias by confessing she had come to ask him questions about Bruce. She also remembered another dagger—one she had found at Governor Huxley's residence in Barbados the night she had first met Bruce. What madness had entrapped her then, with Bruce chasing after her, and when catching her, accusing her of trying to slay him. She could smile now when remembering, but then—

If Don Maximus learned that she had a weapon belonging to his brother Tobias, the questioning of her actions would become as sharp and keen as those of the feared clerics.

No, she thought with revulsion, grimacing as she looked down at the weapon. She best hide it here in the drawer, out of sight—

But her eyes swerved instead to the robe hanging unsuspiciously from the peg. Yes, the robe would suffice better—

She hurried to locate the inner pocket, her head turning toward the door as she listened for the sound of returning footsteps.

Her fingers brushed up against something made of metal, too heavy for a religious item. She removed a pistol.

Her brows furrowed in a moment of confusion, for she had seen this weapon before as well as the dagger. In fact—it had been within her own possession at the governor's hacienda on the Isle of Pearls, the night Captain Bruce Hawkins sacked the Isle. It was the pistol Bruce gave her for self-protection, but had taken back that night in her chamber. . . .

Once again, as when her mother had mentioned the names of Duke Anthony and Lady Marian Bruce, her mind raced backward—

She remembered running across the floor and kneeling before the trunk. With shaking hand she had retrieved the pistol Bruce had given her. In the lantern light she saw the silver-inlaid handle faintly glimmering. But in her haste and fear, she had hardly noticed the initials that were carefully engraved, barely making out in the flickering candle flames the lettering B.A.V. on the handle. "Bruce Anthony." But why the V? Should it not be H?

Holding that same pistol now in Tobias' chamber she thought with a slight intake of breath, *Yes, why is it V and not H for Hawkins?*

She ran her finger over the raised initials, remembering how Bruce had watched her when he had come up to her chamber. That casual behavior of his was beginning to come into focus. She remembered how his eyes had fallen to the boarding pistol in her hand. He had straightened from the door as though just remembering something, and looked at her searchingly. She had wondered why. Now, she thought she knew.

"The viceroy suspects you of having another identity," she had informed him. "Why would he think so?"

He had casually relit a candle that had gone out. "Curious, is it not?" was all he had said. "That pistol, on second thought, Madame, it is too heavy, too cumbersome. Allow me to leave another with you in its place." And he had removed a small French pistol from a shoulder holster inside his shirt. He smiled, when she frowned.

"In my risky ventures, a man cannot have too many weapons. Here, a better exchange. You can keep this one."

Thinking about it now, Devora's eyes narrowed. What had he said? He had smiled, and bowed. "I have already introduced myself. "Bruce Anthony."

"Why is it that I think there is more?"

"A woman is always suspicious," he had said lightly with a smile. "All right; my name is not Hawkins."

"So I thought. What is it?"

He spread his hands. "I have no last name."

"I don't believe you."

"It is true. My father disowned me. And my mother died the eve of my birth. I have taken the last name of my mother— "Bruce"—and the name of an uncle I respect in London— "Anthony."

Devora's breath caught, and her heart pounded so rapidly that her breath came as though she had been running. Her hand tightened on the pistol. It could not be! There *must* be some other explanation.

Of course there was. Why even Bruce said his father had disowned him. Don Maximus doted upon his precious Nicklas. It was Don Favian he had disowned. Then was it only a coincidence that Bruce had the same name as Nicklas' grandfather in London, and his mother, Lady Marian Bruce? Perhaps it was all a vile jest; he had learned about his enemy Nicklas' English parentage and had taken their names, adding them to Hawkins just to infuriate the proud viceroy. But why was it the Viceroy had never brought this up? Surely he knew? Or perhaps he did not?

She frowned, thinking intently until her head ached of whether or not the viceroy had ever called the pirate he sought anything other than Hawkins. Had he ever said Captain "Bruce" Hawkins?

Soft footsteps sounded rapidly behind her and Cuzita's anxious whisper breathed: "Hurry, Señorita, hurry. Two soldiers have come, and many priests are gathering to speak with them. Some trouble is happening. We must get out of here."

Devora, still holding the sheathed dagger and now Bruce's pistol, placed them in the pocket of Tobias' cloak and rolled them up inside taking the bundle with her. In another moment they were rushing out of the chamber back into the darkened court, darting behind shrubs and hiding until the voices faded and the clerics and soldiers had gone inside the Templo de Santo Domingo.

"Quick, away!" whispered Cuzita, and Devora rushed behind her onto the deserted street. They ran to where the coach still waited in the shadows.

"Hurry, Juan," the meztiza cried in Spanish.

Devora, clambering inside onto the leather seat, pulled Cuzita up beside her, then reached over to close the door. The horse bolted forward and the door slipped from her hand and swung backward. Devora leaned out to grasp the handle, but as she did so the horse turned a corner. Her sweating hand slipped. She lost her balance and gasped as she slid toward the gaping doorway. She had a terrifying glimpse of speeding cobbles and felt herself falling. She made a desperate grab as the door swung back, heard Cuzita's cry of alarm, but the next moment Devora's grasp slipped from the door and she tumbled headlong from the coach. A sharp, blinding pain stabbed through her body, the name of "Jesus" whispered by her lips, then—

Devora struggled to open her eyes and saw darkness swirling about her. Bewildering pain engulfed her. The darkness was swallowing her. She was lying on something hard that still held heat from the day's sun. She reached a stiff, bruised hand and touched the street cobbles. She heard running feet, Spanish voices shouting. Someone ran up beside her and fell on their knees, bending over her. Through blurred vision Devora saw Cuzita. Juan's voice could be heard in the warm night crying for mercy as the whistle of a whip sounded.

"Señorita," wept Cuzita. "Soldiers come. And the Dominicans."

Devora struggled to move, but found that after all her agonizing effort she had barely turned her head.

"Do not die," whispered Cuzita desperately.

Devora tried to whisper: "The . . . cloak . . . Tobias . . . hide it."

"Tobias is not here, Señorita, it is too late," and Devora felt the splash of her tears on her face. Devora tried to pray. She reached feebly but desperately for Cuzita's hand. She could hear the soldiers. They had only a moment.

"Hide—cloak—"

Cuzita raised her head, trying to understand, her brown eyes searching her face. Then she looked toward the coach, and back over her shoulder. She ran toward the coach but Devora could not see if she reached it or not. The soldiers' footsteps approached in a rush and Devora was encircled. More guards went after Cuzita, shouting at her in Spanish.

Devora squinted into the face of the cleric she had seen in the cathedral. He looked down at her, the breeze moving his brown robe. "She is English," came his surprised voice.

"The meztiza insists they come from the hacienda of His Excellency the viceroy."

"Don Maximus? Bring her to the cathedral. Carlos! Bring word to His Excellency at once. If the meztiza is lying we will know. She may be the one we saw earlier."

The cleric knelt beside her and crossing himself, began to utter his prayers, as someone was sent for a hammock to carry her to the Templo de Santo Domingo.

Dazed now, numb with pain, Devora relinquished her mind to the warm darkness, hearing the low Latin of the Dominican.

The robe . . . the pistol . . . the initials B.A.V. What if they found it? What if they turned it over to Don Maximus?

❦ 10 ❧

The Discovery of the Pistol

He shall sit as a refiner and purifier of silver...

—Malachi 3:3

Devora awoke within a stone chamber of the nuns' convent, and her first response was one of profound gratitude that she seemed to be in one piece. She shuddered to think how close she had come to being run over by the rear wheels of the coach when she had fallen. *If I'm still alive, then the Lord isn't through with me yet*, she thought, consoled. Although circumstances were turning out badly, she chose to believe in God's sovereign care and His divine purposes for her circumstances.

She groaned, thinking herself alone. At the moment, with plans gone awry and looking worse as time went by, she could see little purpose or good in any of events that had recently befallen her. She did not understand why she found herself in Cartagena, left to the machinations of the Countess and Don Maximus.

She raised a feeble hand, every movement tingling with pain, and discovered a bandage on the side of her head. There were other bandages on her body as well, but as she moved and tested each limb she breathed a sigh of thanks that there seemed to be no broken bones. The bruises would soon heal, and the nasty bump on the side of her head would disappear.

She turned her head and looked toward a small window in the stone wall. Early daylight shone through, offering new reasons to hope again. She listened to pigeons cooing in the olive trees and heard the soft flutter of their wings. She tried to remember being brought here last evening, but had no recollection of it, and decided she must have slept soundly through the night. Had the viceroy been contacted yet? The idea of answering his investigative questions took on the nightmarish face of an ordeal that she shrank from. Had the Spanish soldiers found the weapons in Tobias' cloak? At the time it had seemed wise to take them in an attempt to protect Tobias. Now the action portrayed itself as foolish. Whatever had possessed her to do it? If Tobias had thought it unsafe to keep Bruce's pistol in his cloak he wouldn't have done so. Again she groaned. She had most likely made a shambles of everything, including her own fate.

With considerable effort her sluggish mind dismissed her own dilemma and remembered Cuzita, who had taken such personal risk to help her. A cautious turn of her aching head, and a bleary glance about the isolated nun's chamber, showed that the girl was nowhere to be seen. Devora had a distinct recollection of having heard the lash of a whip, and of Cuzita crying. Were they under detention for breaking the curfew? It seemed a small matter, but Devora had discovered long ago that the Spanish authorities needed little justification for harsh behavior when it suited their purposes.

The nuns, however, had treated her well, and she dimly remembered that there was one older lady who had been especially attentive and kind-natured. As the daylight outside grew brighter and shone in through the window, the light revealed this nun sitting beside Devora on the floor, her rosary beads in hand. Evidently she had been there all along, but Devora had not noticed her in the cloistered shadows. She was a very old woman with white hair and a wrinkled, brown face, whose thin body all but disappeared within the severe, black folds of her hooded garment. There was a smile on her lips and a lively gleam in her dark eyes.

Devora assumed her to be the one who had attended her cuts and bruises and bandaged her head.

"You have been kind to me," Devora's hoarse voice whispered. "Thank you."

The woman made no reply, but kept smiling, a trace of wistful sadness to her wide lips. Devora, thinking that perhaps her Spanish was lacking clarity, repeated her gratitude, asking the elderly nun if she had seen Cuzita. But still, the woman only looked at her, tilting her head, so that the shadow from her hood showed little else except her smile.

"She cannot hear you," said another nun, bringing Devora hot, meat broth in a metal bowl. She aided Devora, who grimaced, into a sitting position and then handed her the bowl. She cupped it between her palms and took a thirsty sip of the hot liquid. It tasted like salty lamb broth poured over cooked maize.

"Our Rosa from Portugal is deaf, and her tongue was removed long ago."

Horrified at the latter, Devora swallowed hard. "Her tongue removed!" she said weakly but indignantly. "How utterly wicked and beastly! Whoever did so dreadful a thing to her should be sorely punished."

"Yes," said the other sadly, "but as you can see, Rosa is not unhappy. Her experiences have brought her closer to the Virgin."

"But—but *why* would the Spaniards do such a vile thing—and to a nun?" She could only conclude that the diabolical deed had been done by the inquisitors.

"It wasn't a judgment of Spain, child, it was the poor savages in the jungles of Peru. Rosa served at a small mission they attacked and destroyed. When the governor of Portobello sent soldiers to retaliate, the Indians were killed and their camp destroyed, but they found Rosa as she is today."

Devora was rebuked into silence. She had been quick to blame every atrocity on the harsh methods of Spain, but the Indians had their cruelties as well, as did the English pirates.

"Rosa spends almost all her time in prayer for others. She has been by your bedside since you were brought here last night."

Devora looked again at Rosa and her heart reached out to her. "Yes," she said quietly, thoughtfully. "I see that pain and suffering can make some bitter, while others have submissive hearts, taking the thorns of life from God who is able to use them for our good."

Rosa extended her hand toward Devora and the sunlight fell upon a small silvery cross with thorns that bloomed into lilies.

"She means for you to take it as her gift. She spends her working hours, when not at her prayers, making many such crosses."

Devora took the small, glimmering pendant, artfully done, and held it in her palm. As she looked at it, she realized she had already learned a lesson she would have missed had she returned to the Valentin house last night without incident. She had seen one of the many other faces of Spain, and Cartagena, in Rosa.

The House of Inquisition remained; but so did this precious, elderly nun Rosa. Her tongue had been removed by Indians, but she was one who could still smile, pray, and show mercy. Rosa, who formed little cross pendants with blooming lilies.

Two days slipped by before she heard from the viceroy. Then a terse message was sent telling the nuns he was coming to collect Devora.

Outside in the plaza the noisy clatter of hoofs intruded into the noonday heat, followed by a commanding voice. Devora, dressed and waiting in a chair the nuns had found for her, braced herself for the onslaught to come and stood to meet him.

The door was thrown open and Don Maximus Valentin barged into the convent as though it were only another chamber in his house, with everything and everyone in it only an extension of his personal kingdom.

The nuns swiftly withdrew as though some fiendish warrior from the pit had burst upon them, smelling of sulfur.

His large frame, draped in magnificent cloth, barred the doorway. He wore a sword, which no one doubted he could use proficiently.

His heavy tread sounded across the floor. He stopped and turned his furious countenance upon her.

Her first thought was to wonder if he had the cloak and pistol. In two days she had not been able to discover any information from the nuns. Either they didn't know, or were told by the Dominicans not to say anything.

"So you thought to run away, to escape."

"I sought audience with Friar Tobias," she said calmly. "Your brother, and if I marry Don Nicklas, my uncle. Is that the vice I am accused of?"

He considered, as though her calm reaction to him confused the issue.

"And in your haste to escape the priests, you fall from the thundering coach and nearly break your neck. I do not see this as religious behavior."

"Do you fault me because the driver feared mistreatment from the hands of the authorities for disregarding the curfew? Where is he? And Cuzita? Have they no reason to fear? Surely they do! And where is your compassion? I heard one of the soldiers using a whip! Such barbaric behavior from civilized Spain!"

His wide, black brows lifted. "I should marvel at your daring agility to maneuver out of your obvious guilt, Señorita Devora. You disobeyed my orders and made selfish use of the slaves to accomplish your desires, yet you boldly look me in the eye and confront me."

She drew in a breath. "I did not disobey. In Barbados I was a free woman. I came and went as I wished."

"This is not Barbados."

"And as long as I traveled about with a guard, there were few who faulted me for impropriety."

"Perhaps you *will* have a guard," he warned.

She pretended that he meant no threat, but offered a service.

"If His Excellency wishes to supply me a trustworthy body-guard, I would find no reason to contend."

He hesitated, then gave a short laugh, scanning her. "You are a remarkable young woman, Devora."

She flushed. She hadn't wanted that response.

"You refuse to cower when trapped. I am not certain yet what I will make of it."

She sank into the chair, and glanced toward the door. "Am I to be brought back to the house?"

"I would not think of banishing you to the fate of a convent." He smiled, a tinge of ruthlessness to his mouth. "Yes, back to the house. You have much to answer for. Since you wish to see Tobias so badly, you will be pleased to know he has gone to Portobello to meet Don Nicklas."

She looked up at him, her surprise showing. "Your son has arrived?"

He took her in. "Yes, and will come to Cartagena in a few days. You should feel stronger by then. There will be a fiesta in his honor. I am sure you will want to join in the praise heaped upon him for his noble military service for Spain."

This was the last thing she wished to do. At least Tobias was safe. Why had he felt it necessary to escape that night, leaving behind his dagger and the cloak with Bruce's pistol? The answer must wait until she saw him again alone.

"Your mother has been asking for you, but her illness restrains me from explaining your actions. She would be upset if she knew what you had done. Come," he ordered, "the coach waits."

He led her from the convent to where several of his men came to meet them, opening the coach door. She gave him a guarded glance as she was helped inside. He climbed in, sitting across from her. She wondered again if he knew anything about the pistol as the horses trotted from the plaza.

"You've not said what Cuzita's fate is to be, or that of the driver who brought us here."

"They will receive just treatment."

"I would like to think so. Cuzita wished only to help me."

"Yes, the meztiza is very helpful," came his retort. "And loyal to you. I do not approve of overly loyal slaves, Señorita. Except to me. As I have learned from my difficulties with Sybella, loyal slaves become a resource for use as personal spies."

So he had troubles handling Doña Sybella. She wasn't surprised to learn this, since meeting her.

"The meztiza I gave you has already proven too loyal for my concerns."

"Cuzita is not to blame, nor is the boy. I would request no punishment for them. Is there not enough cruelty on the Main without more, and for merely breaking curfew?"

"'Merely breaking curfew,' as you call it, is a most serious offense in Cartagena. That is not what worries me, however, but what you were doing out so late."

"I told you, I was hoping to speak with Friar Tobias."

"That worries me even more, Doña Devora. As for the meztiza, she disobeyed my orders. You were not to leave the house while I was away. As for you, since Nicklas will soon arrive I will put no other trial upon you except your recovery. Prepare yourself to be pleasing to him."

"And Cuzita and Juan?"

"The meztiza slaves will remain under questioning by the Dominicans."

"The Dominicans! But why? They have done nothing worthy of such cruelty!"

"Then they have nothing to fear."

Her hands knotted in her lap as she stared across at him. "Why don't you simply ask about the reason I wished to see Friar Tobias?"

"I will, Señorita, but from Tobias when he arrives. Should I tell you what I suspect, Doña Devora? It is," he growled, "that my own blood brother, my beloved Tobias, has betrayed me."

She tensed, believing he knew of Tobias' friendship with Bruce.

"He has argued before the Court of Seville that I and others have done an injustice and cruelty to the Incas in Cuzco. His madness is such that he intends to go to the silver mines and confront me, stopping the production. I could accuse him of more," he said darkly. "Of befriending heretics and owning books of witchcraft defending the Protestant beliefs. This in itself is enough to see him answer to the archbishop of Cartagena."

"But you wouldn't go so far, Don Maximus. Not your *brother*, not Tobias . . ."

His dark eyes rested on her face, searching. "My decision is mine alone to consider, and then take action upon at the appropriate time. You should not be concerned for Tobias, but for yourself. Do not overtire my patience. There are some matters that should be left to the wisdom of Spain alone. Meddling will not be tolerated here, even if you would think to align your beliefs with Tobias'. I will speak to the countess about it. And Nicklas."

So Maximus actually thought she had come to make plans with Friar Tobias on how to bring reform to the silver mines. She might have laughed had the formidable accuser sitting across from her not been Don Maximus. Relief swept over her. She looked away from him and out the window.

Obviously he did not know about the pistol. What had become of it then? Could Cuzita have managed to hide it after all, before the soldiers and bishop arrived? Or was it possible Tobias' cloak remained in the other coach? By now the vehicle would have been brought back to the Valentin stables. She must find it before anyone else did.

"You speak of my mother's illness," she said after they had driven along for several minutes in tense silence. "Was it your idea she recuperate in the healthier climate of Lima?"

"If you think I am romantically interested in Catherina you are mistaken."

"I said nothing of that," she said, embarrassed at his bluntness.

"It is your mother's wish to travel with us. Robert should also arrive by then. There is a cause that brings him to Lima, one that also interests the countess."

She remembered what Catherina had told her about becoming wealthy from the silver at Cuzco.

"She told me of their plans concerning an Inca burial tomb. Is it true?"

He looked at her for a long moment. "Yes. Though I have promised Robert little more than access. His journey inland, and his failure or success, will depend entirely on him."

"And the countess," she said with concern. "From what she tells me, she intends to journey with him on the expedition."

He smiled with sarcasm. "It is Robert who is not likely to last, Señorita."

Her eyes searched his. Why did she tend to read more into his simple words than suggestion? Had he told her the truth when he claimed no interest in Catherina? Or was there something more on his mind that not even her mother had guessed?

When they arrived at the Valentin residence Devora was taken to her chamber and put to bed by the older servant, Florenzia. The doctor, she said, would look at her to make certain she was recovering. And if she felt stronger toward evening her mother had asked that she dine with her in her room.

When the physician came and pronounced to Don Maximus that she was in need of prolonged bed rest, Maximus frowned.

"We will see she obeys," he said. "I do not want a pale and fainting Englishwoman on my hands when Nicklas arrives."

Devora fumed inwardly but said nothing. When he left, Doctor Francisco smiled at her.

"Do not mind the viceroy, Doña Ashby. He is not as stern as he appears."

She wondered. As he gathered his medical satchel to leave she asked him to look into the whereabouts of Cuzita and the stable boy, Juan.

He looked down at her gravely. "I will do what I can. Do not worry yourself. Maximus is right about one thing, though we both may disagree with much that he does. You need to regather your strength, Doña."

When the doctor left her alone in her chamber, her mind remained on Cuzita. She must find a way to see her released. Not only for the sake of the girl, but also to discover where she had hidden Bruce's pistol. If it had been left in the coach, by now one of the stable workers would have found it, and probably reported it to Don Maximus. That left the possibility Cuzita had had just enough time to hide it somewhere on the road before the soldiers and the bishop arrived. If so, there would be no great damage to Tobias, since it might be weeks before anyone happened to stumble across it—unless the authorities forced Cuzita to talk.

The countess was up and seated in a chair in her dressing gown when Devora entered her room that evening for a light supper. Her mother looked elated, as though she were excited about something she had no intention of sharing with her daughter.

"Come, Devora, do sit. Isabel managed to find us some delightsome English tea. I'm weary to death of that dreadful yerba-de-mate brew. The English can hardly call it 'tea.'" She scrutinized her daughter with dismay. "More's the pity, your skin is turning an unbecoming black and blue. And your left eye is swollen."

Devora ruefully touched her bruised head. She had removed the bandage and Florenzia had managed to arrange her hair over the abrasion on her scalp, but evidently not well enough to mask her condition from the scrutiny of the countess.

"Let's hope Nicklas is delayed a week longer, or he might send you back to Barbados."

"Could such fortune be mine?" asked Devora with a touch of wryness.

"Hardly, Devora. Too much is involved now, for all of us. From your point of view it's unfortunate but true—we all need you to further our objectives, including Maximus," she added with satisfaction. "Fortunately this debacle of yours isn't likely to cause him to change his mind about your marriage to Nicklas."

"There is no guarantee Nicklas will feel the way you and his father do," Devora reminded her, but even her own suggestion sounded poor. Whatever the viceroy wanted from his son he was likely to get, since she supposed this ruthless Don Nicklas to be the image of the viceroy.

While the countess sipped her tea she lectured on how terribly Devora had behaved, how she mustn't anger Maximus, even if his plans were set where she was concerned.

"Maximus is not one to duel wits with."

But as her mother spoke, Devora noticed that she appeared absorbed with digressing thoughts of her own. Even Isabel, her servant, watched the countess while she went about her duties serving them supper.

The countess turned toward the half-Spanish/half-Indian woman. "You might as well bring the surprise we have for Devora now. There's no use prolonging her worry."

Isabel's lip twitched. "Yes, Madame."

Devora watched her leave the room, then looked at her mother for an explanation. The countess smiled smugly and tried her Mediterranean soup made from black beans and leeks.

Isabel returned carrying a dark garment. She handed it to the countess, then retreated from the room.

Devora stared at Tobias' cloak. As the countess unrolled it, she produced the silver-butted pistol with the engraved initials of B.A.V.

Devora started to speak, but her mother waved her into silence.

"Intrigue, darling, has always been a part of a countess' life. Luis located it in the shrubs alongside the road and brought it to me the same night you fell."

"But—how did you know?" whispered Devora.

The countess shrugged as though it were much ado over nothing. "Knowing your tenacious ways—due to my own error in allowing Barnabas to have unbridled sway over you these years I've been away—made me think it would be wise to have Luis watch you. I suspected you might try to escape. Naturally I had no idea you would go to the cathedral to find Tobias. Luis trailed you and the servants, and was witness to what happened. As good fortune would have it, he was at his post in the trees when Cuzita managed to hide the cloak there. He retrieved it soon after their arrest, once he knew you were safely being cared for in the convent." She sighed heavily. "For the life of me, at first I couldn't understand why you would go to Tobias for help. Then I quite understood when I saw the initials on the pistol; it wasn't Tobias you sought, but this weapon. Most incriminating, I agree."

What were her plans now that she had Bruce's pistol? "You're wrong, Mother, I didn't know Friar Tobias had it. I went to see him, well—because there were other questions I wished answers to, and only he could answer them to my satisfaction, but—he wasn't there."

"But someone else was there, or had been, perhaps only a few minutes before you entered."

"How do you know someone else was there just ahead of me?"

The countess set her spoon down restlessly and pushed the soup bowl away. "Luis saw someone leaving Tobias' chamber and hurrying across the plaza soon after you and the girl entered the cathedral. Luis noticed that he was anxious not to be seen. He would have followed him, but I had told him not to let you out of his sight."

Devora leaned forward in her chair. "Are you suggesting Luis didn't think it was Friar Tobias?"

"No, since it's certain Tobias left Cartagena early that morning. He was seen getting on board Maximus' brigantine to meet Nicklas' flagship docking at Portobello."

If it hadn't been Tobias . . . Devora frowned. "The viceroy said Tobias had gone, but I thought he might have been mistaken." Then who had been in his chamber just before she arrived? Who had placed the pistol in his cloak, and the dagger on the floor, and for what purpose? To incriminate Tobias?

"I've no idea who it might have been," said the countess.

Devora's alarms grew. She had thought it odd that a man as wise as Tobias would have left evidence of his association with Bruce in a chamber where it might easily be discovered by some monk about his mundane duties. Not when Tobias was aware that his reform ideas were unwelcomed by the Church.

Incriminating evidence. Devora's eyes dropped to the pistol and she was careful to not reveal her inner turmoil.

The countess, however, looked quite pleased with her position in the matter. "Granted, you may not have known this was hidden in his cloak, yet once you saw it, you recognized it. You knew of the potential threat to its owner, so you took it with you."

"Very well, I admit I did. I think kindly toward Friar Tobias, and I feared the viceroy might begin asking him troubling questions."

"Is it only the friar you think 'kindly' toward, or is it also the owner of this pistol?"

Devora grew more uneasy by the moment.

"You have sound reason to believe Maximus would begin asking troubling questions," her mother stated tartly. "The initials would alert him at once."

Devora searched her face, wondering what her mother had in mind. What was she going to do, alert Don Maximus?

"Are you going to give me the pistol to return to Friar Tobias?"

The countess took a bite of the flaky, crust-like dessert thick with nuts and raisins, dropping some crumbs on the front of her satin dressing-gown. "Of course not."

Devora's insides tightened.

"I haven't decided yet what I shall do. Having it in my possession might offer me a bargaining tool in the future, should I need it."

"But why would you need a bargaining tool, as you say," said Devora, her frustration spilling out. "Tobias offers you no threats to accomplishing your wishes in Lima with the silver."

"With all of his spiritual fervency against using the Incas?" scoffed the countess. "Tobias will indeed prove troublesome, but in all truthfulness, my dear, it wasn't Tobias I had in mind."

"Then who?" said Devora in a whisper.

Her mother avoided a direct explanation. She wiped her messy fingers on the napkin and gestured for Devora to refill her empty teacup. Devora did so, her fingers trembling slightly.

"You have much to learn, Devora. It's *always* beneficial to have more than one person to turn to for help in dangerous situations."

"Meaning Tobias?"

The countess shrugged. "I suspect he would find it his duty to show mercy, regardless of his disapproval of my ways, but no, it is not him I had in mind."

So her mother expected danger. Her stomach knotted and her spicy dinner sat on the silver plate getting cold. Danger from whom? And from where? Here in Cartagena, or in Lima and Cuzco? Devora was aware that both of them as Englishwomen were alone in the heart of the Spanish Empire. She had no notion of when Earl Robert and the Englishman loyal to him would return from seeking the *Revenge*.

If her stepfather did not arrive within the next few weeks, they would leave for Lima without him. Don Maximus had already said they would embark on the journey after Don Nicklas arrived, and Nicklas was due to sail into Cartagena in a few days.

Until now, Devora had been too concerned with the matters at hand to carefully consider just how strenuous would be the journey to Lima, or how far removed they would be from English territory once there. Lima was on the Pacific side of the Main, while Cartagena was on the Caribbean. Tobias had said they must sail to Panama, then cross the narrow strip of land called the Isthmus, a long, treacherous, jungle-infested journey on mules and by canoe, before they would again board a ship on the Pacific coast to voyage to the harbor of Callao, near Lima.

"Mother, are you certain you should make the journey with your health as it is?" But when her mother did not immediately reply, she had a troubling moment when she wondered if perhaps she had another kind of danger in mind.

The countess waved a hand, her rings winking in the lantern light. "I must make the journey, but my concerns are not that. One never knows about Maximus . . . he is a rather volatile man with plans of his own. He's not likely to want to see those plans come to ruin."

"I thought you and Robert were working with him, not against him."

A shade descended over her mother's face, so that her expression was unreadable. "I speak merely of taking precautions," she said, but didn't explain what they were. "One must always be careful. And here in Spanish territory, more so. About this pistol. It doesn't belong to Tobias. We both know it. Why it was in his possession is a curiosity."

Could she possibly guess it belonged to Bruce? "Maybe someone wanted it found and brought to Maximus to cause trouble for the friar because of his work of reform in the mines."

The countess was looking at the initials again. "With good reason. Maximus would recognize it immediately."

Devora watched her. "Then—you know who it belongs to?"

The countess raised her eyes, and a glint of amused and smug satisfaction flickered in their depths. "It's quite obvious, isn't it? It belongs to Don Nicklas Valentin."

For a moment Devora did not, could not, respond. She had feared her mother would say the buccaneer Bruce Hawkins.

"The question, however, is not whether it belongs to Nicklas," said her mother, "but whether or not Don Nicklas *is* Bruce Hawkins."

Devora sat still, white-faced, in shock.

The countess smiled vaguely. "That, darling, I intend to find out when Nicklas arrives. If he is the pirate wreaking havoc on the Caribbean and goading Maximus to fury, I shall soon be a much wealthier woman than even I had hoped. Naturally Nicklas will not want Maximus to know." She leaned back against the velvet chair, looking satisfied, but fragile and even innocent.

Bruce? Don Nicklas Valentin?

Devora stood, staring at the pistol on her mother's lap. B.A.V. Bruce Anthony Valentin.

"It couldn't be," she breathed.

The countess' dark brows lifted gently.

"It—it may be the pistol of Don Nicklas, but surely—surely it's a jest, stolen somehow by Captain Hawkins. Yes! That's what it is,

Mother. What better way to goad the Spaniards than to have the pirate they seek with such venom using the pistol of the son of the viceroy!"

"Hardly," she said calmly.

"But—it's possible," argued Devora.

"Yes I suppose, yet the initials cannot be denied."

"But it was you who told me that Nicklas has an English heritage. Duke 'Anthony' is his grandfather, and Lady Marian 'Bruce' was his mother. Is it so unreasonable to think Don Nicklas might have owned a pistol with his family initials before that of Valentin?"

The Countess mused.

"And if the pirate Hawkins somehow got hold of it—"

"But who would give it to him? Tobias?" asked the countess with a rueful smile. And when Devora must have flushed, her smile deepened. "Come, darling, it's quite obvious now you're in love with him."

"I—I've never met him," she insisted.

"No, not Nicklas, but you have met this rogue Bruce Hawkins. What does he look like?"

When Devora remained silent, saying nothing, the Countess studied her face. "So I was right. You are in love with the buccaneer named 'Bruce Hawkins.'" There was no anger in her voice, nor even dismay, but calm thoughtfulness.

Devora rushed to the side of her mother's chair and knelt, laying a trembling hand on her arm. Her eyes pleaded. "You won't reveal this to Maximus?"

"That you have lost your heart to the pirate? Well, I can't say I blame you . . . no, I will say nothing. Not yet. Not until I speak alone with Nicklas when he arrives. He could deny all this of course, but he can hardly deny the truth to you. You will know at once. As soon as you see him. And Nicklas will explain to me what he is trying to accomplish in this outrageous and daring masquerade."

Devora remained adamant. Her heart refused to believe that Don Nicklas, the ruthless son of the viceroy, could be the English buccaneer, Bruce Anthony Hawkins.

"It's impossible," she whispered, as if to herself. "Their very beliefs and character are in total opposition to each other. Why, Don Nicklas has been knighted by the king of Spain. He's been sent to Lima to make certain the silver production is increased for the political and religious ambitions of Seville. And Bruce—vows to sink his flagship to the bottom of the Caribbean."

"If it proves true, he is very clever indeed. And mad, or overly daring, to come here to deal with Maximus. One mistake—like this pistol and my willingness to talk—and he could be turned over to the Church authorities. There would be no escape."

Devora stared at the pistol, her heartbeat thumping in her ears. In a wild moment she wanted to grab it from her mother. But even if she did, how could she silence her?

Their eyes met. Devora's gaze wavered as she guessed that her mother read her mind.

"Perhaps I should be grateful to Barnabas after all that he put the fear of God in your soul. I commend you, my dear. You could easily overpower an ailing woman—and silence her completely if you wished."

Horrified, Devora recoiled away from the side of her chair. Her mother meant it. She believed Devora could do such a thing.

"Do you think I could ever harm my own mother, regardless of what you have done to me?"

"I have done nothing yet," came Catherina's tired voice, watching her through screened eyes as she rested her head on the chair back.

Devora disagreed. She had already hurt her from the time when she was a child and needed a mother to shield her with unconditional love. Her grandmother had been a kind woman, but never affectionate. And she too had been weak in health and confined to her suite of rooms in the Ashby house in England. Sometimes weeks would go by when Devora never saw her. But what good was it to hurl these emotional pains at her mother now? *The past is over,* she told herself. *There is no going back. No way to rid the garden of life of seeds long ago planted and blooming.* Still, she was repulsed by the fact her mother had actually believed she could harm her. She sank into her chair, with little strength left in her legs.

"You underestimate me, Madame. If love bids I harm you to safeguard the one I love, it is not love, but something unhealthy, ugly, and the wisest recourse for such passion would be to put it to death."

The countess considered her words with little feeling of her own. The silence deepened until Devora could no longer stand it.

"What are you going to do?"

"The marriage will go through as planned. And if Nicklas is Hawkins, you should count yourself a young woman upon whom Providence has smiled. Your rogue of the sea has turned out to be a man of power and great wealth, if he does not throw it all away in a moment of hatred for his father."

Devora could not even imagine Don Maximus as Bruce's father, nor yet why Bruce should be planning vengeance against him. Her head swelled with a hundred questions and it was certain she would not get the answers now. Only Bruce could explain the truth—or Nicklas?

It was all so astounding she still could not accept the possibility.

"It isn't true. It can't be."

"Don Nicklas' flagship will be arriving soon. You will be the first one to know."

The Schemes of Sybella

Safety is from the Lord . . .
—Proverbs 21:31

Devora awoke to a great stir within the house and below in the large courtyard. Excited voices filled the morning. Slipping on her dressing gown she went to the window, parted the curtains, and stepped out onto the semi-circular balcony.

Sunshine filled the patio below, and the trees cast their shade on the flagstones. House slaves were rushing about with an air of excitement. Devora saw Florenzia and called down, asking what was happening. The old woman looked up and called in Spanish: "Don Maximus is meeting with the governor. Don Nicklas arrives tomorrow. His Excellency will have all Cartagena welcome his flagship! There will be a processional, a fiesta, and a ball at the governor's mansion."

Nicklas would be here tomorrow. . . . Devora turned away from the balcony as the door to her chamber opened and her mother, who must have already heard the news, entered with her satin dressing gown flowing behind. A nervous Spaniard waited in the corridor, holding what looked to be a hundred yards of lace, ribbons, bows, and silk.

"Nicklas arrives tomorrow!" called the countess. "And your dress is hardly ready for the mascarada at the governor's house. Señoritas from the best families of the dons are anxiously working on their elaborate gowns. Not a one must outshine you." She turned to the nervous man in the corridor. "Come, Diego, come. Lady Ashby must try the dress on. I want it finished this evening, is that clear?"

"Dependably Señora, that I promise. I shall see to the great undertaking myself!"

She turned back to Devora. "These indolent Spaniards move as though time does not exist."

Throughout the day the countess gave long and tedious lectures as to how she should behave in public. She was to speak "just so," and curtsy "just so," and use her fan "just so."

"Much is expected from this rigid society that migrated from Spain. You must do nothing to cast a disparaging shadow on the reputation of English nobility. Remember, you are the daughter of an earl and countess."

"Yes, Mother, of course. I shall try to be the precise 'señorita.'"

Her mother sighed. "If only I were young. Ah, well."

Devora felt that she knew the people and their customs as well as possible without actually being one of them. She learned that normal events in the life of the royal family in Seville, such as the birth of a prince or princess, were celebrated in the principal cities on the Spanish Main with all-day processionals and fiestas into the early hours of morning. "But it needn't be anything having to do with Seville," said her mother. "It might be a tragedy seen as a visitation from God. An earthquake, a volcanic eruption, a plague. These are all events that bring everyone onto the streets. A procession of penitents in long, black robes covered with ashes, carrying candles, walk slowly through the streets behind glittering images of saints. Throngs kneel in the incense-laden air of the churches, while bells in towers ring, adding their deep clamor to that of the chanting priests. The people expect their saints to save them from disaster."

The common people as well as the aristocrats loved a celebration and they found reason to rejoice when the viceroy arrived, or when events in his family were deemed important. There were *mascaradas*—festivals of all sorts. Therefore, Devora was not surprised

when Don Maximus arranged for a great fiesta and parade wel-
coming his son Don Nicklas back to the Main as a knighted emissary of the king. Nicklas Valentin, fresh from heroic battles for
Castile and the sinking of heretic ships, would be received with fireworks and dancing in the streets of Cartagena!

And Devora was to be a part of this city-wide mascarada, an
all-day festival, ending in the evening with the most prestigious
families from Castile attending the residence of the governor of
Cartagena to honor the viceroy and his family.

"It's a formal reception called a *beso-mano*," her mother
explained. "A 'kiss-hand' reception. The slaves and ordinary people
gather in the plaza square to watch the painted coaches arrive,
and sedan chairs bringing guests, carried by Africans in gaudy
livery. The señoras and señoritas have on their best gowns, wear
their most glittering jewels, and, with the proud dons, they all enter
the palace. Strains of music fill the air, and after bowing to Don
Maximus and kissing his hand, they dance Spanish court dances."

Devora had practiced the dance steps as her mother taught
her, alternately scolding her and praising her until she had the
movements down as well as Sybella.

"The dance seems a bit overdone if you ask me," said Devora.
"So dramatic!"

The countess laughed. "When Don Nicklas has you on the
dance floor my dear, and pursues you through the sultry fandango,
from one side of the dance floor to the other—you will indeed find
the moment dramatic."

Devora collapsed onto the bed laughing. "I'll doubtless wish I
could faint first. What if I trip on my lace farthingale!"

Her mother was laughing too, but as they looked at each other,
they both stopped. Her mother cleared her throat and Devora
looked away. There had been a time when she had dreamed of
sharing laughter with her mother over some girlish humor, but
now that it was happening, the moment became awkward. She
clamped her jaw. *Too late*, she told herself. *Why didn't she come
when I was growing up, when I needed her?*

The next day, the grand day, would begin with compulsory religious attendance at the town's cathedrals. All must attend, Devora heard, from the haughty families of the dons to the lowly populace of Cartagena. Devora truthfully pleaded a headache, but it was her conscience that actually forbade her. Sybella entered her chambers that evening dressed in black Spanish lace, her pale face looking serene, but her eyes mocking Devora. She laid a catechism and prayer book on the table before her.

"Refusal, my English cousin, will mightily displease Maximus. You can be certain the archbishop is watching to see whether or not you are obedient to the Church. If he gets wind of your heretical beliefs he will be contacting Maximus."

Devora had known that the time would come when she must confront the frightening issue of whether or not she would attend Mass and kneel in obedience to the Dominicans. She had hoped it would not come this soon. She could not lie if asked about her Reformational beliefs; but neither did she think it wise to openly seek a confrontation.

"I have a headache," she said truthfully. "It's only been a week since I fell from the coach."

Sybella's mouth turned into an unsympathetic smile. "Then perhaps you should go to pray to the saints for healing."

"The day will be long, and the festivities will go through the night, Doña Sybella. If I'm to make it through all the activities, I request to remain undisturbed until we are ready to ride to the harbor for the arrival of your cousin Nicklas."

At the mention of Nicklas, Sybella's little smile froze. "When you arrived I told you I would not stand by and see you marry him. I have not changed my mind."

Devora thought of Bruce. Would the man she met tomorrow be the buccaneer that had held her on the Caribbean beach and promised his love, his return? Or would Nicklas be a dark and ruthless stranger? If it was Bruce she would not give him up to Sybella, no, not if it meant staying in Lima for the rest of her life. "If he cares for you as you claim," said Devora quietly but evenly, "then he is politically powerful enough to resist the will of his father and to refuse me."

Sybella's temper flashed in her dark eyes. "And if he tells you to your face he does not want you, will you go away, back to where you came from, and leave us in peace?"

Devora felt an icy prick through her heart. "Yes."

Sybella smiled coolly. "Is that a promise?"

If Bruce told her he did not want her after all? She hesitated, then lifted her chin with confidence. "Yes. Therefore you have nothing to fear from me. Unless he does not love you."

Sybella drew back a hand to slap her but the door opened and Don Maximus stood there, a dark bulwark blocking the threshold. He took one look at Devora then Sybella, and a knowing look of impatience came to his chiseled face.

"What brings you here, Sybella? Did I not warn you to stay away from Doña Devora?"

Sybella hesitated, then pointed to the catechism and prayer book. "I meant a kindness only. She refuses them. Will the archbishop approve a marriage of Nicklas and a heretic?"

Devora's breath paused. She looked at Don Maximus and saw his black eyes glitter. "A heretic. The daughter of the Earl and Countess Radburn? Did not the Radburn family remain loyal to the English king Charles who was accused of loyalty to Rome? Watch your tongue, you spitting cat."

Sybella turned sharply to Devora. "'Spitting cat', is it? Then ask her. Ask her now. Does she wear the crucifix, or does she have forbidden books among her belongings, brought from Barbados?"

Maximus strode toward them, but it was Sybella who backed away. His eyes flashed as he faced his niece, and Devora, alarmed that he would strike Sybella, stepped between them before she thought clearly of what she was doing.

Maximus looked at her, startled, and blinked. Even Sybella lapsed into a strained silence.

Devora pulled the pendant out from under her bodice and the cross that the elderly nun Rosa had given to her glinted in the candlelight.

Maximus looked at Sybella victoriously. "All your venomous jealousy will be your end one day. Leave us! To your chamber! Do I not hear your baby crying? When will you rejoice in your motherhood instead of scheming for the heart and soul of Nicklas?"

Sybella, tears in her eyes, turned and ran from the chamber.

Devora looked at the religious books Sybella had brought her. Why? Hoping to trap her? She had escaped this time, but for how long?

Aware that Maximus watched her suspiciously, she met his gaze, waiting. The moments crept by. "What books did you bring to the heart of Spain, Devora?"

God help me. "Only one, Your Excellency," she said quietly.

Maximus gritted his teeth and his eyes narrowed. "One book? No doubt, but *enough* book to bring the inquisitors to my house in the morning. Would you be examined? Give me this book now. Lest someone of less mercy than I give a charge of heresy against you."

She sank onto a chair. Sybella? She would never go so far. She was jealous, but not cruel. And from her actions Devora did not think her to be genuinely religious, so why should she care about her faith? Bringing the books had only been a goad to try to frighten her.

"Please, Don Maximus, do not ask. I cannot give what is more precious to me than all the silver of Peru."

His eyes narrowed again as they searched her pale face. He hissed something under his breath. "I knew you would be more trouble to me than you were worth. You have proven it already. And to think I am the one who heartedly agrees with the countess that you should marry my son Nicklas."

He walked over to where she sat and, grabbing her wrist tightly, pulled her to her feet. She stared up at him afraid, yet refusing to cower. For a long moment he glowered at her.

"As you please, Señorita, but I warn you now. If the book is discovered and it comes to the attention of Archbishop Andres, I will be hard pressed to spare even you. You will keep your beliefs to yourself. I will let it be known to Sybella that you have turned the book over to me and I burned it. Know that I do this for causes other than what make you happy. I do it for the cause of my own plans." When he let go of her she sank back to the chair, her knees weak.

"And now," he said gruffly, but quietly. "Go to bed and sleep. Tomorrow you will meet Nicklas and I will not have him disappointed in the woman I have arranged for his pleasure."

He strode to the door and Devora's steady voice surprised even her. "What about the religious services at dawn?"

He looked at her, his face hard. "I will make excuses for you. Your accident a week ago will make a cover. The countess too should remain with you. It is easier to make excuses for two feeble women than one." He smirked and went out, closing the door firmly.

Devora's hands went to her throat and her eyes closed with relief. She had escaped, at least for the present.

At dawn she heard the bells in the towers ringing out the hours of the religious day. She heard the viceroy's coach below in the courtyard leaving through the gate, followed by two other coaches of less dignity, bringing the members of the Valentin household to the cathedral.

Later that morning when Maximus returned and Devora went down to breakfast, she was told that he had made Nicklas' arrival a city-wide celebration. The Cartagena streets and center plaza were decorated and already a crowd was gathering. Devora too awoke on the morning of the arrival of the flagship with excitement, but it came not from the rich, gaudy celebrations to last through the day and night, but from anxiety. True to her temporary promise, her mother had said nothing of her discovery to Maximus, but Maximus himself seemed more thoughtful than usual and had little patience for the antics of his niece.

"You will remember you are the grieving widow of Don Marcos," he growled at Sybella. "And you will conduct yourself in black. You have a baby. Do not forget! It is not you Nicklas comes to see, but Doña Devora."

"Am I a slave?" she countered bravely. "I am a Ferdinand, and if you think to cage me in like a peacock with clipped wings, my Uncle, I shall write to the king."

"Write him then. Perhaps he will call you home to Seville. Then I shall have one less gray hair to worry about."

"If I do write him it may be I shall have much to tell him, Your Excellency," came the warning tone. "Do you think I do not know the plans you have made with the English ambassador to steal silver from the mines? Any thievery will have you recalled as well to answer before his throne."

Devora, seated at the breakfast table, winced as Maximus' fist banged down on the table and the Venetian glassware and silver utensils jumped and rattled precariously. But Sybella remained proud and noble as she sat erect, her dark eyes flashing. Maximus stood, scowling at her. He threw down his napkin.

"You are a fool, Sybella, if you think to intimidate me into succumbing to your will. The plans for Nicklas and Devora will go forward. If you seek to interfere I shall take strong measures."

Sybella's cheeks tinted with temper, and perhaps wise reconsideration, for her dark eyes dropped to her plate and she said nothing more, though Devora could see the flexing of her jaw as she gritted her teeth.

Such emotional outbursts dismayed Devora, who, except for the spoilt ways of the countess, had grown up in the cultured, religious atmosphere of the home of Uncle Barnabas. No one had ever raised their voices, threats were unheard of, and emotions were subdued; here, emotions flamed into bonfires of passion that she feared could erupt into bloodshed. She would be glad when Friar Tobias arrived and added his stable, Christian wisdom to the volatile family disagreements.

It was doubly worse for Devora because she was the one in the middle of the conflict. Except for the morning she had arrived

Sybella had not sought her company. She lived and moved about alone in her world as though planning her own recourse to thwart Maximus and the countess. Sybella looked across the table at Devora now and the animosity that flickered in her eyes was undeniable. She too, stood, threw down her napkin, and lifted her chin at her uncle.

"I shall behave myself as the sorrowing widow, but nothing shall keep me from attending the festivities, or in cheering loudly for the flagship of Nicklas."

"You may cheer all you want," said Maximus with a sarcastic smile, "but you will do your cheering and flower-tossing in your widow garb."

Sybella smiled acidly and turning, left the dining-room. Maximus looked harshly at Devora, taking in her appearance. "I hope, Señorita, that the countess has chosen you a dress fitting for the occasion."

Devora had been involved in the plans for the creation of her dress for the past week, and was about to tell him so when the countess, coming down to breakfast for the first time since her arrival, spoke sweetly from the doorway.

"You need not fret, Maximus. Of course my daughter will be appropriately attired. She is the daughter of the Earl and Countess of Radburn. And it is both her wish and mine to honor the esteemed arrival of Don Nicklas."

Devora looked at her mother, and Maximus turned also.

Countess Catherina was already adorned for the beginning of the celebration, the ride through the streets to the harbor where the throngs had already begun to gather for the welcome. There would be viewing stands set up under royal awnings where the families of the dons would sit. The viceroy had a red awning, edged with gold, and cushioned seats. Refreshments would also be served.

Her mother was dressed royally in a muted rose and blue gown, her dark hair exquisitely done. Sapphires glimmered at her throat and ears. She looked lovely, thought Devora with an ache in her throat, for she could see the fire spring to life in the dark eyes of Maximus as he took her in.

"When will Robert arrive?" asked Devora flatly. "Soon, Mother?"

The countess swished her blue feather fan and laughed softly, as though she saw through her question and it amused her. But Maximus looked angry, and a deepening red flared up in his throat and face.

"Soon, darling," said Catherina, seating herself at the table and graciously gesturing the serving woman to pour her tea. "Too bad he isn't here. He does a most delightful fandango. Don Maximus, my servant tells me you've heard important news from the governor of Cartagena?"

Maximus was still looking at Devora with a furious look on his face. He seemed to squelch his temper.

"Robert has gone to Tortuga to meet with the French pirate-governor there, Fontenay. Robert brings a bribe to force the derelict ruler to tell what he knows about Hawkins."

"Oh dear," said the countess, adding sugar to her tea and stirring daintily. "He will return with some fanciful tales, I'm sure."

"And a good deal more, if I know your clever husband, Countess." He nodded his head graciously, his eyes mocking her behavior.

She raised her brows. "Clever, is he? Perhaps," she said easily. "I always thought you were far more so, Don Maximus. You wouldn't have climbed to the position of viceroy if you weren't." And she smiled to soften the sting of her words.

Maximus watched her evenly. He broke off a hunk of bread from a long roll and took a bite, scanning her.

Devora stood. "I had best prepare my dress. If you will excuse me, Mother, Don Maximus." She turned to go when his words stopped her.

"And do wear the amethysts I gave you. They are from Nicklas, not me."

He gave a small laugh when he must have read her surprise.

"He sent them from Vera Cruz," he said too congenially. "In happy anticipation, Señorita, of dancing with you beneath the Cartagena stars." He looked over at the countess. "And perhaps the Countess Catherina will oblige me with such a dance tonight.'

"Perhaps one, Your Excellency. I fear my illness may confine me to the chairs."

"I shall make certain you have a *par excellence* chair, Countess. We both shall."

Devora, watching them from the doorway, kept her frown masked as he looked over at her to see her response. She believed he was exaggerating his behavior just to infuriate her because he knew she did not approve of him.

Devora's dress was most exquisite, far more wondrous than anything she had owned, let alone seen, in Barbados. The Spanish lace, so minutely wrought and the sweet color of violets so as to complement her eyes, was sewn with crystals and was adorned with love-knots. Her honey-colored hair was elaborately styled and the grand, Spanish headdress went on carefully, placed by Florenzia who clucked and chittered, bringing her hands together in pleasure as she cocked her severe head and analyzed Devora. When the purple amethysts were placed upon her slender throat and ears, and after she had picked up her silver-white fan, she was at last ready to go down and join the countess and Doña Sybella and ride in the viceroy's gilded coach to the harbor.

Sybella turned her back when she saw Devora and shouted something in Spanish to her uncle. She threw off her severe, black lace headdress that trailed to her feet and stamped a foot. Maximus threw back his great, dark head and laughed."You have met your match for the heart of Nicklas in Doña Devora, my pompous, little Señora!" he said. The countess made a gesture of sympathy toward Sybella's widow frock.

"Oh Maximus, do allow the child to be young again. The fastest way you can rid her heart of Nicklas is to let her flirt with a new caballero. Let her adorn herself."

Even Sybella seemed to take the sympathy graciously. "You see? To what hurt my dressing up a little, Uncle?"

"Very well, you bright bird, then go, change. Break the caballeros' hearts. The sooner I marry you off to Favian the more peace I shall have."

Sybella rushed up the steps to her room and when she returned she wore white silk, with red embroideries, and an ornate headdress. No doubt she wore the white of innocence to rebuke the notion that she was to live the life of a forgotten and gloomy señora.

"You look lovely, Sybella," said Devora with genuine warmth, and Sybella smiled, but her eyes held a warning that said she would not release the heart of Nicklas without the bitterest of fights. Flitting her fan, she came down the stairs as Maximus commented wryly on her vanity.

"If Favian has arrived with Nicklas and Tobias, you will have the love-sodden boy singing serenades beneath your window."

It was clear by Sybella's face that it was not Don Favian she wished beneath her balcony.

❧ 12 ❧

The Arrival of Don Nicklas

Take away the dross from the silver . . .
—Proverbs 25:4

The viceroy's coach with its gilt-work and team of white horses bore them down the narrow street toward the open square facing the harbor. Devora's heart thumped with nervous anticipation. The morning air was humid, the day clear and bright. Already she could hear the cannon booming a royal welcome to the flagship of Capitan Don Nicklas Valentin. Her hands were clammy as she knotted her lace handkerchief, casting glances beneath her veil at the robust, tanned face of Maximus. Would his son be a cool stranger, or would it be Bruce, whose gray-green eyes haunted her dreams?

The people were already gathered along the narrow street where Spanish soldiers rode among them keeping order for the upcoming procession. Devora heard them shouting like happy children: "Viva Valentin!"

Every street and balcony was packed. Flags fluttered, roses were everywhere: woven into garlands, worn in the señoritas' elaborate veils, held in the hands of grubby half-caste children, who had gathered the broken buds from the street where they'd fallen. Tapestries sailed in the trade wind with the bright colors of Spain.

Devora had all but given up any thought of seeing him again. *Do not hope*, her heart kept repeating. *It isn't Bruce. It can't be him.*

149

For his sake it was better that it wasn't. To keep up a masquerade of this magnitude would eventually bring his death.

The viceroy and governor's reviewing stand had been set up in the harbor square beneath gold-fringed, red canopies surrounded by a large crowd of the common people. Devora was escorted from the coach with the countess and Doña Sybella to join Don Maximus and the political and religious officials in the stand.

She climbed the wooden steps covered with red carpet, keeping her farthingale from whipping in the wind. Looking out on the blue water she was met by a great, ornate, three-decker galleon proudly bearing the flag of Castile.

A barca longa had already been rowed to the wharf and the men were being escorted toward the square by soldiers in black, yellow, and red, covered with various pieces of armor. Her eyes strained to pick out Don Nicklas in the midst of the inner circle of gallants garbed in handsome Spanish finery, but they were still too far away. She caught only a flash of gold cloth, of silver and black, of ostrich feathers in stylish Spanish hats, of polished leather boots, and the flare of capes.

The deep, ponderous booming of the guns ceased, and a shrill of trumpets cut through the air, followed by drums.

In the reviewing stand, Maximus stood straight in his viceroy uniform, while on either side of him and just behind were other important men that Devora believed to be the general, men from the Church, and dons from the ruling Audencia.

The drums fell silent. An official steward stepped forward and announced: "Your Excellency! May you receive Capitan Don Nicklas Anthony Valentin! Knighted by His Most Catholic Majesty the King of Holy Seville, Servant of God!"

Devora stood beside her mother at the rear of the stand, clutching her fan and standing on tiptoe to see the display.

Maximus lifted his viceroyalty scepter, showing acceptance, and the general and bishop went to meet Nicklas and then escorted him toward the reviewing box.

Devora stared at the tall, magnetically attractive man who marched up the red carpet. In a few brief strides he mounted the steps.

The countess leaned toward her and whispered: "Well my child? Who is he?"

The entourage walked toward the stand with Don Nicklas in the lead, the wind ruffling the hem of his cloak and the feather in his hat.

There was no mistake. The rich, dark hair, the handsome, chiseled line of his features, the molten, green eyes. Her breath caught in her throat as she stared not at Don Nicklas Valentin, but Bruce Hawkins. But he was no Englishman now. This was an arrogant Spanish don, fancifully garbed in a handsome, black uniform with gold, a leather bandolier with pistols across his chest, and a belted scabbard boasting the Valentin name. Nicklas removed his hat and lowered his dark head. "Your Excellency," and when he straightened his gaze met hers with a vague challenge and a brief smile. "As promised, I return—" he looked at his father—"to bring you prisoners for the mines."

"Prisoners, my Son?" His swarthy features scowled. "You promised me prisoners? From where, from whom? Where are the soldiers from the garrison on Granada?"

Nicklas turned and gestured down the steps to Friar Tobias. "I also bring you a gift, my Father," he said cheerfully, and Tobias mounted the steps carrying something long wrapped in a cloak. Tobias unwrapped a scabbard. Nicklas, with a faint smile, whipped out the steel blade, held it up for Maximus to see, then tossed it down at Maximus' feet. "The accursed sword of the diablo pirate Hawkins! I bring you the festive announcement of the death of both your enemy, and Spain's."

Devora's fan ceased swishing; she laid it against her lips to hide a quaver of smile. *The audacious rogue!* She looked at Maximus. He was frozen, staring down at the cutlass at his boots.

A hush descended. Don Favian wore a sullen expression as he looked from his half-brother, Nicklas, to his father.

The silence ended with a ring of exultant voices, of smiles, applause, and a great flurry of excitement. Nicklas bowed graciously. *But to one who might notice*, thought Devora, *there is a hint of amusement in his eyes.*

Don Maximus seemed to have forgotten that Nicklas hadn't answered his questions concerning the soldiers and prisoners. The news of the death of Hawkins had blotted out all else. He looked stunned, even unbelieving, then, snatching up the cutlass, he examined it, noting the name "Hawkins." He stared at Nicklas, who lifted a brow waiting for his jubilation. Maximus threw back his head and laughed. He came toward Nicklas and gave him a hearty embrace, then turned toward the crowd below bringing Nicklas to the rail to stand with him there, cutlass in hand.

"The diablo Hawkins is dead!" shouted Don Maximus. "No longer will he ravage our unhappy Caribbean towns with steel and flame!" He raised the cutlass. "Don Nicklas Valentin has seen to his demise!"

The people cheered the louder. Devora wondered whether or not the humble citizens gathered for the fiesta had even heard of Bruce Hawkins, since he'd never attacked Cartagena, but they responded with cheers and pistol shots as one might expect from a people enamored with the greatness of their masters.

She stood beside her mother as Don Maximus walked up with Nicklas a few moments later.

"Ah, Nicklas, so you have rid the Caribbean of that dreadful pirate," said the countess with a smile, extending her hand. "We are most heartily in your debt. Especially my daughter. She was abducted by him from the Isle of Pearls."

"So I have heard from your husband, Earl Robert."

"You took a great risk in seeing to his death, Don Nicklas. May I present Lady Devora Ashby. This dashing caballero, my dear, as you know by now, is the renowned son of the viceroy. Isn't it splendid he's avenged you for that dreadful business? I present Don Nicklas."

Devora's lashes fluttered downward as she felt his strong warm hand enclose about hers. Her heart leapt as he gave it a secret squeeze. She glanced at his dark head as he bent low and pressed his lips in a real kiss.

"I am enchanted, Señorita." His eyes met hers, a warm flicker in their green depths. "But the Countess is in error. Whatever risk I took in the death of Hawkins only permits me to meet you the sooner."

"I am flattered, Señor," she said, knowing her cheeks were tinted with the warmth that stole over her.

"Then you have known before of this meeting between the two of you?" asked the countess with a smile.

Devora looked up to see Nicklas give the countess a more thoughtful look. He smiled also. "I have known since Seville, Countess. I believe it was you who suggested it?"

Her mother laughed, laying her fan on his arm. "How silly of me, Nicklas, but of course I remember. We shall look forward to talking more with you later tonight at the governor's house."

"It will be my pleasure, Señora," he said gravely, and his tone may have suggested otherwise. He looked at Devora, and his eyes softened. "Until tonight." And bowing again in her direction, then in Countess Radburn's, he departed from the stand.

Devora looked, and saw Sybella waiting for him near the steps down from the stand. There was little doubt in anyone's mind but that she was the picture of loveliness.

Devora fanned herself thoughtfully, watching his response. Did he know Sybella was determined to have him? He looked attentive yet aloof as he caught up her hand and bent over it, said something, then turned and went down the steps to join the viceroy and officials. The processional was about to begin to move to the Plaza Mayor where the fiesta would start at noon, ending that night with dancing and fireworks.

Devora stepped to the edge of the rail, looking below at the gathering horsemen that would lead the procession, all splendid in crimson and silver cloaks, with swords flashing, mounted on fine horses. Friar Tobias looked up at her and smiled. She laughed, showing she understood at last why he had been an ally of the now "demised" Bruce Hawkins. But how long would their laughter endure in the thick of danger?

She continued to watch as Nicklas joined his half-brother Favian, equally dressed in finery. Along with their father, Maximus, the three Valentin men then mounted stallions for the honored positions.

Countess Catherina came quietly up beside her. "You need not tell me who he is," she said. "Your eyes give you away. I must warn you to be careful."

"I have been careful of Don Maximus from the moment I arrived," said Devora, tapping her fan against her chin, still watching Nicklas. "I fear not for myself but for others."

"It is not Maximus alone you need fear."

Devora turned her head and found her mother watching Don Favian. "He does not look pleased at the great notoriety of his brother, Nicklas."

Favian was jealous of his brother, she knew that. His animosity had been noticeable since she had first arrived in Cartagena. He was however, an odd sort, with motives difficult to understand. At the moment she was too overwhelmed with the joy of Nicklas' arrival to think much of Favian. She felt joy, yes, but also fear. Nicklas had come home to the pride and embrace of the viceroy, but if Maximus learned the truth?

She had already discovered that Maximus' volatile moods could be dangerous, that his iron will should not be trifled with. She believed he could swiftly turn against his son if he thought he had deliberately mocked him, had somehow set out to shame the Valentin name. The thought of what might yet happen between these men caused her to shudder. She must bring the matter to God in prayer, lest they all be consumed by one another.

Tobias must know this too. Would he continue to stand with Nicklas? She believed he would, to the bitter end. But Tobias too walked a slippery edge, and somehow she didn't think he agreed with all of Nicklas' plans. Nicklas had mentioned prisoners to Maximus. Devora wondered who these poor unfortunates might be.

She turned her head to look at her mother. Catherina was watching the Valentin men, as most of the women were. Devora's spirit was deeply troubled. She worried about her mother, and the fact she now knew the truth about who Nicklas was. Catherina would say nothing to Maximus as long as her plans went undeterred. But what if they were placed in jeopardy?

She must warn Nicklas. They must escape at once, Tobias with them, but would Nicklas listen to her pleading? He might, when he learned about the pistol and who had it in her possession.

Sybella joined them at the rail, and from her face, Devora could see she was not pleased.

Nicklas, before turning the reins of his horse to ride, cast a glance back up to the reviewing stand, perhaps to see whether or not Devora was under escort. Guards were everywhere, and the señoras and señoritas were already being gathered up to be ushered back into their lords' coaches. He touched his stylish hat in her direction with a gloved hand, and did not look at Sybella.

He still cares, Devora told herself jubilantly. He hadn't changed his mind. Not even the arrival of the beautiful Sybella had been able to alter his emotional course from pursuing her. Not yet. But a glance at Sybella brought a chill to her heart. Her displeasure was plainly written on her face; so was her determination to have her way.

The sun was hot and glaring as she, the countess, and Sybella were escorted across the square to the coaches, reminding Devora of the many agonizing hours before the stars would come out in the sky of Cartagena and she would be with Nicklas again. Hours! When her entire heart beat with the need to tell him of the danger that surrounded him!

❧ 13 ❧

The Procession to the Plaza Mayor

[Wisdom] . . . Better than the merchandise of silver . . .

—*Proverbs 3:14*

Bruce settled his wide-brimmed hat as he watched Devora standing at the rail of the reviewing stand beside the Countess of Radburn.

Maximus noticed. "The daughter of the English countess pleases you."

"She is enough to set a man's heart flaming." Bruce turned his stallion to ride with him to the Plaza Mayor. "I salute you, my Father! You have made a worthy choice."

Maximus slapped his leather reins and they moved forward, following the drums. "A beautiful woman. I have thought of her myself."

"Think no more. A match with the English señorita pleases me well."

Maximus' mouth twisted with irony. "I have not known you to make up your mind so swiftly."

"Do you blame me?"

"No, but I warn you. This one is no well-behaved Señorita. She is opinionated. She reads and writes."

Bruce lifted a brow, as though considering this information disturbing. "Then the fair rosebud is not without stinging thorns?"

"She will need a strong, supervising hand."

"The challenge interests me."

"You will meet her again tonight at the mascarada."

"I would like the wedding before we leave for Lima," said Bruce lazily, glancing back toward Devora. "Yes, next week, I think."

"You may not find her as willing. She has told me she does not wish this marriage."

"Then I shall see she changes her mind," said Bruce, giving nothing away in a tone that sounded as conceited as might be expected from one of his station.

Maximus laughed. He turned back to the crowd lining the cobbled street as they rode past. "In all of the Main there is but one name upon their lips. And before we are finished the Valentin name will resound throughout Seville as well."

"It is enough you are pleased, Father."

The horses' hoofs clopped rhythmically along the cobbled street as the parade wound its way toward the Plaza Mayor. Bruce rode beside the viceroy, while Don Favian and Friar Tobias came behind, astride magnificent horses from Castile. The rolling drums echoed like distant thunder. Banners of glorious Spain fluttered gold and crimson as throngs of people waved and shouted their pleasure until their throats were raw. Although Bruce accommodated their enthusiasm by smiling and saluting, he did so fully aware that his favor was like the sea vapor before the rising Caribbean sun. His true allegiance did not belong to Spain, but to England. Not to the man who had sired him, but to the memory of his mother, abused by Maximus.

Bruce hoped to pay a first visit to his ailing great-grandfather, Duke Anthony, on his way to the Netherlands with the silver shipment. This treasure was desperately needed by the ragged armies of the Netherlands, but whether he would arrive before the duke's death was doubtful. In following his plans through to the end Bruce was aware that he too risked death. It was a troubling thought when it came to Devora. He wondered now whether it had been an error to allow her to come here with Tobias.

"I hesitate to bring up dark news now, but I think it best you know what's happened before meeting the new archbishop of Lima."

Maximus looked at him, his pleasure ebbing. "You speak of Harro Andres?"

"He will be waiting at the residence to have an audience with you when we arrive."

"What ails him?"

Bruce removed a sealed document from beneath his black jacket. "He comes after a stop-over with Governor del Campo. You will know soon enough. I bring you correspondence from there."

Maximus looked puzzled, cautious. "Granada? What does the governor want of me this time?" He waved at the people.

"He wants soldiers."

Maximus shot him a dark look, but Nicklas gave nothing away. He had much to explain concerning his so-called prisoners. Already his brother, Favian, was asking questions.

"Soldiers," repeated Maximus impatiently. "Why does he not ask me for gold and silver as well? I have no soldiers to spare. Davido knows that. Is he seeking a quarrel?"

"He has had more than enough of quarrels," Nicklas said, thinking of Morgan. "The governor of Granada wishes a brigantine as well, and fishing boats."

Maximus said something between his teeth. "And why does he expect such abundance from me?"

"He is in desperate straits," said Nicklas. "It is all in this letter," and he handed it over to Maximus. He looked at the official Spanish seal. His eyes came directly to Nicklas'.

"The letter from del Campo will enlighten you," said Nicklas.

"Suppose you enlighten me now."

"Unfortunately the soldiers at the garrison will not be serving as guards at the mines."

"What! Did Davido refuse you? They were authorized by the king."

"He did not refuse me, and I would not have taken no for an answer. The soldiers that have not fled are either dead or slaves to pirate dogs."

Maximus stared at him astounded. "Soldiers fled? What is this you say?"

Nicklas accepted a rose from the señorita who ran up beside his horse. "Yes, pirates—that scoundrel Morgan."

Maximus said not a word, but slowly the veins on his neck bulged. He rode stiffly in the saddle, a look of thunder on his brow. He ripped open the seal and read the correspondence while the celebration in the streets grew with noisy enthusiasm.

Nicklas watched him with affected gravity. Don Favian edged his horse up on the other side of his father. "Troubling news, Father?"

"Morgan," hissed Maximus, crumpling the letter in rage. "He has sacked Granada."

Favian looked at Nicklas almost suspiciously. "You encountered this prince of demons?"

"A great misfortune you were not there to aid me, my Brother. You might have killed this diabolical prince, while I ridded the Caribbean of Hawkins."

"Morgan will burn for this act of brutality," said Maximus. "I will light the faggots myself."

"A just fate, my Father," said Nicklas.

"By now he's returned to Port Royal to share his plunder with the English pirate-governor, Modyford."

"If I could raise a fleet, Favian and I would lead the attack upon Jamaica," suggested Nicklas, "and capture Morgan."

Favian looked at him with wonder as Maximus considered in silence. Nicklas pressed: "All that is needed is a letter of request to the king. Turn it over to me and I will see it is aboard the galleon when it sets sail."

"The annual treasure fleet does not arrive for six months," said Favian. "Why do you wish the letter of request now?"

"Why wait for the capitan of the treasure fleet? Is there not cause to send a ship to Spain now? Your ship, perchance, my Brother."

"My ship is in repair," said Favian sullenly, and looked briefly at Maximus.

"Ah? A battle perhaps?" asked Nicklas innocently.

Favian looked uncomfortable. "No, storm damage. I was in hot pursuit of the *Revenge* when a hurricane thwarted me."

"Ah well," said Nicklas, smiling at his brother. "It is just as well you did not duel Hawkins."

Favian's ego was ruffled. "Why so? I, too, could have killed him."

Nicklas considered. "Perhaps. But it is best you did not find out."

"Do you mean to dishonor my swordsmanship?"

"Still your tongue, you peacock," growled Maximus. "Hawkins is already dead. Are there not enough other pirates devouring the Main upon which you may prove your skills?"

"True," agreed Nicklas to Favian. "There is Morgan. He now sits in the taverns of Port Royal boasting of his raid on Granada and Villahermosa. We ought to teach Jamaica a bitter lesson, my Father."

"And you will lead an attack on the island?" asked Favian.

"Impossible," said Maximus. "The treasure fleet will arrive from Seville in six months. Nicklas is under orders from the king to double the production of silver bullion. Or have both of you forgotten?"

"There is nothing to hinder an attack on Jamaica once the fleet returns to Seville," argued Nicklas. "I happen to know Jamaica has no standing army, and Commodore Mings has been called back to England to fight the Dutch. If we attacked Jamaica we could recapture the island for Spain."

"You seem to know much about the doings at Port Royal," said Favian.

Nicklas waved an airy hand. "Spies are easy to come by. What do you say, Father? If I draw up the letter to the king explaining why an attack on Jamaica is expedient, would you sign it and send it to Seville?"

Maximus considered. "And you would lead this attack? You and Favian?"

"And others, yes. As soon as my duties at Lima are fulfilled."

"Very well, write the letter. I will review it. It will need to be done before we depart for Lima. *Maria* sets sail for Madrid from Portobello in a week. I will send a *petacha*," he said of the small but fast vessel used for carrying dispatches and mail, "to its captain. An answer should arrive on the treasure fleet."

Nicklas restrained his satisfaction. He would arrange for a copy of the letter to be given to Henry Morgan to help convince Governor Modyford of the need to commission Morgan. It would also provide the governor the excuse he needed to save his own neck should he be called in to answer to King Charles if Morgan attacked Portobello.

The coach carrying Devora and the countess wound its way down the avenue toward the Plaza Mayor. On either side of the avenue large trees joined branches to form an overhanging arch of shade offering reprieve from the midday sun.

The countess, her face flushed with recurrent fever, wearily leaned her dark head against the leather seat and fanned herself, shutting her eyes.

"It's moments like this when one remembers girlhood days in England. The dewy morns, the cool spring weather that carried a whole world of expectation to the heart. How age and time make one cynical."

With Devora's anxiety over the identity of Don Nicklas past, she was becoming more troubled by the evidences of her mother's declining health. So far, nothing she said could convince her to set sail for England.

"I wish you wouldn't go to Lima, Mother. The journey will be so difficult. You have no strength to endure it."

"I should be stronger by then. Maximus seems to think Nicklas won't be prepared to leave for several weeks. If all goes as I plan, your marriage will occur first."

Marriage to Nicklas ... would he accept the arrangement made for him by Maximus, as she was to accept the will of the countess? She was certain his eyes had spoken his remembrance of their brief romance aboard the *Revenge*.

"I'm sure the viceroy could arrange a ship to bring you to Jamaica or Barbados," persisted Devora. "You could return to London and wait for Robert there."

"Twaddle. We've discussed this before. I have no intention of leaving Robert to handle our plans at Lima by himself."

Devora's unrest over the royal Inca tomb had been growing. She had been unable to discuss the disturbing matter with Friar Tobias. If Nicklas had spent his boyhood in Lima he must know about the Indians. Hadn't there been an Inca Indian aboard the *Revenge*, a friend of Bruce Hawkins? What was his name? Tupac, yes, that was it. So then, perhaps Nicklas knew as much about the treasure in the tombs as did Maximus, perhaps more.

"I want to make absolutely certain Maximus doesn't cheat us out of what he's promised," said the countess. "Robert should have been here by now."

"What do you mean? You're not suggesting the viceroy has deliberately detained him somewhere?"

The countess' fan stopped in midair and she looked rather surprised, as though the idea startled her.

Devora hurried on: "Don Favian suggested that Robert has voyaged to Tortuga to meet the French governor, thinking Captain Hawkins had gone there. Once he learns differently, Robert is bound to return here."

The countess' eyes reflected amusement. "Nicklas, that clever rogue. Imagine the audacity of telling Maximus he had killed his enemy. Even bringing Hawkins' sword." *But even more dangerous,* thought Devora, watching her alertly. There was no doubt now that her mother believed Nicklas had sailed the Caribbean as Hawkins. What would he do when she confronted him with the pistol bearing those infamous initials?

"You still intend to speak with Nicklas about the pistol?"

"But naturally. Nicklas will be of tremendous help in locating that royal tomb should Maximus decide to show any reluctance about it."

"Yet there is no proof linking the two men together as one," argued Devora. "He could simply deny ever owning the pistol."

"Not as long as you're in Cartagena," Catherina said thoughtfully.

Devora wondered what she meant. After all, he had sent her here under the care of Tobias. "Me? Why does that matter?"

"'Tis simple. If Nicklas' double identity is discovered, Maximus would have him arrested. Except for Tobias, you would be left in Lima without protection. Nicklas must know there are any number of dons who might like to take his place in claiming you. He's too gallant to put you at such risk by refusing my request. Which is why I won't leave you and voyage to London until all matters are settled here. There is more at stake than your marriage. Robert must arrive at Lima, and Maximus must pay according to promise."

Devora should have been repulsed by the calmly stated strategy. Had it come from Uncle Barnabas or Tobias, she would have been shocked. Coming from her mother she felt only sadness over the apparent death of her character, which had occurred many years earlier. That she was bargaining away her daughter's future and manipulating circumstances of great risk to herself and others, didn't appear to trouble her.

Devora had lain awake in the darkness of her chamber considering the possibility that she might be united in marriage to some don other than Nicklas. The thought had brought such revulsion that she'd shut it from her mind and turned instead to quoting the Psalms. Now, with the arrival of Bruce, hope dawned, but she was seeing anew that the road they must travel was marked by dangerous turns. Much could go wrong.

Their coach neared one of the public viewing spots along the route. The countess leaned toward the open window and ordered the guards riding along beside them on horseback to pull away from a long line of other gaily painted coaches and park beneath the trees. Her servingwoman, Isabel, riding in the open seat at the back of the coach with her husband, Luis, came around to see what might be disturbing her lady. The countess, feeling ill and dreadfully thirsty, requested one of the fruit beverages sold at a nearby stall. Devora left the coach and aided her mother up a brief flight of steps onto a raised adobe walk where the guards chased away the crowd. Here, Devora sat the countess on a bench and they enjoyed the deep shade and hoped for a breeze.

Isabel returned with citrus and banana drinks and Devora and her mother sat sipping the tangy juice while the procession wound slowly forward. It was still a good distance to the Plaza Mayor, where every festival either began or ended.

Devora watched the gaily costumed merrymakers march by, bowing and waving toward them. They were followed by members of the craftsmen's guilds. The silver workers, gold smiths, painters, and carpenters were dragging carts on which were built shimmering castles, ships, horses with wings, and great birds. Last of all came the Virgin surrounded by singing angels, trailed by a pageant of priests in black robes following slowly behind the glittering images. Devora saw the humble throng of people who served the aristocrats kneeling in the street while the incense-laden breeze carried the peal of bells from the towers.

Devora sniffed the incense, the Caribbean, the smell of horse flesh, of donkeys, of unbathed bodies, and, as she swallowed the tangy citrus juice mingled with banana, she felt headachy and nauseous. The hectic morning that had brought the clamor of carnival and religious sobriety had also brought Bruce and the imminent prospect of marriage. It was all overwhelming.

Devora watched a second coach stop in the shade. A guard came around and opened the door. Devora's curiosity was awakened. An elderly woman was helped out, a woman with a cane who was dressed in sedate black. The breeze blew her black lace mantilla, revealing contrasting silvery-white hair.

The woman was treated gently by the guard as he walked her over to the stall and brought her a refreshment. She piqued Devora's curiosity because she appeared to be an Englishwoman.

"Who is she, Mother? Do you know her?" asked Devora.

The countess remained silent a moment too long. Devora looked at her, wondering. Her mother watched the elderly woman meditatively.

"Yes," she finally admitted. Devora waited, expecting some breathtaking account of the woman in black.

"She is Lady Lillian Anthony Bruce. Nicklas' English grandmother."

Devora, stunned, looked back at the woman, then stood and picked up her trailing skirts to hurry toward the woman to meet her, but the countess snatched firm hold of her wrist.

Devora looked down at her, surprised. She searched her mother's eyes and found there something very troubling.

"What is it?" asked Devora quietly.

"Do not disturb her."

"But—why should I not go and meet her?"

"It is not wise, nor the right time. Do sit, Devora."

"But she is Nicklas' grandmother! And English at that. Why— she must be a daughter to the duke," she said, with a little awe.

"She is, and the mother of Nicklas' uncle Lord Arlington. One rarely sees her in public. She must have come out to see Nicklas' grand arrival."

"I don't see why we both shouldn't go speak with her—"

"Because Nicklas would not approve."

Devora frowned, bewildered. "I don't see why not. She looks to be a very great lady."

"She is. I shall let Nicklas explain. When he wishes you to meet his grandmother he will bring you to see her."

"She lives here in Cartagena?"

"She does now, I am told. She left Lima a few years ago. Come, we best be on our way."

As their coach pulled away, Devora looked out the window at Lady Lillian Anthony. She felt a strange but growing affinity with the woman, and couldn't wait to ask Bruce to introduce her. That she lived in Cartagena somehow made Devora feel a trifle more at home. She not only had Bruce, but now his dignified grandmother. It was curious that her mother had forbidden her to go near her. Odd, indeed. She would ask Bruce about it tonight.

❧ 14 ❧

Favian Uncovers a Secret

That we may buy the poor for silver..

—Amos 8:6

At the governor's palace on the Plaza Mayor, the aristocracy were arriving by coach and sedan chair. The haunting strains coming from Portuguese guitars drifted up to Devora, who stood with the countess in the upper corridor with its wrought-iron rail.

"Every worthy event includes a bullfight," the countess persisted, as Devora continued to resist any notion of attending.

"I can easily believe that immature aristocrats like Don Favian take pleasure as the matador confronts the bull, but I simply refuse to attend. It's barbaric and disgusting."

"I have no quarrel with your not wishing to go," her mother told her, "but if you don't, Maximus will not be pleased. He tells me you are too contrary."

Devora stood her moral ground. "Do you wish me to go and cheer for the bull?"

The countess groaned, fanning her heated, flushed face as they prepared to meet the Valentins in the receiving gallery below. "Yes, I believe you might . . . well, I am simply too ill to find the energy to argue. I blame your ways on the teachings of Barnabas."

"You blame Uncle Barnabas for everything. It's not fair, you know. He did his best to raise me."

Her mother's face hardened. "Yes I know. I've failed you as a mother. That's what you keep insinuating at every opportunity."

"I have never said that."

"You don't need to. It's obvious you feel that way. It's quite unfair, I might add. You forget there was a war going on in England and across Europe. The safest thing I could have done with you was send you to Barbados."

"Could have done with you." It almost sounded to Devora as though her mother were discussing an interruption in her schedule. Devora looked below the rail at the señoritas in their flashing gowns but made no comment.

"Devora—" For the first time she could hear the anxiety in her mother's voice. She expected Devora to rush to deny her mother's selfishness and make her feel more comfortable with the past, but Devora deliberately remained silent. At the same time she denied her own resentments. *I do understand her. And I am not bitter toward her. I do have love for her. . . .*

"If you are not feeling well, Mother, perhaps you should lie down in your room."

"No, no, I'll be all right," she said petulantly. "If anything did happen to me, I don't think you'd care at all."

"Mother, please don't say things like that—"

"You are indeed difficult. I always sent money to Barnabas. You lacked nothing in the way of frocks and pretty things. You behave as though I didn't care about you at all."

Devora sighed and plucked at her glittering fan. "I'm sorry if I made you feel badly, and I know it's not good for your health to be upset—"

"Never mind. Oh well, I suppose I can arrange for both of us to miss the silly bull fight since I've no liking for it anyway. At least my poor health is good for something; it allows me a ready excuse. You can trouble *me* with your stubbornness, but not Maximus. The more you contest him, the more difficult you'll make matters for me and your father when he arrives. We'll want to conclude our business at Lima and be on our voyage to Seville. You should think

of your father's obligations to King Charles as English ambassador."

Devora swallowed back the desire to retort. She could easily
scoff about Robert's *duty* to King Charles when he was willing to
sell secrets to Maximus to pass on to the king of Spain. *Duty, indeed.*

"I believe the viceroy waits for us below," said Devora tone-
lessly.

She walked beside the countess down the upper corridor. The
wrought-iron railing overlooked a wide receiving hall with black
and white tiles, potted palms, and many mirrors of glimmering
gilt-work reflecting the flaming candles. The wealthy display of the
guests dazzled her: men's outfits and women's gowns were made
from cloth of gold, or dyed silks and plush velvets in vivid colors
of purple, red, and yellow, with contrasting embroidery in silver
thread or twinkling jewels. Nor had she ever seen so much jewelry.
Heavy gold and silver bracelets flashed in the candlelight. They
wore necklaces and brooches encrusted with precious gems. Rings
weighed heavily on the slender, uncalloused hands of young gallants, whose chief expertise appeared to be in fencing or attending
the bullfights held in the plaza.

Devora was no less adorned in her second gown of the day
than those señoritas below who were daughters of the dons. Her
dress had been created especially for her formal introduction by
the Valentin family to Nicklas. There would be dancing with him
afterward, and a stroll on the plaza where there were foods of various kinds and all sorts of refreshments and sweet dainties, the
long day and evening ending with fireworks.

Her dress was of sumptuous pearl-colored lace cunningly
embroidered with silver thread, with matching slippers of silver
cloth. Her honey tresses were woven with an invisible silk netting
sewn with small amethysts that caught the light like purple-blue
winking stars. She carried a silver-lace fan and a small, choice bouquet of sweet-smelling white roses. Each glance down at the vel-
vety petals thrilled her heart. They had been delivered to her
according to custom, sent by the man whom she soon would meet.

The calling card had contained a simple sentence written in his own hand: "I have dreamed of this moment."

Devora could see Don Maximus waiting below. He came forward to meet them, garbed in a distinguished uniform. As he took the countess' hand and bent over it, Devora glanced toward the receiving chamber where she was "officially" to be introduced to Nicklas, but did not see him. Had he arrived yet?

Other members of the Valentin family were there, however, along with Favian and Sybella, who stood beside him.

The countess raised her fan. "You'll need to watch that hungry tigress," she whispered about Sybella. "She'll devour you if you allow her an advantage."

Devora turned her head away from the intemperate gaze of Sybella, noting as she did, that Favian's mouth was sealed sullenly beneath his ribbon mustache. His brooding black eyes were fixed on Maximus as he walked up with the countess and Devora. Devora supposed that Favian was upset because Sybella seemed to have little interest in acknowledging his attentions. He held a red rose limply at his side, which appeared to have been spurned by Sybella, who was looking pointedly at the white rose bouquet Devora held. Sybella must know where it had come from.

Devora greeted Sybella as though unaware of the underlying tension, then offered her hand to Favian, then to other male Valentins who were the epitome of Spanish civility as they bent their heads. Her mind grappled to remember the numerous titles, names, and relationships of these men to Nicklas. Most of them were cousins. Except for Sybella, who was a Ferdinand, there were no Valentin women present. Either there weren't any, or Maximus didn't consider them important.

I won't remember any of their names an hour from now, she thought, distressed.

There was only one name that persisted to claim her attention and all her heart. *Where is he?* she wondered again. *And where is Friar Tobias?*

For the most part the Valentin family members were owners of large, inland sugar estates. She noticed one man—a newly arrived older brother of Maximus, Don Roman Valentin, who had been sent out from Spain by the king. As he bowed over her hand Maximus explained to the countess that Don Roman was the new president of the Audencia in Cuzco, the capital of the Inca Empire.

"The Audencia?" repeated the countess, as though taken with the desire to understand Spanish rule on the Main.

"A legislative body administering affairs under the will of the viceroy."

Under the viceroy. Maximus' authority ensured that the Valentins continued to gain wealth from the region of the mines. As president of the Audencia in Cuzco, Don Roman would be certain to follow the will of his brother.

When it appeared as if nothing more would happen because Nicklas was delayed, the others drifted toward the ballroom. Favian turned to Sybella.

"You would favor me with this dance, sweet cousin?"

"No," she retorted. "I am in mourning for Marcos, remember?"

"You do not appear to be in mourning. You dress as gaily as the other señoritas who are enjoying themselves."

"Nevertheless, I will not dance," and she left, calling to one of the señoras walking by. They entered the ballroom together and Favian's eyes smoldered as he looked after her and threw down the red rose.

"Where is Nicklas?" demanded Maximus of Favian.

Favian appeared to find something that at last brought him a look of satisfaction. "He is not coming," and he looked at Devora with a smile. "Perhaps Doña Devora will permit me to take his place and escort her to the ball?"

"Not coming?" repeated the countess, troubled.

"What do you mean by this!" said Maximus, frowning. "He must come."

Devora watched Favian with secret concerns that went beyond her disappointment. Why did Favian appear to be pleased? Surely it was not because of any interest in her. He was enamored with Sybella.

"He was called aboard the *Our Lady of Madrid*, and is delayed there for the evening," said Favian.

"Your hopes prove vain, my Brother," came a voice from behind them.

Devora turned with secret relief. It was Nicklas, dressed in black velvet and silver, his gray-green eyes sparking with restrained anger as he watched Favian. He retrieved the red rose from the tile floor and with deft fingers placed it in Favian's embroidered caballero jacket studded with gems.

"You should stick with wearing roses, my Brother, and leave heretic prisoners for me to handle."

"What is this about?" demanded Maximus. "What prisoners?"

Nicklas was watching Favian. "The next time you set foot aboard my ship without permission I will be there to stop you."

"You have reasons to fear my presence among your prisoners?" challenged Favian. "Look how he treats me, Father. He returns home like a king and demands I bow to him."

Maximus lifted a hand to silence him, measuring Nicklas with a glance, but Nicklas showed no evidence of backing down.

A group of men stood across the hall and turned their heads to look as Favian raised his voice. Maximus shut the door and faced his two sons.

"Do I need to ask again what this is about?" he growled, hands on hips.

"A minor inconvenience delayed me," said Nicklas. He turned to look at Devora and bowed his head. "My pardon at keeping you waiting, Señorita."

"Minor inconvenience?" scoffed Favian. "He will not tell you, but I will."

"Was it not your reason for coming on board?" said Nicklas. "You wished for something to run to Father with."

"Explain!" said Maximus impatiently.

"I had word the prisoners were not that at all, but well-fed and armed sea devils," said Favian. "I found it my duty to see whether or not it was so."

Nicklas smiled wearily. "Your duty, Brother, is self-imposed. You can thank Uncle Tobias for coming to me in time." He looked at Maximus. "Favian nearly got strung up on the yardarm. That will teach him not to unexpectedly enter the hold of a ship without permission."

Maximus turned sharply to Favian. "You went aboard the *Our Lady of Madrid*? What for?"

"I did," said Favian sullenly. "I had the authority."

"You had none," said Nicklas. "If you were not my brother I'd have you arrested."

"How generous of you to refrain. It so happens I had all the authority that I needed." He smiled. "The Archbishop Harro Andres." He looked at Maximus. "He went with me. His presence was wisely not challenged by the soldiers on guard as we boarded." He looked back at Nicklas with a smile of satisfaction.

"The archbishop," said Nicklas, "is no more welcome aboard my ship, searching my cabin, and interrogating the king's prisoners than you are."

Don Maximus said something between his teeth and slammed his hand down against the table. "This is Cartagena," he gritted at Nicklas. "Here, the archbishop is law."

The countess sank breathlessly into a chair. Devora went to lay a hand on her shoulder, all the while watching the three men.

"I thought you were the viceroy, my Father," said Nicklas with pretended innocence.

Maximus' eyes narrowed. "You know well enough the authority of the Church. Not even I contest the archbishop and Dominicans. You have yet to tell me who these prisoners are, or why you brought them. If they are to stand trial—"

"They are not to stand trial," interrupted Nicklas. "I will strike canvas and set sail before I turn them over to the archbishop."

"You see?" said Favian. "One might ask him why that is so. He has yet to explain to the archbishop why he has these heretics safely aboard."

"He has yet to explain to *me*," snapped Maximus. "What about them, Nicklas?"

Devora watched tensely, but Nicklas' expression did not change. He looked calm enough as his gaze found her, and softened and warmed as it took her in. "I fear we are frightening the Señorita and her mother. Much more of this and they will be asking Earl Robert to sail with them to Barbados."

Devora's eyes lowered as she read his real thoughts. The countess spoke, "You have no cause to think so, Don Nicklas. I find it all most interesting. Heretics aboard your ship?"

Devora's fingers tightened on her mother's arm, warning her. Nicklas pondered her thoughtfully, then Devora's face, and she wondered if he guessed her mother might know who he was. Did he possibly think she had told her?

Nicklas bowed toward them. "I confess it is as Favian says. There are heretics aboard the *Our Lady of Madrid*. I might also hasten to assure you, Madame, that they are well under guard— as my dear brother will admit if he were honest."

"One was not," countered Favian. "And since we were interrupted in our search, I cannot attest to the security of the others. They may all have been free and carrying weapons as far as I know."

"If that were so, you would know," said Nicklas dryly, "since the archbishop would likely be dead now, and you'd be chained in the galley."

"The prisoners will be interrogated," said Favian to his father. "Archbishop Andres says so."

"Any further questions asked, and any dealings with the prisoners, will be done through me alone," stated Nicklas.

"Is there something you do not wish the archbishop to see perhaps?" said Favian with a smile.

"It is not what he may see, my Brother, but the foolish and intimidating manner in which my soldiers were challenged."

"They refused us access. They insulted us."

"With good reason. They were under my orders. Your barging aboard was simply a display of arrogance. Religious arrogance and Valentin pride."

"Enough, both of you," said Maximus, who had been unusually quiet during the exchange. He had watched Nicklas with a thoughtful frown. Devora believed he was suspicious, but he was not accusing him. If anything, he appeared tense, even a bit anxious. This was not Maximus' typical behavior.

"I do not know what is going on, but I want a clear explanation. Favian, was it you who contacted the archbishop about these prisoners?"

"He already knew about them. How, he didn't say. I saw him riding in the procession and rode back to speak with him about another matter. He asked about the prisoners. He intended to board the ship to interrogate certain men said to be among them. It seemed wise to accompany him."

Nicklas laughed. "Wise because you wished to search my cabin. What did you expect to find?"

"Ask him why, Father, these mad dogs were loose and walking freely about when we surprised them."

Nicklas calmly removed his gloves and dropped them on the table. "He exaggerates. The debacle may have convinced him they were free. The man in question is a feisty Irishman. Favian was no match." He looked at Favian, scanning him with a smile. "I can see how a gallant with my brother's sensitivities might think all the world was arrayed against him, but in truth, my Father, it was but one lone Irishman."

Favian colored angrily and stepped toward Nicklas, but Maximus restrained him with a firm hand on his arm. "There will be none of that."

"He was caught? This 'lone Irishman?'" he demanded of Nicklas.

Nicklas smiled. "What chance would a single heretic have of hoping to escape Cartagena? And you may be certain that I will deal with him according to his offense in the morning."

Devora's gaze swerved over him. He didn't mean it, but did Maximus believe him? It was important that he did.

"One would think they were not prisoners at all," said Favian. "They are all well-fed and there were no whip marks."

"Favian thinks every prisoner should look half dead," said Nicklas with sarcasm. "And is it my fault their previous captain pirated the best of our cattle and wine?"

Devora tensed. She glanced at Maximus.

"And," said Maximus, "how is it you expect to double the silver production in Lima?"

Favian smiled. "A good question, my Father."

Devora glanced from one Valentin to the other. Her admiration for Nicklas grew when he remained calm.

"I shall tell you how I do *not* expect to increase the silver production. With half-dead prisoners so diseased and weak from lack of nourishment that they won't be able to carry their own packs on the rigorous journey over the Isthmus. If they don't have their strength now, they'll be useless by the time we reach the mines."

Favian laughed. "Now he sounds like Uncle Tobias."

"Silence," snapped Maximus. "I must have answers. Nicklas, were these heretics free of chains or not?"

"They were under guard by armed soldiers, and that was sufficient—I use bonds only as a means of punishment. And as Captain, I am responsible for both my crew and the prisoners."

"And if it does not please me?" growled Maximus.

Favian smiled, satisfied.

"I need not remind you, Father, that I shall be held accountable for the production at the mines under a commission from His Majesty—and I have every intention of using my prisoners effectively in order to carry out that obligation."

Maximus' dark eyes squinted at him. Nicklas looked back evenly.

"Just who are these prisoners that you have brought here?"

Nicklas smiled coolly. "Hawkins' crew."

Devora held her breath. *How could he? How dare he!*

Maximus looked stunned. "What? *His* diablos?"

"Can you think of a more fitting end for them than to serve out their remaining days in the mines in humble service to the king of Spain? You must convince the archbishop."

"I can convince him of nothing, nor do I agree. I want them brought to the plaza to stand before the Dominicans!"

"A waste, my Father!" Nicklas walked forward. "I did not capture them alive and bring them to Cartagena just for their carcasses to fill the plaza air with stench. Morgan robbed me of the soldiers needed for Lima. Now these English and French dogs will be my slaves. His Majesty will have his increase in silver bullion on the blood and sweat of Hawkins' crew."

Devora considered the cunning and passion of his words, and feared. She looked at Maximus to see his response. The viceroy considered, and did not appear as furious as at first. Perhaps he was beginning to believe him?

"If the treasure galleons do not bring more silver to Seville, the failure will reflect badly not only on me, but also on you, my Father. Does the king not know that you are in command of the Main? If I remember, he made clear his orders to both of us."

"You need not remind me," Maximus snapped. "I am well aware of the danger to my life should the king become displeased." He began to pace. "How many are there?"

"Fifty. There were more, but some were killed before Hawkins met his end."

Maximus ceased his pacing and looked at him. "It may well be as you say; that these dogs may be used in the service of Spain. But, I will see them myself before I speak to the archbishop."

"You may see them anytime." Niklas looked at Favian, who had retreated to a divan and remained sullen. "Had Favian come to me first, instead of making his appearance as though boarding an enemy ship, the matter would not have gone so badly."

Favian smirked. "If that is true, my Brother," he stated doubtfully, "then I am heartened. For I wish to board yet once again to arrest the dog who dared to strike *me*, a Valentin."

"Patience, my Brother. As an emissary of His Majesty, I am to keep the heretics alive until they have accomplished their service to me and to Spain. After that you may take vengeance upon the offender as you see fit."

Devora moved uneasily. He sounded like a stranger. A ruthless stranger. *But Nicklas is behaving thus for a purpose,* she kept reminding herself.

Maximus turned to him. "You say these men are in good health, and strong?"

"The way I intend to keep them, Father. It is not mercy but wisdom that requires it. I feed my horse and it serves me well. And Hawkins' men will have no choice but to serve me better than soldiers from the Granada garrison would have—I shall get all the labor from them possible. Within six months the treasure fleet will arrive from Seville. If then, after they have served their purpose, you wish them delivered to the inquisition fires, you may do so."

Devora looked at her mother. The countess was pale, but her eyes were alert and keenly fixed upon Nicklas.

"I will have them sent to Lima within the week," Nicklas was telling Maximus. "Just as soon as provisions for travel are arranged."

"May I suggest, wise Brother, that you at least surrender the one prisoner who attacked me?" said Favian. "Turn him over to me, and the archbishop will make certain he talks."

"I will need every man, and since Hawkins is already dead, the prisoner will have nothing to confess to the archbishop."

"Let me be the judge of that," said Favian.

"Yes, he may know something of Morgan," said Maximus. "I want this prisoner, Nicklas."

Devora wondered what Nicklas would do now. He wouldn't turn over a loyal crewman to the Dominicans?

Favian watched him with a satisfied gleam. "You have heard what our father requires."

"Yes, and it won't help my task, but I suppose I can afford to surrender one man. He will be turned over in the morning," said Nicklas.

Devora was disappointed. *He couldn't mean it. . . .*

"By the time the flota arrives from Seville there will be more silver than ever before. And the glory will go to you as the viceroy," said Nicklas.

Maximus' smile was thoughtful. "I will see these prisoners tomorrow."

"Then tomorrow I will have them brought to the Center Plaza."

There was a lapse in the conversation before Devora became aware that Maximus was speaking to the countess, offering an apology for her having to endure a matter of political concern.

"On the contrary, Maximus, there is no need. I'm sure Devora found the politics of the thing as interesting as did I. After my horrendous ordeal on the Isle of Pearls, I can hardly be said to have sympathy for a crew of pirates, even if they do have English blood. I can see my daughter will marry into a strong family."

"May I remind you," said Devora, "that neither Don Nicklas nor I have yet agreed to the arrangement?"

A slight frown appeared between her mother's brows, and Maximus fixed her with a wilting look, but Nicklas sounded congenial for the first time that evening.

"Then I suggest that the Señorita and I be left to ourselves to discuss the matter. One can hardly blame her for restraint when an evening of celebration has turned into a sordid discussion of prisoners."

"I quite agree," said the countess breezily and stood from her chair, swishing her fan. "It's dreadfully warm tonight, Don Maximus." She held out a hand. "Do you think you might lead me for a breath of air in the garden while Devora and Nicklas become acquainted? And you, Don Favian, I do believe I saw Sybella loitering about the door to the ballroom. Isn't that the *curanto*?" she asked of the dance music coming from the ballroom. "Sybella will certainly have changed her mind about dancing and wish to be led out."

❧ 15 ❧

"You Have Won My Heart . . ."

Set me as a seal upon thine heart

—Song of Solomon 8:6

When the door shut behind them, Devora looked across the room at Nicklas. Their eyes held. The silence deepened, as though they were indeed strangers. Then he stood and approached her until they were but a few steps apart.

His eyes searched hers as if to know her mind, her heart. He smiled, and lifted a questioning brow. Devora, despite the danger of their secret, found that she was smiling too.

"You rogue," she whispered with mock dismay. "How could you? How could you come like *this*? Don Nicklas Valentin! Why did you not tell me who you were?"

"And that would have made all the difference?"

She knew it would not have, that knowing who he was would have opened the door to a hundred new questions that even now he was not able to fully explain.

"I told you I would come. That you loved the English scoundrel Hawkins was more satisfying than you know. A pity I had to end his life and give his sword to the viceroy, but it was the only way I could come to you. While he still lived, my life here would be in even greater jeopardy."

"Oh Bruce, I—" she stopped, her eyes darting toward the door, but he quickly stepped toward her, laying a warning hand to her mouth.

"Never, Señorita, say his name."

Her eyes closed as she realized just how careful she must be. One slip in front of Maximus or Favian, and—she felt his arm slide about her waist, drawing her close, and when her eyes fluttered open she gazed up into gray-green eyes that sent her heart racing as they drifted down to her lips.

"So you cared for the English pirate, did you? Perchance he will live again, another time and place, but in the meantime, you will love a worse rogue—the ruthless Don Nicklas." He caught both her hands in his and brought them to his chest, gazing warmly into her eyes. "Your loveliness takes my breath away. How many dons have been after you since your arrival? For you, I will duel a dozen."

"You flatter me. I have seen no one except Maximus and Favian, and I wished it so."

"Enough then. I came as promised, because I intend to marry you. The countess has offered me her fairest jewel in trade for mere silver. Neither personal danger nor your refusal to marry can keep me at bay now."

He bent, kissing her possessively, his arms enfolding her.

Heavenly, she thought. The moment was everything she had not dared to dream about.

When he withdrew the world seemed a warmer place. Even the frightening experiences earlier melted away in the ardor of his embrace.

"Nicklas. . ."

"I love you," he whispered, and kissed her again.

"Stop—" she whispered, weakly turning her head away, trying to calm the pounding of her heart.

He held her for a long moment in silence, the side of his face against hers.

"Then . . . like my mother, and Maximus, you wish to . . . to go through with this arrangement?" She knew it sounded foolish, but she didn't know what else to say. When he laughed softly, she blushed, and buried her face into his chest.

"Ah little English Señorita, do you need to ask such a question?"

No, she didn't think so. She kept her eyes cast down and toyed with the soft velvet of his black jacket, tracing the silver threads. "For a time, I thought Maximus might have changed his mind about me, Don Nicklas."

"He would have a difficult task changing mine, Madame."

"Well, I—"

He lifted her chin gently and she saw that he wore a brief smile while he studied her face. "I thought we had our hearts already pledged."

"One can change his mind."

"Yes, one can, but I have not. And if you mean to suggest you have, I'll not take no for an answer. You see," he said with laughter in his eyes, "I have all the advantage."

She knew he was teasing her, but there was a seriousness to his manner as well.

"Then what is there left for me to say?" she whispered.

"You may say anything you wish, as long as it is yes."

She thought how compelling his gaze was, how his touch thrilled her, but did she know him, *truly* know him?

"I leave you small choice," he said, and brushed his lips against her forehead. "After all, I am playing the role of an arrogant don who takes little concern for the will of his señorita. Should you refuse to marry me, I will claim you anyway, and how would you stop me?"

"I could run away—Tobias would help me," she said half-heartedly.

"You dream. Tobias is loyal. He would simply lead you to my ship. And once aboard? You would find me waiting in my cabin to sweep you away again."

Her fingers sought him, touching the side of his face. He brought them to his lips and kissed them.

"Will you fight against my will, and that of Maximus and the countess? You are beaten," he jested. "Tell me you love me, because I wish to marry you before we leave for Lima next week."

He meant it. A week! She stepped back, staring at him. "A week! Nicklas, we need time!"

"Nicklas—I never liked the name he gave me until this moment, when you spoke it."

She looked up into his eyes, her expression troubled and questioning. "And isn't it better to wait, to know each other?"

"We have a lifetime to know each other, and we will. Say yes, and I will inform Maximus I want the marriage ceremony next week." He tilted his head, watching her. "However, my heart wished for a little more certainty on your part."

She had dreamed of his arrival, never believing it possible. She had longed for him, prayed for him, and now that he was here and her fingers touched him and he was not a wish, she feared the answers to the questions that remained unanswered. How little she knew about him!

His arms encircled her. "Oh, Devora, say yes. You have won my heart . . . I would have come for you as Hawkins if there had been no other way to capture you. It seemed wiser for me to marry you here in my own home, but now I wonder—but it is too late to reconsider that. We belong together. I have wanted you from the moment I first saw you. I cherish each moment we are together as a special gift from Him. The Lord knows what's best for us, and He knew that having you as my beloved is precisely what I needed. From the moment we fell in love, I knew it too—my heart is settled."

"I do love you, Bruce—oh no, I said it again!"

"Nicklas, Nicklas, my angel, unless you wish to alert the inquisitors!"

"Oh don't even say such things. If anything should happen to you I would not be able to bear it. Oh Nicklas! Let us escape now, tonight. Let us sneak aboard the ship and leave before someone finds out the truth about you!"

"The time will come for us to leave, I promise you as much, but not yet. My work in Lima is crucial."

"How long?" she whispered.

He hesitated. "Until the treasure galleons arrive—six months from now."

Six months! Her fingers dug into his arms, her eyes pleading with his. "What work? Won't you tell me what it is? It has to do with those prisoners, doesn't it? Your crew—oh how could you dare to bring them here? What if Favian finds out, or the archbishop? Favian knows you have a second identity. He's hinted so to Maximus."

"No, if he did have suspicious about me, I have put an end to them. It was Hawkins who had a second identity. But I acted before he could, before Maximus could. Hawkins is dead, remember? Whatever identity he was suspected of having has died with him."

Devora wasn't as certain, but were her doubts based on fact or fear? "Yet you heard what Favian said. Archbishop Andres was suspicious of the prisoners. Why else would he board your ship?"

"I intend to find out. It may be that Favian misled him."

She thought again of Favian's jealousy. "How far do you think Favian would go to oppose you?"

He appeared thoughtful. "That remains to be seen. He would withhold truth to influence the archbishop in his favor, but betraying me—I've wondered. There are other reasons for the tension between us."

She believed he was speaking of Sybella. Now was an opportunity to discuss his past relationship with her, but was it wise?

"He wishes the love of Sybella," she began casually, "but she grieves for someone else."

"She does not grieve," he said, nothing in his voice.

Was he thinking of himself?

"Had she been wise, she would have remained in Madrid as I asked her to do."

Alert, she turned to face him. "You asked her to stay in Spain? When? When did you see her?"

He studied her face in the candlelight. "I suppose she has spoken to you about me. I hadn't given it much thought, but I see she probably has. Sybella is a proud woman, a Ferdinand through her deceased father. Her mother would have been my aunt, my father's half-sister. There was a time when she came to visit and the stay lengthened into five years. We were both young; children, actually. I was attracted to her as most of the boys were." He began to say more, then he must have decided against it. "She was sent back to Spain to marry a cousin, Don Marcos Ferdinand."

She did not know why but her heart sank. *If she had stayed . . . if she had not been sent away to Spain. . . .*

"Another arranged marriage?" she inquired, a slight sarcasm in her voice. "And if she hadn't been sent away you would have married her."

Alert in his turn, he looked at her with lifted brow. "Maximus would have never arranged anything between me and Sybella. And I would never have accepted it. Do you think I'd have gone along with the scheme by your mother and Maximus had I not greatly wanted you myself? They could have *arranged* all they wanted to but I would have eluded their plans."

She smiled unwillingly. "Yes, I think you would have. Tell me about Sybella—about you and her."

"You want all the details, so after we're married you can lie in my arms and bring them up again?" His eyes hinted some amusement.

"Do not forget she will be in Lima. Should I not know the truth?"

"The *truth* is that there is nothing 'breathtakingly scandalous' to tell. She sought me, more than I sought her. And if there were some kisses, she instigated them all."

Devora stamped her foot. "I don't believe you—how much did you love her? Were you pained when she was sent to marry Marcos?"

He laughed.

"Tell me. Is that why you followed her to Spain? To see her again from afar?"

"My dear, I did not 'follow' her to Spain. Is that what she told you? Never mind, disregard her saga. This is all foolishness. I went to Madrid to the riding school, to the military academy. I had plans to excel for reasons of my own. She was there, yes, and so was Cousin Marcos, a young man I happened to think highly of. I probably grieved more for his death in the war than she did."

"And after his death?"

"After his death," he began easily, "I saw her a few times at some of the functions given by the king. I had little choice."

"And she wanted to renew the romance with you."

"I wish we can discuss this *once* and hopefully never again. Yes, she wanted marriage. But Maximus had other plans for her. He has been her guardian since her parents died. She has a child by Marcos, a boy I think. I have not seen him yet. Maximus wants her to marry Favian. She has wealth and political connections in Spain, everything Maximus finds desirable. The arrangement between Sybella and Favian suits me well enough since the only woman I want stands before me."

"But Sybella feels differently."

"Yes, unfortunately, but she will need to accept life as it is, not as she wishes. She saw me in Spain recently when I was called before the king. She insisted on coming to Lima against my wishes."

"Then you had no understanding with her about marriage?"

"None. Before I ever met you in Barbados I told Sybella there could be nothing more between us."

"She is determined," she said, troubled.

He frowned. "We won't stay in Lima permanently. After a few months we'll leave there."

She did not understand all this, for it seemed realistic to her that Nicklas would wish to remain near the Valentin family. Did he have plans to return to Spain? And if they did, how would an Englishwoman be received? Of course, her parents were there, but that notion raised another problem she hadn't told Nicklas about as yet; that Robert, as English ambassador, was passing secret information from London.

"Where will we go?" she whispered, "What will you do?"

"I've made plans. We need to discuss them, but not here."

"You are serious about marriage within the week?"

He smiled. "Who am I to thwart the wishes of the viceroy and Countess Radburn?" He drew her toward him. He was so compelling that her will at last merged with his. "This may be the first time I've agreed so heartily with my father. It will probably be the last. All but the day and hour is settled. I will leave the choice to you."

"You are very generous, Don Nicklas," she whispered teasingly. "Then, I shall have a Sunday wedding. And Tobias will oversee."

"Five days." He turned thoughtful. "In the meantime there are serious matters to take care of where the prisoners are concerned. The archbishop may wish to question them about Hawkins, but his main interest is to force them to become reluctant converts. Not that it would do them much good."

"What do you mean? Why not?"

"What they call 'New Christians' are not considered fully pardoned. They would escape death by torture, but they would still be placed in a dungeon—especially known pirates. And a trial would most certainly mean death by hanging. In Spain," he continued, "Jews and those of the Reformed faith who convert under inquisition are not permitted to own land, nor to sail as colonists to the New World. They are under watchful eye for years. Which makes one wonder why the Church sanctions torture as a means of so-called conversion. The Dominicans themselves, those who inflict the cruelty, look upon those who recant as suspect in faith."

She thought about that and knew that the Scriptures teach that salvation takes place the moment one trusts in the finished work of Christ on the cross. His resurrection proved that His payment was acceptable to God the Father. "He *has* delivered us from the power of darkness and translated us into the kingdom of the Son of His love, in whom we have redemption through His blood, the forgiveness of sins."*

"I don't think Archbishop Andres suspected them of being Hawkins' crew, nor did Favian," Nicklas was saying.

"Was it wise to tell them?"

"My dear, I take few unnecessary chances with men who would lay down their lives for me. Their safety lies heavily upon my conscience. It was distinctly wise to admit it. If Favian or

---

* Colossians 1:13,14.

Andres found anything in my cabin, or on the crew, I've disarmed them from rushing with it to Maximus. I've also earned his respect, for what it is. I know him well," he said flatly. "As long as the 'great man' believes his son has honored the Valentin name by killing Hawkins and taking his crew, he will stand with me against the archbishop."

She had noted the slight inflection of bitterness in his voice, and wondered. "Then that's why you did it, to gain the support of Maximus?"

"I will need his authority to stand against the Dominicans, otherwise they'll work to keep the prisoners here in Cartagena to stand trial. The religious authorities are nearly impossible to thwart in pursuing their aims; but a viceroy's authority also wields a sharp sword."

She shuddered, thinking of the inquisitors. She could see now why he had decided to admit who the men were. By doing so, he had turned what might have been a death-blow to his masquerade into one of advantage. If any evidence of Bruce Hawkins had been discovered in his cabin, it could be accounted for.

"Had I waited for them to reveal it, Maximus would raise questions not easily explained away," he said.

"But Maximus has demanded to see the prisoners. What if one of them confesses your identity?"

"I have chosen them well. They would die first."

She wondered about the loyalty of such men. They either loved Nicklas, or they were courageously bound heart and soul to whatever cause he was pursuing at Lima. Perhaps it was both reasons.

"I will do whatever it takes to protect them."

She believed in him too, but life had a way of unexpectedly making sharp turns in the road and overthrowing the best-laid plans. Anything could happen to them all once at Lima, yet she believed Nicklas had made his plans well enough to take danger and risks into account.

"I have one regret," he admitted softly, taking hold of her by the waist and looking into her eyes. "I should have taken you to Barbados and married you there. You would now be safe with your uncle at Ashby Hall."

"The hurricane," she reminded him gently. "You had no choice."

"I should have tried harder. I was selfish. I wanted you here when I arrived, since I knew I would be such a long time in Lima. Now, you will be part of the risk there—unless I can send you away from Cartagena before we set out."

"No, I won't leave you, not now, not after we marry."

He smiled ruefully. "We could postpone the marriage . . ."

She stepped closer to him and placed her hands on his arms. "Nay, I will not hear of it."

"Sending you away from Cartagena is possible, but the arrival of your mother complicates the issue. She will wait for Robert. And I suspect he will bring ill news from Tortuga where I'm concerned. Not that he can prove anything. I've heard your mother intends to journey to Lima with us."

"There is so much to tell you about what she plans."

"I've suspected she might know something. Hold off on your information. We can't discuss it here."

"What do you intend to do with the prisoners once they are in Lima?" she whispered. "You can't turn them over to the task masters at the mines. I've heard of the atrocities done there."

"I know better than anyone of the atrocities you speak of. I cannot explain everything to your satisfaction now, but I will later. You will need to trust me. Do you?"

She nestled into his arms. "Yes, but I'm afraid too."

He held her closely, embraced and kissed her gently, then walked with her to the open balcony. They looked down on the plaza that was lit with brightly burning torches and a crowd of Cartagena citizens making merry. There was music and dancing, the sound of guitars and laughter.

"You intend to bring them to the mines don't you?" she whispered, troubled by the path that wound into the unknown future. She was not certain where it would lead them, or what would be the outcome. More was involved than her own well-being. What of Nicklas? What of his crew members? What of Tobias? Yes, Nicklas was a loyal captain, the men were also loyal. But what were they about? Somehow she believed it had something to do with his father, and she found the idea frightened her.

"It's just as you told your father, isn't it? The prisoners are being risked to work in the mines. But why, Nicklas? Why would you bring them to produce silver for the king of Spain?" She turned and looked at him. He was looking below, but she knew he had heard her.

"You ask me to marry a man who is determined to remain a mystery."

He laughed her off, turning to face her in the silvery moonlight.

"I am under sworn duty to King Philip. First, to rid the Caribbean of Hawkins, which I have done. Secondly to ensure the double production of silver bullion for the next treasure fleet to arrive from Seville. That is all I can tell you."

"You mean it's all you wish to tell me."

"Yes. For your sake and mine."

"And you will use the crew of the *Revenge* at the mines?"

He looked at her, unsmiling. "Yes."

"And when you have the silver bullion," she said cautiously, her eyes searching his, "what then?"

For a moment she tasted their first test of wills.

"That, my dear, is not an issue I want to discuss."

She knew little about the process of hauling the silver by mule train to the treasure galleons that would arrive here at Cartagena Bay, but her suspicions troubled her. He might be Don Nicklas now, but she had known him only as an English buccaneer with no liking or propensity for Spain. She was almost afraid now of knowing the truth, afraid it would strengthen the division between them she was sensing.

As their eyes held, the same question arose. Did she trust him or not?

She trusted him, but did it mean she believed in what he was doing?

She turned from him and walked to the railing, her fingers tightening around the band of iron. She could see a bonfire blazing in the plaza and a throng of ordinary citizens dancing, the skirts of the señoritas swirling.

There was more to his relationship with his father than she knew. What was it? Her mind went over the trail of what she had been told about his English mother, Lady Bruce. There was his grandmother too, the daughter of Duke Anthony. There was so much to ask Nicklas that she didn't know where to begin.

"Don Maximus is a determined man." She glanced at him. "There were times tonight when you looked at him—when I thought I saw veiled dislike in your eyes," she whispered.

She saw his jaw flex. She proceeded carefully. "But I must have been wrong. He is your father."

The steely silence that settled between them turned her heart heavy. Then it was so. He disliked Maximus, but why? Surely not only because of Maximus' overbearing personality as he insisted on his own will in matters. There was something more, something deeper.

"He is your father," she repeated, searching for a response.

He turned and looked at her, the silver thread in his jacket glinting as hard as his inflexible stare. For a moment she believed herself looking into the face of a handsome stranger.

"As the countess is your mother," he said bluntly.

The evening concealed her flush. She turned away. "I didn't know my feelings about her were so apparent," she said quietly.

"That you resent her? I have known that from the moment you told me of the arranged marriage. Naturally you felt betrayed. You were. She had no idea how our relationship would work out. Neither did Earl Robert. They arranged this for their own benefit, as did Maximus."

She remembered with a start what the countess had told her and turned to Nicklas, concerned now only with explaining matters to him.

"You are in more danger than you might think! Even if Don Maximus does not suspect anything, the countess does. If only we could escape now, but you will not listen!" She tugged at his arms. "Why won't you listen and go tonight!"

"Devora, darling," he embraced her, soothing her sudden fears, "no need to quaver. I understand the dangers, the risks, and have planned everything with the greatest care. We will leave here as you wish, but only when the work is accomplished. And now," he lifted her chin. "Be brave and tell me about the countess. You say she has suspicions?"

"Oh yes, yes!"

"How do you know?"

"Because—I had some questions about your name," she admitted.

"I gathered as much aboard ship. It was why you came to my cabin."

"And when my mother arrived from the Isle of Pearls she told me your great-grandfather was Duke Anthony, and your mother, Lady Marian Bruce. I remembered then—the initials on the pistol you gave me. They were B.A.V. 'V' for Valentin. I had noticed them earlier, at the Spanish governor's residence, but that was when the pirates were entering the residency and I was too afraid to give it much thought."

"Yes, I remember . . ." he smiled. "You were easily distracted when I gave you a smaller pistol. But this does not explain why the countess is suspicious."

"It does, Nicklas, because when I went to see Tobias there was a dagger on the floor, and your pistol in the inner pocket of a cloak. At the time I thought Tobias had gone out for a few minutes and would return. But later I realized that was wrong. He wouldn't have needed to depart in such haste. And I was right. Because my mother informed me he had left Cartagena with Favian early that day to meet you."

"Wait." He was alert. "Impossible. Tobias would not have left either weapon behind."

"I tell you it is so. Someone was there just before I arrived. I do not know what they were doing, but someone else was seen leaving the cathedral in great haste just as I entered."

"Someone else? Who told you so?"

"The countess. Oh Nicklas, that is not the worst—"

"Wait, who was this person leaving Tobias' chamber? Do you know?"

"No, and neither does Luis."

"Who is Luis?" he asked patiently.

"The bodyguard of the countess. I do not know his last name, but he is a Spaniard. The husband of her serving lady, Isabel. Mother trusts them implicitly."

"Ah, a danger in itself."

"I don't think so. They are devoted. At least Isabel is."

"So Luis saw someone but he does not know who."

"But it's likely the person I disturbed by arriving to see Tobias."

"Go on. What about the pistol?"

"I was going to hide the dagger inside the cloak, afraid Tobias might be called in question if a superior saw it on the floor. But when I reached into the cloak pocket I found the pistol. I took it with me."

"Then you have it?"

"No, that's the dreadful part. I wrapped it in the cloak and ran for the coach, but the boy was not accustomed to driving and in our haste to escape—it was past curfew—I well, fell out of the coach."

"You what!"

"It was nothing," she said, embarrassed at the debacle. "But they caught us. A bishop and several priests and some guards."

"Devora," he breathed with frustration. "You should never have risked going out at curfew! The guards arrest at the slightest infringement of the law."

"Cuzita failed to inform me."

"*Who* is Cuzita?"

"She is my maid. And now being held by the inquisitors. So is Juan. That's another dreadful matter I must talk to you about—"

"One thing at a time. The pistol. What about it?"

"I was injured, and I couldn't move to hide it in time, so I told Cuzita to do so. She did, in the bushes, but we were all taken away. I had intentions of going back to search for it, but I was in the convent for some days. When I returned to the house the countess called for me. She told me she had been suspicious I might try to run away back to Barbados, so she had Luis watching me."

"And this Luis found the pistol, is that what you're saying?"

"Oh Nicklas, and now my mother has it."

Although he said nothing, she could sense his grave concern as he walked to the rail and looked thoughtfully below. Her heart thumped painfully. After a moment he turned. "What did she say to you?"

She swallowed. "She knows who you are."

"The only proof she has is that pistol."

"Yes . . . she had the horrid notion I might destroy her for it. Imagine, she thought that of me." She sank onto a balcony chair.

"It is the recourse she might have sought if she were in your dilemma."

"Please, do not even say that. She is indulgent and compromising of her character and beliefs, but she is no murderess."

"No, but an extortionist perhaps. Well it looks like I will need to deal with the Countess Radburn. What does she want for her secrecy, did she say?"

She looked away, ashamed. "Wealth, naturally."

"Ah, silver, of course. She knows about my commission from the king and the work in Lima."

"Oh Nicklas, what can we do?"

"I'll play her game. It is all I can do. If she wanted my neck she'd have gone to Maximus by now. But it isn't your charming mother who worries me. Others know of the weapon also. You say Luis found the pistol and brought it to her. That means his wife is likely to know as well. If I'm a judge of human character, they too will have silver dreams."

Devora hadn't thought of that. Worried and afraid of the long months ahead of them, when time gave chance the opportunity for something to go wrong, she stood quickly and went to him, taking hold of his arms. "If we left tonight. . . ."

"Softly, querida, we have already talked of that impossibility. And even if I wanted to leave my ship is now being watched by Maximus and the archbishop. One move of panic and they'll all be down on me like a fruit bat on a ripe fig. We must stay calm and cool."

She admired him, for he was never more coolly relentless than when facing a tight and dangerous situation that would make almost anyone else panic.

"I will make arrangements to speak with your mother tomorrow," he said. "But first I must deal with the religious authorities about the prisoners. For that, I need the backing of the viceroy. After tonight, I think I will have it."

"What of Tobias? Will you ask him anything about who might have been in his chamber that night?"

"Not only who was there, but why. It may be he will have a few suggestions. I would also like to know how someone got hold of it."

"Then you gave him the pistol?"

"Yes." A minor frown appeared. "Yes, along with a sword and scabbard from an English uncle, Lord Arlen. The pistol was to safeguard you here to Cartagena."

"You think someone other than Tobias may have the sword?"

"An astute question." He smiled. "It remains to be answered. I will see him later tonight. And now, with little more to be done about that, what is this about your maid and a coach driver being hounded by the Dominicans?"

She explained, pleading for his intervention. "I asked Doctor Francisco to look into the matter of Cuzita and he promised he would do what he could, but I have heard nothing."

"I will find out. In the meantime, the fiesta goes on. There is no more we can do tonight. Let us forgo the ball. I shall bring you instead down to the Plaza Mayor." He took her hand. "Come, I will give you a small taste of Spain."

She knew it was a custom that they could have the night before them uninterrupted by social obligations. Normally there would be a chaperone, but she suspected Nicklas was avoiding that requirement. That too suited her very well.

A Small Taste of Spain

Beloved thou art fair
—Song of Solomon 4:1

Nicklas led her unnoticed out a side door, down the steps of the governor's palace, and across the large central plaza. Soon they mingled with the throng of merrymakers, leaving behind the severe grandeur of the Spanish aristocracy where each man was mindful of his high degree.

Every Spanish city on the Main had a large, central plaza, a cultural idea brought from Spain by the colonists.

"The people of Spain have always been city lovers," Nicklas told her. "Even in the mighty ranges of the Andes, you find the conquistadors had visions of more than gold and silver. They occupied Cuzco, the capital of the Inca Empire, but they built Lima where there was nothing. They dreamed of the great cities of Spain— Cordoba, Seville, Madrid—and built their miniatures to commemorate their own glory, mostly with slave labor—Indians, Negroes, and heretics."

The irony in his voice told her he stood with Friar Tobias where the Indians were concerned, instead of his father, and once again she wondered about his plans at Lima. But it did not seem a night for danger and she opened her heart to receive the music, dancing, and laughter filling the trade wind. Everywhere she looked there were blazing torches. The tropical night was hot and alive with excitement, like her heart.

And like the cities of Spain that Nicklas had mentioned with their paramount plazas, here in Cartagena the Plaza Mayor was adorned with marble statuary, running fountains, and flowers. There were all manner of flowering trees; and the sweet blossoms of orange and lemon filled the air with their fragrance. Olive and fig trees mingled with native palm, banana, and chirimoya. An abundance of tropical flowers perfumed the night.

Strolling the plaza was also a custom from Spain. Nicklas told her the evening paseo was popular among the aristocracy, where young dons strolled round the plaza in rich clothing, conversing and exchanging bits of gossip with friends.

"What kind of gossip?"

Mild amusement reflected in his eyes. "Oh, most everything important—men's pretty new fashions or which bold señorita was willing to toss a rose from her balcony should you go there and hide among the bushes until her dour mother retired."

"I see. And how many roses did these bold señoritas toss to you as you hid among the bushes?"

"Hiding in bushes has never held much charm for me. I would more than likely fall asleep waiting for her mother to retire. The gardener would catch me in the morning with the sun beating upon me. I prefer more bold approaches."

Devora tore her eyes away from his, tapping her fan on her chin, and looked around her as though curious to see where they were, a smile trembling on her lips.

"Then again, if *you* had been that 'bold' señorita who tossed roses, I might have reconsidered the art of bush hiding. It is more likely, however," he said thoughtfully, "that I would have grown impatient and risked the climb to your balcony."

Now they were walking through the coffee houses and shops.

She was pleased that there had been no one else, not even Doña Sybella. His heart had been unconquered until now. The thought was inspiring. However, she changed the subject, intending to learn more about him, though she was learning much already as to what a tease he was. "Did you, um, like Seville?"

He considered. "There were times of pleasantries. I liked the Mediterranean Sea. For the most part my days and nights were consumed with military studies, with riding and fencing, with winning what in England they call accolades."

"I have heard you won more than your share."

He plucked a leaf from the tree they were walking under, examining it as though it were of some interest, but she could see his mind was elsewhere.

"I had reason to desire such. When a student has a cause he believes in, no sacrifice is too great. I wanted to impress the king of Spain."

As they walked on, the heavens displayed their glittering treasure, more fair than any diamonds spilled across a carpet of black velvet. Devora sighed. For this brief interlude, completely happy and content in his presence, she was willing to pretend there was no danger.

"And did you?" she asked, knowing he had, but wanting to hear more. She had heard about his appearance before King Philip for his knighthood.

"Did I what?" he asked evasively, tossing the leaf aside and stopping beneath a laced arbor of branches. The moon slivered through like speckled, silver beams.

"Impress the Spanish monarchy." He certainly was not over-weaned on self-pride. So what had driven him?

"I accomplished my goal, but the acclaim means little to me. The king would hang me tomorrow if he knew the purpose for which I am here."

His casual attitude only thinly concealed the fact he too was a dangerous man. What was his real relationship with the Valentins? And why would there be any underlying current of unrest and resentment? Was not he the favorite of Don Maximus?

"Don Maximus takes great pride in your having sunk several ships," she stated, trying to learn more. "When he first told me of your military exploits, I told myself I could not endure being given in marriage to such a haughty Spaniard." Although music filled the air, she lowered her voice. "I suspect they were Spanish ships you sunk, not English."

A faint smile touched his mouth. She felt the stormy power that was just beneath the veneer of his restraint.

"Were they?" she whispered.

"I think you already know the answer. You suspected that aboard the *Revenge*. The name of my ship says much."

"Don Favian continues to bring up the subject of the straits of Florida. And each time he does, your father rebukes him."

"Does he?"

"You were there, in Florida?"

"Yes, nearly two years ago. I sailed there on a matter for the king, but also to the English colony of Virginia in North America to see if I wanted to settle there."

She wished to pursue Florida but could see he did not. Due to even more pressing matters, she let it slip by to join the many other things in his life that she did not yet understand.

"If Don Maximus should learn of your true allegiance—" she could not go on, her chest tightening with fear.

"In six months or less we shall both be gone from here. He will be left with the mockery of his empty boasts of greatness. The Valentin name will haunt him with the brutality it is known for."

Her eyes searched his and found anger, though carefully leashed. What was it between him and Don Maximus that bade him do this?

"Why do you wish to ruin him, Nicklas?"

"I expect to do to him what he has done to others better than he," he stated without apology. "As he has destroyed the innocent with his selfish brutality, he will drink of his own cup. And when I am done with the Valentin name, he will know why I set out to accomplish its ruin."

"And if you ruin your life in order to destroy him, what then? What of us? Does it matter?"

"You know it matters. We will always be together, nothing will be permitted to ruin that."

"Seeking revenge may destroy more than the Valentin name. A root of bitterness growing in our hearts will choke out everything else. Oh Nicklas! I don't want to lose you to bitterness!"

He took hold of her. "You won't lose me. Not to revenge, not to anything else."

"What then do you want, Nicklas? Do you take after your father, or Lady Marian?" It was the first time she had mentioned his mother in conversation and she noticed he reacted to it with a new reflection of sobriety.

"I am a mixture of both, but unlike Maximus I want justice. Unlike my mother I will not be the victim of his overpowering will! This time, *he* will learn humility, *he* will bend the knee to defeat."

She trembled, afraid of what his plans might do, not to Don Maximus, but to them.

"If I dream, it is of you," he said more gently, "of what we will do when this is over. I dream of the Caribbean, of aiding the victims of Spain in Holland. I'm a sea captain, and a soldier. It is a way to fight back at injustice."

"If you do aid Holland, know that any future here will be thrown to the trade wind forever," she warned. "Is that truly what you want? You wouldn't miss the West Indies? Or Lima?"

He was quiet for a long minute as if giving her question serious consideration. "There were some good times, with Tobias, with friends among the Incas, a life with horses, but I've never considered it my home. I suppose it sounds like treason to prefer another country, but I do—the English colonies in North America. What would you think of settling there?"

She had personally hoped he would return to Barbados, to Uncle Barnabas and Ashby Hall, but she also felt it was unfair to expect it.

"You know I would go anywhere with you, Nicklas."

He turned to her, slipping an arm tightly about her, an almost wistful look in his eyes. "Would you, Devora?"

"Do you doubt my love?" she whispered. "I would escape with you now, even tonight."

He looked off toward the Caribbean, the trade wind tugging at his dark hair and the wide lapel of the exquisite jacket. The breeze touched her skin and gently lifted her lace skirts. As she looked at him she thought her love for him was so great it would break her heart.

"You sorely tempt a man," he said softly, "but others are involved. I must go to Lima." He lifted her fingers, pressing them to his lips. "What kind of ring do you want?" he said, changing the subject.

"Oh," she said a bit breathlessly, "I don't know . . . the countess has brought one that's been in the family for a century, and I think I heard the viceroy also mention a Valentin ring."

His mouth turned with boredom. "Then I will choose a different ring for you." His eyes held hers. "Do you have a preference? Diamonds, or some other stone?"

Her gaze warmed beneath the desire in his eyes and drifted against her will to his lips. "No . . ."

He slowly drew her toward him and she tilted her head to meet his kiss. He slid his arms around her. The sound and images of the fiesta grew fainter, and dissolved.

Soon the sound of prancing horses forced them back to the moment, and his hold loosened.

He smiled. "Come, let me show you the bull that will meet the matador tomorrow."

She drew back with exaggeration. "You too!"

He laughed. "So you feel sorry for him!"

"Yes!"

"It's just as I thought. If you had your way you would turn him loose."

"Bull fights are cruel. And the men who antagonize them are not gallant."

He smiled. "What! The other señoritas share great excitement over the graceful toreros. They swoon to see the skillful attack on the bull by daring caballeros on horseback!"

"You mock. But I do not swoon over such men."

"It's just as well." He slipped an arm around her shoulders and walked away with her. He smiled down at her. "If there's any swooning to be done, you will do so in my arms. But there was a time as a boy when I thought the toreros were brave and gallant. I planned to fight a bull to impress Maximus. It's my good fortune Tobias put a quick end to it."

"Did you always do daring things to impress the viceroy?"

"I was always trying to prove myself," he admitted, but would not elaborate.

She wondered, glancing sideways at him. "Strange, it's Favian who is bullied by his father."

He said nothing, as though he did not wish to talk about it. "So you cheer for the bull. Well, we share a secret. There came a time when I did too, much to my father's disdain. I even released one once, the night before the fiesta. Tupac was with me. We climbed a tree and enjoyed the spectacle of the free bull thundering across Maximus' courtyard. Other than destroying the cook's garden, no one was hurt."

"Did you really! Did he find out it was you?"

He smiled. "I blamed it on Favian."

She laughed.

"What would you like to see, or do?"

"I would like to walk through the Mentidero."

The Mentidero was a raised walk under a lattice roof where stylish booths and coffee shops offered a rich assortment of foods, wines, and coffee. Below the walk were shops displaying the newest fashions, offering everything imaginable, from the newest fashion in ladies shoes to jewelry and daggers.

"Do you see anything you would like?" he asked as they passed the various booths. She had little appetite. He smiled at her hesitation. "The world is yours. What looks good?"

"What's that?"

"Spanish coffee with cacao and cream."

"I'll try it."

It tasted black and strong, with a dose of chocolate. "It's bitter."

"A typical English tea drinker," he teased. "I should have known."

She found his gaze disconcerting and chose a small, gilded tin of chocolates. He tossed some silver coins onto the counter and they moved on.

"Oh—look," she said, partly because she could no longer endure the steady look of his gray-green eyes, or the admiration she saw in them as he studied her. "Who are they, Nicklas, do you know?"

A cavalcade of gaily dressed young men of the nobility rode by, prancing through the street, garbed in fancy dress and pieces of armor. They were followed by other Spaniards in turbans, looking deliberately foreign.

"Players for the mascarada. Would you care to watch it?"

"What is it?" she asked cautiously.

"Tonight, it's a game. It is the old Spanish historical play of Moors and Christians. Are you acquainted with it?"

"No. What is it about?"

"The men wearing the turbans represent Moorish knights. They will gather in a wooden castle and try to fend off the attack of the brave Catholic knights arriving in boats."

She could see the boats being dragged into the plaza on carts.

"After a furious battle, the infidel Moors surrender and are carried off by the victors." He smiled. "Naturally the Spaniards win."

"I wish to see it," she said with a smile. "After all, my husband-to-be has also been knighted."

"My knighthood will soon tarnish," he said wryly.

The colorful scene was busy and noisy, but after being practically locked away behind lattice windows for weeks, and now in the stimulating company of Nicklas, she felt the freedom of release. After it was over, they continued their walk. "That building, what is it?" she asked. "It's not a church."

"It's a *cabildo,* where the town council of the same name holds its meetings. Every city has jurisdiction over its outlying territory," he explained. "The king, through his Council of the Indies, controls the details of all the affairs of the empire, which is linked together by cities, by passing his wishes to the viceroy in Lima. My father, as you may have learned by now, is like a small king. Yet—that is not all he wants. He has plans to gain the title of Count of the Realm, which will secure his riches and holdings permanently throughout as many generations as Spain holds the Caribbean."

"Yes, but do you know how he expects to attain the title from King Philip?"

He looked at her, alert. "He told you?"

"Yes. Our marriage has much to do with it."

"Our marriage will have nothing to do with bringing his devises to pass," he said firmly. "I will see to that. Though, of course, he expects it to. I've known from the beginning why the countess wanted this arrangement."

She was surprised. "You know about my stepfather giving information from the Private Council of King Charles to Don Maximus?"

"He's a spy, yes. I've mentioned it to Lord Anthony, an uncle. He is aware of what's going on, but we have no proof yet."

The knowledge that her parents were involved in spying for personal gain troubled her greatly, and she could not bring herself to tell Nicklas that her mother was the main instigator.

"Don Maximus has told my mother of a royal Inca tomb in Cuzco. She and Robert both believe they are entitled to carry away certain items. Do you think it's true, about the tomb?"

"There are royal tombs remaining. How they escaped the greed of the conquistadors is rather difficult to explain, but what Maximus says is true. I remember such a tomb. When we were boys, Tupac brought me to one in the mountains around Cuzco. But if Robert believes Maximus can be trusted, he is in for a disappointment, not to mention great danger from the Indians themselves. There are groups who live in the mountains who try to continue their Inca culture unmolested by Spain."

Learning this only compounded her concerns. She looked at him gravely. "Don Maximus has impressed a great many people, but he has not impressed you, his son. You are very angry with him."

He was silent for a moment as they walked slowly through the throng. "'Angry' is not a word I would have chosen, but I suppose you are right. There is anger. I would have more love for him if he were man enough to humble himself before God. If he showed even a little humility over his serious faults, I could understand, and even ... forgive. But his pride encases him in rage, allowing him to ridicule others who do not measure up. I remember his rejection. His thoughtless cruelty to others who were vulnerable to his authority. I remember those days as though they were yesterday. I have relived them so often. One always remembers his childhood."

Incredulous, she searched the side of his face as they walked. "Reject you? Maximus boasts of no one else but you."

"Now, perhaps, but even that is questionable. Believe me, he would hang me tomorrow if he knew I had shamed him. He does not know what it means to love anyone for what God made them to be, but only if they measure up to his god-like standards of grandeur. He has always loved Favian more, but scorns him now because Favian is not the soldier Maximus wishes him to be. He is not proud of *me,* he is proud of what I have accomplished for Spain, for the grandeur of the Valentin name."

"And that is why you excelled?" she whispered.

"Yes, but to win his respect was not my end. What he thinks of me no longer matters as it did when I was a boy. His respect is merely useful to attain my goal; because it will bring about the ruin of his pride, his little empire."

"Then you have no sympathy for him at all? I cannot believe it of you."

"He does not want sympathy, but absolute obedience."

She considered, and agreed, Maximus was inflexible and demanding; yet she wished for the misunderstanding between them to be solved. She changed the subject, hoping the viceroy's responsibilities would gain sympathy from Nicklas.

"It must be a difficult task for him and his officers to sort out and obey all those royal orders."

"They arrive with every ship from Spain! But with the king so far away, it is easy for him to ignore them for any reason. I can remember seeing him receiving one of those royal papers. He kissed it, placed it on his head in a sign of respect, saying, "I obey, but I do not execute.""

She smiled.

"The cumbersome system is so crowded with petty officials determined to make money from their positions, that there is corruption throughout the governing system. Is it any wonder the earl and countess think to carry away treasure from Cuzco? And now an uncle from Seville has arrived to oversee these matters, serving under Maximus."

"Yes, I met Don Roman tonight."

"Maximus has him under his thumb."

"Is that why you spoke of interest in Virginia, why you wish to leave for America? Because of unjust rule?"

"Partly. I have other reasons as well."

It was obvious he would not explain now. She believed his plans, whatever they were, were dangerous, and the less she knew about them the more at ease he felt.

She settled into silence. The journey to Lima, and his work there, grew more foreboding by the moment.

They left the Mentidero and strolled in another direction away from the main fiesta. They walked in silence now. She was aware of some great barrier between them and she wondered about it painfully.

❦ 17 ❦

The Authority of the Viceroy

He that loveth silver will not be satisfied. .
—Ecclesiastes 5:10

The sky was a hard, pearly-gray above the sun-baked stone court rimmed with gnarled olive trees. Devora had spent the night at the governor's palace with the countess and the Spanish aristocracy that had not yet departed for their homes. She slipped out of her room unnoticed and came silently downstairs. From outside, she heard a tumult filling the morning air. She sped across the lower floor into a chamber facing the front court. She went to the window, parting the heavy curtains. In front of the palace in the wide, paved Court of Judgment the governor had arrived with Archbishop Harro Andres and several Dominicans. General Alfonso and soldiers from the Cartagena garrison were also arriving, herding the prisoners forward.

Devora heard the echo of horse hoofs on stone and the shout of commands from guards, followed by the crack of a whip.

She left the window and stepped out onto the semi-circular balcony. She looked across through a screen of blooming honeysuckle. Although she was partially hidden, she could see a large section of the court.

She winced, watching some sixty English and French pirates, many of them Nicklas' own crew from the *Revenge*, being driven forward into the square by soldiers riding on horseback. One of the soldiers cracked his whip across the back of a prisoner moving too slowly.

Her anxious gaze searched the throng of officials and onlookers for Nicklas, but she did not see him. Favian, however, had arrived and stood beside the governor.

More men on horseback were arriving. With relief she saw Nicklas ride up with Friar Tobias. To her surprise she could see that the viceroy also rode beside Nicklas on a sleek white horse with a silver-ornamented saddle. Don Maximus was in uniform, as was Nicklas, who appeared authoritative in black and crimson, wearing a sword, and carrying pistols in the criss-crossed leather bandoleer across his chest. An elite band of royal soldiers separate from those under the governor rode with them, carrying the flag of Castile beside the flag of the Viceroyalty of Peru. Friar Tobias, with a large silver cross glinting bright and awesome in the sunlight, rode on Nicklas' other side.

Devora smiled. She never thought she would experience such feelings of pride while seeing the flags of a political and religious system contrary to England waving in the breeze, but now, the three Valentins represented justice and she believed might also was on their side. Nicklas had indeed been wise and even clever to get his father to back him in the confrontation.

The governor stood upon the hastily constructed Judgment Platform and came down the steps to meet them. Devora could make out the uncertainty on his face. Favian too, looked surprised as he stared at his father. Evidently he had not expected him to support Nicklas' cause to protect the prisoners.

Archbishop Harro Andres stood waiting with the Dominicans, the breeze ruffling their long, clerical robes. She could see his hard-boned, tanned face showing signs of impatience, as though he knew he had come up against an equal, but opposing, force. He walked forward, but remained on the steps.

The viceroy dismounted and climbed the steps to Andres, while Nicklas and Tobias remained on horseback.

Devora strained her ears to hear, but the voices were distorted on the breeze by the din of snorting horses and the murmur of the curious throng of onlookers.

Nicklas appeared calm, confident and coolly intimidating. He was clearly showing himself the legal emissary of King Philip, and as such, he was claiming the right to commandeer the prisoners he had taken from the pirate Bruce Hawkins. *It is all cleverly done,* she thought. Don Maximus' voice now sounded forth strongly: "The will of His Most Catholic Majesty must be done." And he turned toward Nicklas, arm extended. The sun's rays caused the jewels on his hand to flash.

Nicklas drew something from beneath his jacket and gave it to the capitan who rode up beside him. He, in turn, brought it to the viceroy, who handed it to the governor. The governor handed it to the archbishop, who removed the ribbon and unrolled the official-looking mini-scroll and read.

It must be Nicklas' orders from King Philip, she thought, watching intently. *Would Andres feel his authority superseded?*

A few minutes later Nicklas was called forward. Devora watched him mount the steps, and bend over the hand of the archbishop. The Church official laid his other hand on his head.

The confrontation had ended peacefully, she thought—until Favian stepped forward and said something to Don Maximus. Then two soldiers hauled a red-headed, brawny man forward. Devora's breath tightened in her throat. It must be the Irishman whom Favian had accused of striking him aboard the *Our Lady of Madrid.* Was he to be sacrificed to save Nicklas' plans with the other prisoners?

There was a movement, and her gaze swerved to Friar Tobias who was riding forward, his great voice booming: "Alas, my Lord Bishop! May I speak a word in your ear! This man cannot be tried as a heretic! I can myself avow to his faith. Look and see!"

The Irishman's shirt, already tattered, was torn aside by one of the soldiers and a silver cross glimmered boldly.

"I have knowledge this man was exiled from Ireland because he was Catholic! He has confessed to me at dawn this day his sins!

He knew not Don Favian Valentin was the esteemed son of the viceroy!" Tobias gestured to Favian to walk forward. He did so, looking down at the Irishman with disdain.

"Then down, Irish dog!" demanded Favian.

The Irishman got down on one knee before Favian. After a moment of prideful satisfaction, Favian walked away. The soldiers grabbed the Irishman by the arm and hauled him back toward the other prisoners, where he was again shackled in chains.

Devora's breath slowly released. She wondered about all that Nicklas and Tobias might have had to tell the Irishman before they could convince him to bow the knee to Don Favian.

Words were exchanged between Nicklas and the officials, then the archbishop turned and left with the Dominicans, and Maximus joined Nicklas and walked down the steps toward Tobias. The prisoners were being led away back toward the harbor, evidently to be rowed out to the *Our Lady of Madrid* where they would remain until the overland journey to Lima.

Devora stood, relieved, and became aware that someone else was in the chamber with her. She heard the rustle of skirts and turned.

Countess Catherina Radburn stood behind her, her lips set in a calm, but determined, smile.

"I think it is time I spoke alone with Don Nicklas about the pistol. You may go to your chamber, my dear. Wait for me there. I have sent a slave with a message to Nicklas telling him to meet me here."

❧～❧

Nicklas entered the chamber, and seeing Countess Radburn seated in a high-backed white chair with red velvet, swept off his hat and bowed. When he straightened there was a brief smile on his handsome face that reflected his amused scorn. He had met the countess on several occasions in Seville. He had been taken aback the first time he learned that Devora was Catherina's daughter. The two women could not be less alike, except in appearance. The eyes . . . but the countess had blue-black hair and, though old enough to be his mother, was boldly flirtatious.

"Your servant, Madame!"

She greeted him with a charming smile. "You sometimes sound so English, Nicklas. Duke Anthony would be proud if he could meet you before he passes away."

"Perhaps his wish will know the blessing of Providence. You wanted to see me?"

"Yes, I promise not to detain you for long. I understand the severity of the pressures placed upon you, with getting the prisoners ready for the journey to Lima. I wished to speak with you about certain matters, the wedding being one of them."

He walked into the chamber where a breeze entered through the balcony, and turned to study her. She appeared to be in poor health. She had lost weight since he had last seen her in Seville, and there were faint bluish marks beneath her eyes. The journey to Lima would be difficult for her. It was unfortunate that Robert was not here to care for her. She was a shallow woman, from Nicklas' viewpoint, and spoiled by the comforts of her title. That she desired only silver and not political power was an advantage.

He had spoken with Tobias last night about the pistol. Tobias had hidden both the pistol and the family sword in his chamber at the casa Valentin. Evidently someone had come across the pistol while searching Tobias' chamber and planted it in his robe at the cathedral. But who had done so and why? More troubling was the question of his English sword. Had it too been taken? The dagger, however, had not belonged to Tobias, who had carried his own on him when he sailed with Favian to meet the *Our Lady of Madrid*.

"Your willingness to take my daughter to wife pleases me well, as it will Earl Robert."

"I'm content to hear it of you, Madame. It is even more pleasing to me that the arrangement suits Lady Ashby."

She smiled. "Of course, Don Nicklas. It causes a mother joy to learn the match she believes so accommodating for her daughter is desired also by the gallant in question. And does it suit you to have this ceremony here in Cartagena before the journey to Lima?"

He bowed lightly, restraining his amusement. "It suits us both quite well. Will five days be long enough for your preparations, Madame?"

"They shall suffice," and she languidly fanned herself. "I am also pleased to see that matters turned out well this morning in regards to the prisoners." She wrinkled her brow. "Whose crew were those buccaneers from? Hawkins' wasn't it? Captain Bruce Anthony 'Hawkins'?"

Nicklas smiled blandly. "I think you know quite confidently whose 'buccaneers' they are, Countess Radburn."

"Yes, very intriguing. Amusing, actually." She laughed softly behind her fan.

His brow lifted. "Amusing?"

"Don't you think so? It was quite sporting of you, Nicklas, to be able to gain the support of the viceroy like this. Imagine, bringing these buccaneers to Lima to the mines. It's rather like the viceroy bringing a viper into his own bed, isn't it?"

"That depends. I am more concerned with your reasons for going to Lima—the environs of the mines. Could it be you and the notable English ambassador have interests of your own?"

"It could, and I suspect you know why I wish to go, and what is to be gained. The question remaining, my dear Nicklas, is whether or not you will cooperate with my wishes, or whether I must turn the pistol over to Maximus. It seems a pity to do so, you having managed thus far to be so rarely clever. As I said, I find a certain amusement in the entire matter since, despite my efforts to the contrary, there remains within me a loyalty to Whitehall."

He suspected she was admitting the truth, that it had not been easy for her to encourage Robert to sell secrets to Spain. That it did trouble her, however, in no way lessened his scorn. If anything, he respected her less. Had she done so without qualm, he would have judged her as merely a selfish and rather silly woman. Knowing that she could sell both her conscience and her daughter in order to sustain the glittering lifestyle of a countess in London only unveiled her lack of discretion.

"Do you actually have the pistol?"

"Oh come, Nicklas, would I bring it down with me? How easy for you to simply take it from my hand. Not even you are gallant enough to refrain. But do not be concerned. It is well out of sight in a safe place that will both guard your secret and mine. Once we are in Lima and you're able to make good on my behalf, I shall hand it over to Devora."

"And naturally, Madame, I can trust you," he said wryly.

"You have no choice, really, do you?" She smiled when he deliberately remained silent. "So you see, we must make a bargain. My silence for your generous cooperation. Say—enough silver to make me an extremely wealthy woman in London."

There was no point in trying to intimidate her—to perhaps frighten her into backing off and surrendering the pistol, especially when time was on his side. He would not do so to Devora's mother, anyway, in spite of herself. As for the loss of silver—if he did cooperate—it would be negligible compared to King Philip's loss. If he were successful, the bulk of the treasure would be brought to Holland.

He bowed again. "How could I bring myself to refuse you, Countess Radburn?" He straightened, the green of his eyes amused. "After all, you will soon be my mother-in-law."

She smiled, and stood elegantly, holding out her hand for him to kiss. "Then our little secret remains permanently concealed."

He bent over her hand, and straightened, his mouth turning with irony. He watched her walk to the door with head held high and sweep out, leaving a trail of too-sweet perfume.

~18~

Tomorrow's Dreams

Devora's joyful heart saw the noonday fill with jewels: the gloriously hot sun burned in an opal sky; the distant hills appeared like hazy amethysts. Every plant and vine flaunted vivid hues of the rainbow, from the scarlet blossoms of the bougainvillea that entwined the balcony rail to the orange trumpet flowers. Mynah birds, like ebony with golden eyes, were chattering happily, and iridescent humming birds flitted and darted among scores of tropical flowers.

For the present, the whole world was like a spectrum of fragrant beauty declaring God's great goodness. Devora stood on the threshold of seeing some of that blessing upon her own life. Within a week she would be Doña Devora Valentin. In less than a year, she and Nicklas would be sailing the Caribbean on their way to a new beginning, perhaps in the Virginia colony.

On their way they would stop and visit the island of Barbados where Uncle Barnabas waited at Ashby Hall. When she saw him again she would tell him his prayerful intercession for her had indeed been answered by a faithful God with good intentions for His redeemed. She would be wearing a wedding ring on her finger, and Nicklas would be at her side—a handsome and daring buccaneer. They might even voyage to England to visit Duke Anthony!

A mynah bird squawked and flew from a branch, casting a brief shadow across her face. Trouble too would come, like the shadows which inevitably fell across the path of life. But for now, she refused it entrance to her heart. She was on the threshold of marriage! She hummed as she gathered her things to go downstairs, hearing the coach pull up in front of the governor's palace. She glanced over the balcony rail and saw that her mother and the Valentins were already waiting below in the court for the return trip across town to the family residency.

Devora turned and snatched up her silk shawl and handbag to join Nicklas. She knew he loved her. She was even more confident in the love and faithfulness of the One who was like a refiner's fire. He would ordain their steps to keep them from departing into the way of shame and ruin. Whatever awaited them in the future, she and Nicklas would meet it together. She would walk by faith, looking unto Jesus, who in His sovereignty had ordained her path to merge with His plans for Nicklas. Who knew where the road would lead them?

"Now we see through a glass darkly, but then face to face." Until then. . . . Her own silvery dreams cast a hopeful glow on the long and adventurous journey to Lima.

Harvest House Publishers

For the Best in Inspirational Fiction

Linda Chaikin
TRADE WINDS
Captive Heart
Silver Dreams

Lori Wick
A PLACE CALLED HOME
A Place Called Home
A Song for Silas
The Long Road Home
A Gathering of Memories

THE CALIFORNIANS
Whatever Tomorrow Brings
As Time Goes By
Sean Donovan
Donovan's Daughter

KENSINGTON CHRONICLES
The Hawk and the Jewel
Wings of the Morning
Who Brings Forth the Wind
The Knight and the Dove

ROCKY MOUNTAIN MEMORIES
Where the Wild Rose Blooms
Whispers of Moonlight
To Know Her by Name
Promise Me Tomorrow

CONTEMPORARY FICTION
Sophie's Heart
Beyond the Picket Fence

Virginia Gaffney
THE RICHMOND CHRONICLES
Under the Southern Moon
Carry Me Home
The Tender Rebel
Magnolia Dreams

Maryann Minatra
THE ALCOTT LEGACY
The Tapestry
The Masterpiece
The Heirloom

LEGACY OF HONOR
Before Night Falls
Jewel in the Evening Sky

Lisa Samson
THE HIGHLANDERS
The Highlander and His Lady
The Legend of Robin Brodie
The Temptation of Aaron Campbell

THE ABBEY
Conquered Heart
Love's Ransom
The Warrior's Bride

Ellen Gunderson Traylor
BIBLICAL NOVELS
Esther
Joseph
Joshua
Moses
Samson
Jerusalem—the City of God
Melchizedek